She Ruined the
A Historical R

By:
Anna Macy

The following text is a work of fiction. All the characters, organizations, businesses and events portrayed in this novel are products of the author's imagination or are being used fictitiously.

She Ruined the Marquess: A Historical Romance

Table of Contents:

CHAPTER ONE   5

CHAPTER TWO   18

CHAPTER THREE   35

CHAPTER FOUR   52

CHAPTER FIVE   68

CHAPTER SIX   87

CHAPTER SEVEN   107

CHAPTER EIGHT   130

CHAPTER NINE   155

CHAPTER TEN   173

CHAPTER ELEVEN   194

CHAPTER TWELVE   210

CHAPTER THIRTEEN   233

CHAPTER FOURTEEN   255

CHAPTER FIFTEEN   275

CHAPTER SIXTEEN   295

CHAPTER SEVENTEEN   300

CHAPTER ONE

William Huntington, the Marquess of Mansfield Park, was exhausted. He hadn't seen his two closest friends in months, and their reunion tonight had set him back a few hours of sleep.

When he finally did pour himself into bed, he could barely be bothered to undress. William knew that his long-suffering valet, Simon, would be all aflutter in the morning at the state of his master's clothes. But the liquor and the ungodly time of night demanded he just passes out where he lay, on top of the pile of feathered, overstuffed blankets and pillows in his expansive guest suite, this one decorated in a mind-numbing shade of green.

"Oh, thank god," he whispered, pushing his head deep into the downy pillow, his dark hair flopped over his eyes as he settled his body into the blankets with a grateful sigh.

He was lying prone, his long legs half hanging off the mattress, his liquor swirling brain relaxing into what he knew would be a sweet, blissful sleep when he was ambushed.

One moment he was lying there, spread eagle and wonderfully half-conscious; the next, there was the warm, substantial weight of another human clambering right over him.

Almost apologetically, a pair of hands felt their way across his shoulders, while painfully bony knees connected with a susceptible area that had him flying off the blankets with alarm.

Groaning thickly, he suddenly found himself nose to nose with a woman, her face shrouded in the early morning darkness that encapsulated them both. The scent of lavender washed over his dulled senses.

Skin like hot silk slid against his cheek. Her fingers traced his cheekbones to the edge of his jaw, a ghost of a caress. There the phantom nails drew lazy circles against the sharp stubble.

Exhaustion or not, every flight or fight instinct in William's body was beginning to fire. He wasn't expecting a woman in his bed.

Gripping what felt like a fine-boned wrist in one of his hands and the smooth curve of one delicate hip in another, he sent up a silent blessing that he hadn't accidentally latched onto an even more feminine body part. In his state of mind, even this passing touch had fogged his mind with a passion he didn't need.

Regardless of how he could feel his body responding to her attentions, he knew he had to get in control of the situation. Summoning his wits, he rolled the both of them across the bed, grabbing for a hold of his sweet-smelling bedmate.

Williams bucked his body off the bed with practiced ease, uprooting both of them and landing in a heap, his body now across the intruders. The woman below him let out a soft gasp of surprise.

Growling, William pressed his weight against the body below him, using the weight of his thigh to pin her down while he attempted to sort out whatever madness had just flown to him.

"What the devil? Who --," he started before, to his boundless surprise, warm, soft lips cut him off with a tentative kiss. He reeled back, shocked and even more confused, letting go of his mystery woman's wrist as he tried to put some healthy distance between the two of them — namely distance from the caressing lips that stole his breath and would've quickly taken his sanity.

However, his new guest had other plans for the two of them. Her newly freed hand reached up to grab at the undone collar of his linen shirt, her fingers dancing lightly against his bare chest.

Gripping the fabric tightly, she pulled herself back up to him, fastening her lips once more over his in a hot, velvet press of her mouth. Confused, and with more than a little liquor still clouding his usually sharp mind, William lost track of the moment when the attack turned from surprise to seduction.

He smiled against the pair of insistent lips pressed to his. Whomever she was, he still couldn't see in the near-black darkness of the guest suite; she was like putty in his hands.

Her hands untangled themselves from his shirtfront. William immediately felt disappointment as humid summer air filled the minute space between their bodies.

He was trying to distract his mind from the feeling of her lush body curling perfectly around his hard edges, which were growing dangerously harder. William's mind scrambled to identify her.

Had one of his friends taken a mistress and not told him? No, it couldn't be, William thought dully, striking that option from his list. While she would earn points for sheer enthusiasm, the woman under him acted with raw instinct, not the well-practiced seduction that a mistress would've used.

She had to be a sorely misled guest. It was the viable only answer.

Her sweet lips broke from his, skimming their way over his jaw to where they pressed at his pulse, which was speeding out of control. Long legs had wound around his legs like curling ivy, and he could feel her full breasts arched up into his body.

Every part of her begging to be touched.

Her body spilled over the bed and around him, intoxicating him. The soft sighs that slipped from her lips as she addressed the thick column of his throat were enough to shred any preconception about his chance at a good night's sleep.

His darkly handsome face, paired with the generous title and family reputation among the aristocratic sect, meant William had never had to beg for any female attention.

But this, this was a whole new experience, and it heated his blood instantly. This fiery, surprise visit was setting his skin aflame, and his mind was fumbling at an explanation when her voice broke the moment like ice water on his back.

"Robert, I'm so glad you changed your mind," a low, throaty female voice spoke, just a breath from his lips. Trepidation ran through his veins, devastating whatever feelings of passion he might have had moments ago and replaced them with dark, cold dread.

Robert. She had said, Robert.

William gulped audibly. Robert, as in Robert Wains of Devonshire, his closest friend, with whom he just been downstairs sharing drinks. That's who she believed him to be.

William knew that Robert had changed his plans at the last minute to meet everyone at their mutual friend Nicholas' country house to enjoy a few days' retreats from the suffocating heat that was August in London. Robert was staying exactly one door further down the hall.

"Oh, bloody hell," William said, sucking in the warm night air as he managed to detangle himself from his new bedmate. His heart was pounding in his chest, and his body desperately tried to bring equal function to all its limbs.

This time, he successfully set her aside, keeping a desperate hand on her shoulder to block her from coming any closer. Panic wrecked him, his breath short in his lungs as he began to piece together the only identity possible for this intruder.

Weeks ago, Robert had written to him the short letter getting to William as he dutifully performed his annual check at his family's historic estate, Mansfield Park. When he had read the note from his friend, something in his chest had twisted.

Resentment, ugly and clawing, had risen in his belly.

At Eton and in the blissfully unencumbered short years after, William, Robert, and Nicholas had been the closest of friends in school. Thick as thieves. More brothers than any friend William had ever had before, or since.

Like Robert, William had spent most of his youth preparing for this transition of power and responsibility, yet it didn't make it any more manageable. Robert had been burying himself in work, as his father, the Lord of Devonshire was slowly stepping back from the immense shipbuilding empire that had been in their family for generations.

It had been understandable, Robert's aversion to the London social scene, much to the chagrin of his mother and sisters, who aspired above all else to secure the perfect bride for their beloved Robert.

In a desperate act to please his parents and siblings, Robert had agreed to attend a few society events. At the same time, his focus stayed on the only thing that mattered to him right now, maintaining his family's legacy as the premier shipwrights in the region. The minute Robert stared down the actuality of his future as a Lord, he broke down and allowed his family to arrange a match for him.

Dear William,

It has finally happened. My mother and sisters have finally achieved the marriage match of the utmost importance. I am to be married to the only child of the Earl of Greystone, Miss Juliet Sonders. She is not challenging to look at, but I know little else of her, other than her evident breeding and wealth. Two things we at Devonshire are always sorely in need of, or so the ladies of the house have informed me.

Her stepfather has been agreeable, and we will be married at the beginning of the winter holidays. Until then, I plan to avoid the poor woman for as long as possible so that she does not become aware she is marrying an ungrateful monster who has no interest in the wife, house, or the domesticity that comes with either.

While it will not be the most fashionable event, I'd like you and Nicholas to be there to be sure I get through the ordeal with as little drama. With Marian at the helm, you can only imagine how impossible a task that is.

I hope to see you and Nick at Lakeview at the end of the summer. It has been too long, friend.

-Wains

After everything they had grown up promising each other, those blood oaths they took as children. Maybe it hadn't meant something to Robert, or Nicholas, but to William, those promises had been a lifeline to a brotherhood, a family, he craved.

So much for strength in numbers, William had thought bitterly. He was used to being alone, but never before had it cut so deep, so permanent than in that moment.

After William's father passed away just over a year ago, it left not only a seat in the House of Lords vacant for William to assume but a powerful, sprawling estate to manage. Learning about his land and his new role had consumed every waking moment of William's life. He had begged off attending much of anything this past year, hiding behind the perfectly acceptable excuse of grieving

However, he had not been grieving for his long-estranged parent, but for his former life of frivolity. His father had never offered William a single reason to believe he cared for his only child in life. When he died, William felt only anger at his passing.

He had struggled to author letters to his friends this past year. After all, how does one politely explain that his life had been turned upside down? Yet he cherished each letter his friends sent to his apartment in London, or even to Mansfield Park, where he had been attempting to get a solid grip on life as Marquess.

Regardless, he now regretted several of his decisions to stay away now more than ever. Perhaps if he had been more involved, he would understand why his best friend's fiancée was sprawled across his bed.

William could feel the sweat breaking out on his brow at the possible outcome of the situation he was in. Praying for sanity, William attempted to process this situation.

First and foremost, this woman thought he was Robert, and based on that could assume that she was, in fact, Juliet.

It was too dark in the room for her to know she had gone astray. His mind whirled in an attempt to smooth over that catastrophic detail.

Sleeping precariously close to this suite on the second floor of the vast Lakeview Manor, on either side, to be exact, happened to be some of the biggest gossips this side of the Atlantic. They would pounce on this *small* misunderstanding faster than a starving barn cat on an unsuspecting mouse.

His heart suddenly skipped, realizing that the formerly writhing woman below him had grown impossibly still during his analysis. Too still. For a fleeting moment, William prayed he had imagined her entirely, a curvaceous figment of his dreams that had quickly gone from fantasy to nightmare.

Then slowly, with an educated and very polite tone, his nightmare incarnate spoke again.

"I'm a little confused," she said, her body shifting slightly under his, her knees brushing up against his torso in a tortuously slowly caress as she sat up against the pillowed headboard.

William couldn't tell if it was intentionally seductive or accidental, but regardless, his blood flared again. He clamped his jaw hard, focusing hard on the predicament he was in. He cleared his throat once, then again, and shifted his clothing, including his trouser pants, slightly to offset any unintentional touching between him and who he feared was his best friend's fiancé.

"You, I'm afraid, are not the only one confused," William said, speaking in what he hoped was his calmest, least panicked voice. He wasn't used to dealing with hysterical females. That said, if a situation ever called for hysterics, in his opinion, this was it. He wouldn't blame her in the least.

Gingerly releasing her completely, he rocked back on his bare heels. As if brought on by fate, a thin blade of moonlight shone between the heavy brocade curtains on the far side of the suite. William felt it flash across his face, clearly displaying his distinctive features.

For a long moment, the world stood still, as if drawing both of them to a precipice of impending chaos. Then William was shoved backward hard, legs and arms akimbo, he toppled off the bed with a grunt and a string of curses. Disorientated, the woman launched herself off the bed, the sheets trailing after her bare feet.

Making a split-second call, William lurched upward, making two quick strides across the bedchamber where he grabbed for the floor-length curtains and swept them back, letting moonlight pour into the room. Capitalizing on nature's luminescence to confirm everyone in the dark room's identity.

Jerking his head back around to lay his eyes on his fleeing intruder, William found himself staring into wide, dark brown eyes. A quick look told him very quickly that all his fears were entirely well-founded.

The woman in front of him stood tall, back ramrod straight from either decades of proper breeding, or more likely, an overly strict governess growing up. Her flowing white nightgown reached the floor, but the neckline was stretched from their tumble, revealing a view of smooth skin, the color of ivory cresting across a graceful neck above lush breasts.

She was panting too, from passion, panic, or exertion, he wasn't sure. He also didn't want to waste his time wondering or staring, God help him, as her chest heaved.

The look on her lovely face was pure horror. Slowly, as if mesmerized by William's appearance, so different physically from Robert's, her fingers climbed her neck to cover her kiss-swollen lips.

William opened his mouth. Desperate to try again to calm the situation before he lost control of it completely. Or rather, lost control of it again, he thought to himself.

She cut him off, her voice stiff, with no trace of the passionate, seductive creature who had first spoken. "You must be William," she dropped into a hasty curtsy that had him raising one eyebrow, "I know I owe you a proper apology and an explanation."

She took a rattling breath, her fingers still half covering the lower half of her face. The half he could see pulled at his chest, making it ache for some reason. Robert was a lucky man indeed. Her delicate brows were dark, shaped, and graced a face that looked as if it had been carved from marble in its sleek beauty. A round stubborn chin cast in a heart-shaped face that remained hidden as she surveyed the scene she had been cast into.

He could almost see her thoughts flying across her face; the expressions were so vivid, so transparent. He could tell instantly she wasn't the type to be driven to hysterics. Drawing a deep breath, William patiently for her to come to a final resolve, watching that lovely face flutter with emotion.

William was having a hard time forgetting the feel of her body twisted into his. Physically William shook himself free of the scalding memories and stomped out the remaining fire coursing through his body.

Slowly the horror of her mistake subsided from her expression, replaced with the pink flush of embarrassment. To his surprise, she didn't falter a step. She almost grew taller under his scrutiny, that stubborn chin rising as she resolved her plan.

With a voice that left no questions, she finally said, "But not now, I cannot be in here a second longer. I bid you goodnight, my Lord."

Relief swept through William like a tidal wave, and he could feel his body sag at the prospect of this night finally coming to an end. He needed a few moments, or a few days, to at least sort out what had even happened.

"Yes. I understand." His eyes were drawn to her slim form as the soft moonlight illuminated the curve of her body against the thin lace-trimmed nightgown.

Her slender bare feet made tiny slaps against the polished floors as she hurried to the door. William walked up to the elaborate four-poster bed and leaned onto one corner. His shoulder burned at the unusual position, but William welcomed the clarity that came with the pain.

He couldn't help but stare after the beautiful young woman who had gone from a burning volcano to a polite, soft-spoken maiden who ran from his room.

What a night.

Shaking his head at the incredibility of the night, William felt his knees threaten to give. William plopped ungracefully onto the end of the bed, casting his eyes wryly over the mess they'd made, the blankets pulled every which direction.

Lady Juliet hesitated with a single step to go, glancing back at him, her swirling dark amber locks caressing the exposed skin of her shoulder. For just a moment, their eyes met, and a half-smile curled those sweet lips, the same that he could still taste against his skin.

"By the way, my name is Juliet," she said softly, her eyes smiling at him as she turned back to go. Her pale hand reached for the large brass doorknob to make her exit, only to be suddenly shoved hard back into the room by the force of his bedroom door being opened inwards from the hall.

Juliet went sprawling to the floor, her gown fluttering up to reveal trim legs up to her knees. She landed with a thud as William automatically sprung from the bed to aid her, dragging his eyes from the slight of his best friend's fiancé's limbs.

He gripped her shoulders in the dimly cast light, kneeling behind her to get her feet back under her. It was then he realized how light the room had become.

William couldn't move at first, as he noticed the warm candlelight now circling the pair of them on the floor. He knew in his heart that the door opening, coupled with the newly lit room, could mean only one thing.

They had been caught.

CHAPTER TWO

Not just caught, but as William's eyes adjusted, he looked up at a petite young woman towering over them with her mouth hanging open. They had been captured by *Marian Wains*, Robert's eldest sister, and truthfully, one of William's favorite people.

When William was an only child, with his parents otherwise engaged, Robert's family had been his second home, making Marian, Robert, and their youngest sister Laura, the only siblings he had ever been blessed with.

Beyond the initial slack-jawed expression on Marian's face, the burning glare he was currently being pinned down by rivaled any punch he'd ever taken.

"Juliet? William? What's going on?" Her steady voice betrayed nothing, but her light eyes continued to hold him pinned to the floor. The question hung in the air, twirling between them like the seeds of a dandelion.

With a breathy snort out of her delicate nostrils, Marian fluttered her lashes shut. "I heard Juliet's voice and thought-," she hesitated, "Well, I'm not sure what I thought, but not this."

While Marian held the candle with one hand, the other pointed at first Juliet, then William in a palatable move of disapproval.

William's legs finally seemed to be working again. He rose with a slight grunt, gently pulling Lady Juliet to her feet after him. He meant to let go of her as soon as she was standing, but his hands lingered just a half a second too long, and when he removed them, they tingled slightly at the loss of contact.

Guiltily, William stepped back, wiping his suddenly sweating hands on his thighs as he put more distance between himself and both ladies. Dejected, William realized he was about to be in a significant amount of trouble. Robert's smiling blonde face flashed in his mind, as did his ferocious right hook.

Marian watched him like a hawk, sharp eyes easing over his face. William could practically see the speech she was composing in her head. Ever polite, ever elegant, it had been Marian who kept him and Robert in line all those years. Her speeches as to his inability to be a proper gentleman had been lengthy.

He could see her composing another, damned if they weren't both adults. Based on his suspicions, it would be lengthy, it would be painful, and he would have to sit and listen to every word.

But perhaps, at the end of it, Marian might come out an ally instead of an instigator. William knew from experience that she could be swayed. Or at least bribed. Taking a deep breath, he settled a polite smile on his lips. Perhaps her finding them wasn't the worst possible outcome for any of them.

William stepped towards Marian; he was ready to take his punishment, especially if it meant these two ladies would be out of his room, and he would be able to finally crawl into bed and put this ridiculous day to rest.

"Marian, please understand. This is a simple misunderstanding." William looked between the dark-headed beauty who had crawled into his bed and the tiny, fair woman he loved like a sister. Neither moved nor even breathed as he wracked his mind for the right way to explain how she had just found him in bed with an untouchable young gentlewoman.

William tried to catch Juliet's downcast eyes, to beg her to give that explanation she had mentioned earlier a try right now. But she seemed transfixed again, staring at her bare toes just peeking out the bottom of her nightgown. Marian looked from one to the other and back again, clearly desiring a more detailed response.

Marian crossed her arms over her robed chest, "A misunderstanding William? I know you think you have a way with ladies, but this is Juliet Sonders of Greystone. The same Juliet, who is Robert's fiancée! What on earth are you thinking?"

William cringed away, not just from the implication, but the volume of her voice cutting through the quiet of the manor's upstairs hall. He held out his hands, trying to find a way to quiet her, but without garnering more of her ire.

It didn't work, and William saw those perfect, fair arched brows rise a deadly fraction. A sure sign that her speech on his apparent lack of decency and misuse of gentlemanly charms was quickly on its way.

"It is my fault, Marian. Please," Juliet suddenly broke in, that raspy voice, solid as stone, cut between William and Marian.

Juliet stepped forward, facing down the stern-faced blonde woman who was effectively blocking her escape from William's room. With a smile, Juliet reached out, gripping one of Marian's hands in her own.

"This was all my doing, don't be upset with -," Juliet turned back to him for a quick look, "William. It was such a horrible idea in the first place. I'm dreadfully embarrassed by all of it. Please don't extend that embarrassment by making William a part of my mistake." She turned her almond-colored eyes back to Marian, and William could see the slight flush across her cheeks.

Marian tilted her head a bit, looking hard at Juliet. After a soberly long moment, she leaned to look around the tall, young woman to find William again with her bold blue eyes.

"This is not over, for either of you." Marian pointed at both of them again, narrowing her eyes before raising her candle and turning to leave the room. "But right now, both of you need to get back to bed now. Separately, may I suggest?"

Juliet immediately darted around Marian. William guessed she would've been down the hall in a flash of that white nightgown if she had not run face-first into the broad chest of none other than Robert Wains, the future Viscount of Devonshire.

Letting out an *oomph* of surprise, Robert gently caught Juliet's slender shoulders in his large hand, his face filled with confusion as they stared at each other. Robert was dressed casually in a deep red velvet robe belted around his slim waist. His thick blonde waves were rumpled as if he had been sleeping.

His head was moving impossibly slow, looking from his fiancée to his older sister, to his best friend. Each moment was darkening the fair man's expression.

Setting Juliet from him, Robert's intelligent eyes snapped from William to Juliet and their matching guilty expressions, straight to his sister, who was making an extraordinary impression of a gulping fish, her lips opening and repeatedly closing as she moved towards Juliet.

Robert and his sister shared a likeness, their bright blonde hair was curling, and they tanned easily and quickly in the summer sun. Robert was never one to shirk away from the outdoors, and he and William had spent many, many summers holidays hunting, fishing, swimming all across his family's estate.

On the other hand, Marian had always been forced to wear her bonnet and stay indoors during the best of the summer sunlight for fears of freckles ruining her prospects at an advantageous marriage. It had been a woe William had heard long and often during his stay with their family in his youth.

Other than their fair complexion and intense blue irises, the siblings were very different figures. Robert was abroad, a barrel-chested figure of a man who looked like he'd be far more comfortable on the back of a horse, or even in a boxing match than he'd ever be behind a desk.

On top of the previously mentioned tricky right hook, Robert was a natural swordsman and a horrible poker player. William loved him like a brother.

Marian, Robert's sister, younger by three years, was a petite, delicate creature who had been the bane of their existence when they were children. While she might be a great deal smaller than Robert, William, or their third, Nicholas, Marian needed no man to defend her.

Her brilliant mind and wickedly sharp tongue kept her brother and his friends right where she wanted them. She also used that tart mouth to keep Devonshire, and those associated with it, up to date with the latest gossip and chatter amongst the peerage.

William met his friend's eyes steadily, "Rob, I'm so sorry," he blurted out. All formalities and explanations were far out of reach at this point.

To his surprise, Robert's handsome face turned sheepish, almost ashamed as well. "Not as sorry as I am."

Stepping aside, taking Juliet with him, William noticed that it hadn't only Robert who had joined their strange little party in his suite. Standing in the shadow of Robert's form was the human who William feared most in the entire country. Perhaps the world.

Lady Catherine of Devonshire stood as still as a statue, her tiny figure draped in a voluminous bed robe the same deep, blood-red her sons. Her length of silver hair was twisted into a long braid draping over her shoulder and the eager face that watched him with rapt bemusement.

Suddenly the green shade of the room's walls reminded William vividly of the churning ocean, something he intensely disliked because it gave him such horrible seasickness. Something he was starting to feel here, too, even with his feet on solid ground.

"Oh sweet, merciful-," William began, his hands raking through his dark hair as he bent at the waist to take a long, deep breath.

"That is quite enough, Huntington," Lady Catherine cut him off, her familiar voice ringing through the room with painful clarity and authority. For a moment he was nine years old again, getting scolded for the trouble that he and Robert consistently got into as boys. The woman had boxed his ears more times than he wanted to remember.

William's stomach churned, and he straightened, looking down his nose at the Devonshire matriarch, who undoubtedly now commanded the situation. Robert had released Juliet awkwardly, and somehow despite the space constrictions, they shifted until they were all inside William's temporary rooms. The elaborately carved and gilded door may as well of been a jail cell.

"This is most unusual, William," Lady Catherine scolded; her aristocratic features molded into a mask of cold indifference. "Only you would find this to be an enjoyable way to ruin yourself, to ruin our treasured Lady Juliet."

"Ruin me?" William stammered, his voice catching as he tried to process what was coming out of Lady Catherine's mouth.

Clearing his throat, William tried to speak again, "Nothing happened, Lady Catherine. Lady Juliet simply turned and ended up in the wrong room. It could have happened to anyone." There was a long pause where Marian glared at him as if trying to squeeze the truth from his body with only her eyes. He looked away quickly, knowing it would've worked if he kept her gaze.

Lady Catherine sighed deeply, releasing her son's arm, she moved into the room and closer to William. "Now, William, stop gaping at me like a fish. It's very unbecoming."

"Wait, hold on. *Your* treasured Lady Juliet?" William said in disbelief, looking from Robert to Juliet. Lady Catherine ignored him, pushing further into the group until she was right in front of him, Juliet at her back wearing an expression of dread that must have matched his own.

"Lady Catherine, I beg of you, please listen to reason. She mistook our rooms, which all look the same from the hall. It could've happened to anyone."

"But it didn't, young man. It happened to you." Lady Catherine said, ignoring his questioning and somehow managing to look down at him, even with the vast height difference between them. Even now, that look took him back to being caught sneaking frogs into the manor to scare the governess at Devonshire.

Rolling his eyes back, William found himself avoiding direct eye contact with her, instead of looking back to Robert for his reaction. And again, William was confused to find his friend looking on rather serenely as the scene unfolded.

William knew that Robert and Juliet were not a love match, but his lack of interest was offsetting in the least. A hint of suspicion crept up his spine, but it was squashed as the bright flame of Lady Catherine's candle was thrust upwards, illuminating his face for her perusal.

Lady Catherine was looking intensely at him; her expression unreadable, the crinkled hand holding her candle was steady. "I'm going back to bed. I highly suggest all of you do the same," Lady Catherine said, looking around at the group meaningfully.

Juliet reminded William of a startled doe, prepared ready to flee at the first sign of danger, and he couldn't blame her. William understood the notion completely, but he could feel the air changing, and he waited.

There was no way that it would be that simple. Not with Lady Catherine. William glanced at Juliet, his heart skipping a beat.
No, this would not be a simple dismissal; he was sure of it.

Lady Catherine turned and began to walk out of the room, sliding her delicate hand back into the crook of her son's elbow with a dignified sniff. Bending at the door, she stared straight into Williams' soul. And for a moment, he considered making a run for it, as he always had as a child.

"You will need all the sleep you can get before we negotiate the terms of your wedding."

Robert looked down at his mother, then over at Juliet, who had paused just outside of the bedroom door. Confused, Robert opened his mouth only to be shushed by his mother. Lady Catherine's face slowly split into a smile. "Oh no, not your wedding Robert. I meant William, dear."

"What did you say, Lady Catherine?" William said cautiously. Juliet gasped, her pretty face pulled tight as both hands covered her cheeks in shock.

"Yes, William, you heard me correctly. *Your wedding*. Actions have consequences. I believe I've taught you that a few times over the course of our relationship. Quite a bit more than a few times if I remember correctly, young man."

William felt faint. He closed his eyes hard and waited for a breath. Then he opened them again to see the group still standing there in his room. Still very real. Worse, Lady Catherine and Robert had made it to the doorway now.

"This isn't happening." William knew his voice was a mix of anger and disbelief.

"Oh yes, yes, it is," came the stern reply. "I'll write to the Earl at first light. I don't think he will have any concerns about his daughter marrying into the Mansfield Park estate." There was a pause as William let his chin fall to his chest, one hand ran through his dark hair, tugging as he considered what implications were now quickly headed his way.

With a sweep of cloth and shuffling of slippered steps, William knew that he was finally, at long last alone. He had gone to bed a bachelor, blissfully and wholly unconnected, with limited responsibilities and very little concern about his future; yet somehow, he had woken up an engaged man with not only his mantle upon his shoulders but hers.

It should shock and horrify him, but all he could think about was falling straight back into bed and dreaming away this whole confounding night. Yet, as he stripped off his shirt and trousers and flopped back into the mussed covers, his mind and nose were filled with memories of lavender-scented skin and warm, insistent lips.

***

Marian waited until her mother, still clinging dramatically to Robert's arm, turned the corner at the far end of the hall before she dragged Juliet down the opposite corridor. Juliet's bare feet scuffled against one of the beautiful woven rugs that covered this portion of the manor's cool wooden floors as she and Marian headed straight towards their chambers.

Arriving rapidly at Juliet's door, Marian ducked in, dutifully pulling her dear friend behind, and immediately relit several candles along the armoire's shining top. Taking a large, exaggerated breath, Marian turned to Juliet, her bright blue eyes practically glowing in the dim light.

"Juliet, what were you thinking?" Marian hissed. Her lovely, petite features were worried and clenched. Juliet walked to her bed, dazed, folding one leg under herself so she could curl on the edge.

None of this felt real. Juliet reached out, gripping the rounded bedpost in her hands. Heart pounding, Juliet raised her eyes to meet Marian's inquiry.

"I swear, I heard Amelia say that Robert would be in the green suite, and William in the blue. I had no idea that they had switched." Her voice sounded dejected, almost melancholy as she stared down the path she had set herself on with just one stupid idea.

She saw Marian's face soften marginally. "You were supposed to be in Robert's room. Do you have any idea how long I waited outside of there to discover you? Only to realize that the only person out for a midnight walk was my insomnia ridden Mama."

"Not only was I waiting forever out there, but I had to do it practically hiding behind that coat of arms," Marian exclaimed in a loud whisper, her voice vibrating as the humor of the situation broke through her serious nature.

"I've probably caught a chill because of you. And got far too familiar with Sir Ironarms out there." She crossed her arms and tried to glare at Juliet but failed as a manic grin broke out on her small, curling lips

Juliet dropped her head, biting her bottom lip hard as she considered the significant ramifications of her rendevous. But it was getting harder by the moment to stay sober, especially once she saw Marian's smile.

In the whole of her young life, Juliet had never broken any rules. And in one fell swoop, she had broken not only the cardinal rule for all eligible young brides of the ton but dragged in an entire flock of people with her. Who would've thought? The irony was not lost on her

"I feel awful, Marian," Juliet said, her hysterics finally calming, "What am I supposed to do now?"

"What do you mean?" Marian said.

"I can't stand by while William is forced to marry me out of obligation! I couldn't live with myself."

Marian gave her a stern look. "I'm not sure what you were expecting. When you asked me how I could convince my brother to keep to the original wedding date, this was our best idea. And it's not as if you and Robert were a love match."

"We might have been. Someday," Juliet finished wistfully.

"Maybe you would have. But there are no guarantees in love. When we talked, you asked for a guarantee." Marian's voice held a chilly quality that caused Juliet to shiver involuntarily. Marian must've noticed her friend's reaction and her expression changed quickly, turning to one of understanding.

"I know this isn't what you were hoping for. But William is a wonderful man. Not to mention devastatingly handsome. When the ladies hear of his engagement, there will be a celebration. Or a riot, depending on who hears first." Marian feigned a faint moment, swiping one hand across her forehead dramatically.

Juliet gave her friend an exasperated look. "You know that's not what I'm looking for. If I were, I would've picked up any one of those peacocks I danced with during the season. I'm looking for a home. A family." Her voice almost cracked over the last words.

Robert had been willing to marry her, and with him came the chance to build a future she could be loved in. If this morning's rendezvous was any kind of evidence, William wasn't looking for a wedding, a wife, or the family she so desperately desired.

"The whole plan was to make sure Robert didn't back out on the Earl's agreement like you heard he wanted to. Not to accidentally ensnare Robert's best friend in a marriage plot."

Marian brushed her hand over her friend's linen covered shoulder in a gesture of comfort, "I know, Juliet," she paused thoughtfully, "Let's find out what my Mother's plan is in the morning. Then we can sort out William and Robert."

They sat in silence for a long minute, both sighing deeply as the weariness of the night settled over their bodies.

Suddenly Marian snorted. "I wish you could've seen William's face. I've been waiting my whole life to startle that man the way you managed to do so within five minutes of meeting him."

"Oh, don't remind me." Juliet groaning, thinking back to the shock and panic that had taken over William's striking face as he had startled at Marian's entrance.

"What did happen? Before I barged in, that is."

Juliet choked, coughing as she looked at Marian.

Marian rolled her eyes, "Easy there, if it was that good, then maybe I don't want to know. He is practically my brother, after all."

Juliet blushed bright pink, glad not to have to explain the heady rush that had coursed through her body when he'd begun to respond to her. The tangy taste of him still lingered on her tongue, and she could remember the hard, heavy length of him against her, pressing her into the mattress.

Juliet could feel her body flush at the thoughts that rushed to her mind. Wicked thoughts that sent tingles straight to her core, where her thighs twitched and tightened.

Marian turned and paced a few steps forward and back, her tiny slippers making no noise against the polished hardwood floors. Juliet watched her with drooping eyes, waiting on the advice she knew would be distributed momentarily.

"Alright, here is what we have to do." Marian sat back on the edge of the bed, smoothing out her nightgown's fabric down her legs, the pinnacle of ladylike behavior, even in a moment like this.

"We keep going forward. The plan was to set you up with my brother, who would've been a lovely husband, father, partner. But the bottom line is that we must get you out of that horrid house. William may resist a little initially, but it is because he's afraid of making the same mistakes his parents did."

"He might be a little rough around the edges, but that's nothing you couldn't polish up with time. And he's still more put together than Robert is, God love him."

Marian leaned back on her wrists, surveying Juliet's questioning face. "Now you have secured my mother's interest, something is guaranteed to happen. She would've adored having you as a daughter-in-law, but with William, she will act as an agent on your behalf, I'm sure of it."

Juliet let out a sad chuckle. "Did you mean to have your mother also join in on the discovery?"

Marian shook her head, "Oh no, that was total happenstance. I had seen her pacing the halls a few days ago, but I thought it a fluke. Now I know that she can always be counted on to provide additional witnessing eyes in the chance we need to hook another marquess someday." Marian elbowed Juliet, forcing a small laugh from her willowy friend.

"And don't you forget that woman may be the one person out there who William truly fears."

"For good reason," Juliet joked back, a smile finally pulling at her lips. Marian smiled back at her, taking her hand between two of hers.

"From the first time I met you, I knew that you were the sister I was meant to have," Marian said earnestly, her eyes searching Juliet's face, "It doesn't have to be blood to be permanent."

Juliet leaned onto her friend's shoulder. "Again, I am sorry I made such a mess tonight."

Marian just tightened her fingers around Juliet's hand once before gently setting it back on the bed.

"Get some rest, Juliet. I'm sure William will want to talk tomorrow. And you owe him that."

Juliet's face became worried. "You've never told them about my life at home, have you?"

"No, never. That's your story to tell." Marian stood slowly, her fingers smoothing the edges of her nightgown. "Goodnight, my friend."

With a last quick wave of her fingers, the ever-proper Devonshire daughter slipped from Juliet's chamber, silent as a mouse and twice as fast. Juliet fell back onto the bed, closing her eyes tight, already dreading breakfast where she'd be faced with both her fiancé and now ex-fiancé. The shame was suddenly overwhelming.

She, the girl who always followed the rules, had gone and made a horrible mess of her life. Groaning, Juliet sat up only long enough to blow out the remaining candlelight before tumbling back into bed and falling fast asleep.

CHAPTER THREE

Thankfully, someone must've told Juliet's handmaid, Amelia, to let her sleep in because it was far past breakfast time when Juliet finally pried open her eyes. For a shining moment, Juliet didn't remember the night before and all the events that had transpired since.

She was simply visiting with friends in the country, one of which happened to be her fiancé. Yet now, only a day after arriving, she had turned her entire future on its end and had significantly altered another's as well.

And she didn't mean Robert. She doubted very much that Robert was that upset about any of this.

Although she and Robert had got along well enough, he had never expressed much interest in putting their engagement into action.

Juliet's stepfather, Marshall Pinecrest, the Earl of Greystone, had taken a shine to the arrangement. The Wains family were shipwrights. Their company produced a large portion of the cargo ships that the Greystone estate needed for their involvement in newly organized shipping investment.

Juliet knew that when Marshall looked at her, his stepdaughter, he saw only monetary opportunities, not the woman behind them. With no other children, and Juliet's mother, Lady Elizabeth, in her forties, Marshall couldn't count on any other children.

Juliet was his best option for making the most profitable and advantageous match possible. The moment Marshall had realized who Robert and the Wain's family was, he wanted to sign off on her engagement.

Marian had warned her up front that Robert was fiercely independent. But after spending night after night on the arm of dowry hungry second sons at all the summer events, Juliet was wholly swept up in the idea of Robert. He had marched in one evening with his no-nonsense words, wide smile, and infectious laugh.

Juliet had never met anyone like him and knew in her heart that he would be an honorable husband, a loving father, and his title would be enough to protect her from the life she would be leaving behind.

Marian had fanned the flame of their innocent, quick courtship, whispering to Lady Catherine and Robert's father, Robert Sr., and within weeks it had been official. Juliet could remember the relief, the day that Marshall had ridden into Greystone, his sneering face as he handed over the documents.

At the bottom, his scrawling signature announcing her as an engaged woman. He had practically spat the words at her. "You're welcome. Glad that you are finally fulfilling your duties as a Greystone."

Shaking the memory off, Juliet slid her long legs out from under the now too-warm bedding and pushed off, her long nightgown falling behind her. In a moment, a red-hot flush swept through her body, remembering exactly how far she had been willing to go to assure both herself and Robert that the wedding would go forward as planned.

Finding a seat in front of her small mirror, Juliet stared into it at her reflection, fanning her heated face with both hands.

The familiar girl staring back at her from the mirror looked worried. Her lips were a little too tight, her forehead furrowed, but a lovely blush was still gracing her strong cheekbones. When she noticed that, Juliet smiled, making the darkness in her eyes brighten, and the little flecks of gold in their rich brown depths glow with possibility.

Unbidden, Juliet's fingers gently caressed her lips, remembering what it had felt when William had kissed her back, those warm lips plying her own open, a sweep of his bold tongue against her own. Maybe she had been the instigator, but she hadn't forced him into that response; that was ultimately his own.

Amelia appeared, her immaculate maid's frock starched and pressed to perfection. With a disapproving glance at her mistress, she clucked her tongue. "Out late, my lady?"

Juliet dropped her fingers from her lips, and sheepishly smiled up at her long-time maid. "You've already heard?" Amelia's eyes narrowed, and she propped her fists upon her plump hips.

"Lady Juliet, everyone in this manor, and probably this county, has heard about what happened last night," Amelia said, her tone scolding. While Juliet knew she was exaggerating, a tendril of dread throbbed in her mind.

Amelia walked behind a somber-faced Juliet, picking up a hairbrush. Even if her voice had been scolding, the expert fingers that smoothed her long dark hair were familiar and caring. Amelia had been with Juliet since she was a child and had been the one person Juliet had ever really been able to depend on.

When Juliet's father had died in a horrible carriage accident when she was nine, Amelia had been the comforting, warm arms that had held her for hours. Juliet's mother had never shown her only daughter a fraction of the affection or guidance that Amelia demonstrated every day.

When the first Earl had passed away, Elizabeth, Juliet's mother, had disappeared to the city and back into the socially elite circle that all but swallowed her whole.

She hadn't come home for months, and when she finally did appear, it was on the arm of Lord Marshall Pinecrest. Marshall was everything her father hadn't been. Showy, loud, and at least ten years younger than his new bride. In Juliet's mind, Marshall Pinecrest was nothing but a dark mark upon the Greystone title.

Marshall and her mother had a pitifully short engagement followed by a chaotic, disorganized wedding that turned Marshall Pinecrest into an Earl. And then things had changed completely. Not just for Juliet, but the whole Greystone estate.

Juliet had been shipped off to boarding school in order to allow the newlyweds to revel in their love uninterrupted. Greystone itself began to slip into disrepair, large portions of the land and assets disappearing over the years.

Thinking of her home, the one her father had made for her, made her chest ache, and she quickly pushed those sobering thoughts aside.

At least her stepfather wasn't here at Lakeview. For the time being, Juliet could try to forget the dark shadow, he cast over her life at Greystone. Swallowing hard, she tilted her head forward to give the much shorter Amelia access to the back of her head as she set pins there.

Amelia reached down to pat her shoulder, and quick as lightning Juliet reached up, gripping her maids' hand. Amelia's gaze found hers in the mirror. "I am sorry, Amelia if I disappointed you." Juliet wanted to apologize further, but her throat suddenly felt thick. The words barely got past.

Amelia's face softened, her fingers brushed gently against her shoulder. After a pause, Amelia gave a tiny smile. "You could never disappoint me, my Lady," she said carefully, "Now, let's get you dressed."

Quickly working her magic, Juliet was dressed, her thick hair pinned to the crown of her head, and she was making her way downstairs. The tea and pastry that Amelia had brought up for Juliet since she had missed breakfast now felt like lead in her belly. She knew she was dragging her feet, but every footfall was taking her closer to the conclusion of a situation she never wanted to be in again.

More than anything, Juliet was dreading looking into the face of William and realizing that she was ruining any plans he may have had prior to her nighttime escapade. Even more so she was dreading the unconcerned look that Robert would be sporting.

She understood that she had put them in an impossible situation, but a small part of her still wished that Robert had expressed horror at the fact his fiancée had been found in another's bed. Instead, he had looked relieved. The conclusion that he hadn't wanted her to marry her, to begin with, hurt her already tender pride.

Worst yet, it would be a face-to-face conversation with Lady Catherine, who was as duty-bound and dignified as any lady in all of England. No matter who she walked into that room as, she would walk out a certified scandal, a woman found in a man's bed who was not her husband.

Finding a way to contain news of her nighttime activities would be the first thing that needed to happen after her conversation with Lady Catherine. Closing her eyes, she dreaded not just the whispers, and the judging looks at the last summer ball of the season, but the possibility that Lady Catherine had written to her stepfather or mother already.

Taking a deep breath, Juliet paused at the base of the stairs, knowing that her future was seated just around the corner, waiting for her to arrive. Raising her chin, she murmured to herself, "I am Juliet Sonders of Greystone, and I make my path." Nodding to herself, she smoothed her hands over her deep red bodice and walked into the parlor.

Immediately, her wide eyes were drawn to the swarthy skinned man who sat across the parlor. His almost black hair was neatly combed back from a tall forehead and below that, a square jaw that had begun to twitch the moment she had walked into the room. He barely looked like the roughed up, the dangerous-looking man she had encountered last night when she sneaked into the guest room.

This man was polished, aristocratic, looking closer to someone serving in the House of Lords than the wild man child Marian had always talked about. She had been right about one thing, though; he was devastatingly handsome. But his tense shoulders under his grey jacket made her wary; reminded her why exactly they were here this morning.

She hoped she would be given a moment to explain herself. Juliet hadn't met William during her short time out in society, but she had seen the way other ladies had acted around young, wealthy bachelors. At the time, Juliet and Marian had looked down on those women, with their desperate smiles, coy glances, and cunning mothers.

Marian had already begun to sow the seeds of a potential marriage between her dearest friend and her brother, but after Robert waffled on the wedding dates, a feeling of desperation she had never known had crept into Juliet's veins.

William rose from his chair, standing with his back to the windows, showing the darkly contrasting lines of his cheekbones and the lowered brows that almost hid his slate-colored eyes. If she hadn't already been transfixed by his lovely olive skin and dark hair, his eyes drew her in like bees to honey.

They were stunning and almost silver in the bright morning light, flashing with an emotion she couldn't place. The corresponding bright white linen of his shirt and cravat only emphasized the man's darkly handsome looks, his thick hair just long enough to curl lightly over the edge of his collar.

Juliet distinctly remembered running her fingers through that hair just hours ago. She flushed pink with embarrassment.

Suddenly, all Juliet wanted to do was apologize, and the words built in her throat, overwhelming her, filling her mind. Explanations, stories, apologies. Anything to clear the air between them and start fresh. Her lips fluttered open, her breath catching in her lungs. "My Lord," Juliet began, pausing just beyond the thick double door entrance.

Robert stepped into her vision, halting her train of thought. He must've been sitting directly across from William, but it was only now that Juliet noticed the man.

Dear, sweet Robert, whose face usually smiled so quickly, looked at her now with a sort of uncomfortable brotherly fondness.

Until now, Juliet had resented that non-romantic affection he seemed to hold for her, but today it felt right. Even if it was a bit sad, his bright blue eyes quickly dashed between William, who still stood at attention, jaw clenched and twitching, and Juliet, whose eyes couldn't seem to get enough of the darkly handsome man. A small half-smile tugged at Robert's mouth.

"Lady Juliet," Robert began, giving a small bow as he gestured to the plush pair of settees in the center of the room. "Please come in, join us."

Juliet snapped her mouth shut, realizing that not only were Robert and William in the room but Lady Catherine as well. The older woman was dressed for the day in a stylish gown of pale green, emphasizing the light tones of her eyes and the softness of her still perfect skin.

And while she didn't smile or greet her, Juliet had a suspicion that Lady Catherine spent the moments that she crossed the room carefully evaluating her every move.

Juliet dropped into a full curtsy, bowing her chin to Lady Catherine until the older woman politely cleared her throat, and said, "Please sit, Lady Juliet, we have much to discuss, and I'd like to get started."

Juliet sat quickly, her red dress pooling around in a way that she hoped would make her appear voluminous and powerful, instead of the nervous, heart-pounding anxiousness that she feared everyone could see.

Juliet returned Lady Catherine's calculating gaze, so much like her daughter Marian's, with her own. She folded her hands on her lap to hide their shaking.

Without another word, Lady Catherine went straight to the heart of the matter, "We were all there last night, so there is no need to keep the small talk going." Both Robert and William sat hurriedly, almost comically. Their faces turned to their mutual maternal figure with rapt attention.

"Much as I believe that Lady Juliet would be a fine match for you, Robert, I cannot ignore the obvious and blatant disregard for propriety that we have stumbled into." A uniformed staff member of the Lakeview manor walked into the room, discreetly dropping a tray of biscuits and tea between the two women, and quickly disappearing back out of the room.

Lady Catherine dropped her sharp eyes to the tea set; the message abundantly clear. Juliet immediately gripped the teapot and filled a delicately curved cup and passed it smoothly to Lady Catherine. The woman who bobbed her grey head in approval. Juliet suppressed a small smile. She was still a Greystone, not some heathen.

"No matter now, though. I have acted as a parent to William for many years, and while his dear parents are not here to advise on it, I believe that you may potentially make a better match for him."

Juliet focused on placing the teapot back on the table, biting into her bottom lip to avoid immediately staring in Williams' direction. Every fiber of her being was desperate to see how he was reacting to Lady Catherine's statement.

Juliet looked carefully up through her thick lashes and could just catch the flash of a pained emotion across William's handsome face before it was replaced with a mask of disinterest.

"Lady Catherine, whatever you think you saw that night, it was a small, easily correctable misunderstanding," came the smooth, caressing voice from William.

"It will be days before the rest of the invite list descends upon Lakeview." He leaned back in his chair, crossing one leg over another with casual nonchalance born of a lifetime of privilege.

Juliet was not as in control of her emotions, and a flash of anger colored her smooth skin as she set her cup down with a clatter and shifted to face William. Her mouth opened to serve the Marquess with a scalding retort when Lady Catherine beat her to the punch. "Don't take that tone with me, William. You may be a Marquess now, but you will always be the wild little boy who ran naked across Devonshire's lawn to me."

Robert snorted. Juliet's jaw dropped, and she could feel her ears turning red at the imagery. Shockingly William remained unmoved as Lady Catherine stood, her tiny frame emanating an almost palatable wave of austerity into the room.

"You will do what is right, William. If not because you respect both myself and Lady Juliet; it will be because I have already written to several prominent newspapers in London to correct the wedding announcement between Robert and Juliet. As soon as I have confirmation from Lady Juliet's father, it will run across the page on every member of the peerage's breakfast table. Can you imagine? Greystone's daughter and the *mysterious* Marquess of Mansfield Park. What intrigue."

Juliet flinched, biting her lip again at the severity of the tone coming from Lady Catherine's rouged lips. In many ways, she appreciated the woman's plight to save her modesty. But it seemed aggressive to her, considering that Juliet had been the instigator.

"Lady Catherine, I don't think you understand," Juliet began, sitting up straight and tearing her eyes away from William.

"It was me, not William, who set this into motion. I understand if you do not want me to marry Robert, but William is a victim here as well. Please don't force me upon him, not like this." Juliet flinched at the irony of her own words, seeing as she had only recently jumped on the man. "I am sincerely sorry for the distress I've caused you."

She stole a glance at the two men. Robert was looking down, his expression relaxed, his shoulders dropped, and his fingers brushing lightly against the fabric of the chair. He was more adept at taking a verbal assault from his mother than the rest of them. William, on the other hand, was utterly still, his face frozen in a handsome smirking mask, his body unmoving.

But those silver eyes flashed with frustration. With clear intention, they rose to gaze at her. A shiver ran down her back as she recalled the way he had returned her kisses; at the way his body had felt covering her down.

"I'm not sure *distress* is how I would explain what I feel." William's icy response cut through Juliet's heart like a hot knife through butter. Juliet blinked rapidly, hating the flood of tears that threatened, making her eyelids tremble.

Looking back to Lady Catherine for any hints at how to salvage this conversation, Juliet dug her fingers into the deep scarlet fabric of her skirts.

"I don't know how to explain." Juliet kept her face cast downward, giving her traitorous tear ducts a moment to withdraw.

"Don't know how? Or won't?" William's voice was chipped, bitter, frown pulling lightly on his full lips. Juliet raised her clear, dry eyes to his, scowling at him for a moment.

"Your time for explanation and avoidance has passed. Step up. Both of you." With a flourish of her skirts, Lady Catherine stood and swept from the parlor with such dramatic flair that Juliet found herself wondering how Marian had turned out so easy-going, let alone Robert.

Staring at her feet, Juliet couldn't decide what to do next. Part of her was brainstorming a saucy reply, which she could throw over her shoulders as she followed the powerful woman from the room. The other half of her longed to stay and talk, to explain. This may be her only shot.

One look at Robert sealed her decision. His face was serene, calm, but he looked back at her with grave concern in his eyes. He was a good man, and he deserved her explanation more than anyone else.

William could wait, Juliet decided; she needed to tackle these two issues separately. And, as it turned out, she and William might have a lifetime to discuss her impropriety.

"Robert, May I speak to you privately?" Juliet startled slightly at the way her voice carried so efficiently across the room to where the pair of gentlemen sat silently. William looked sharply at Robert, and an unsaid moment passed between them.

Nodding, William turned to Juliet, and with something akin to a grimace, he bowed to her before marching from the room with such force that it created a light breeze that caused her skirts to billow slightly against her legs.

Once he was gone from the room, Juliet felt like she could finally take a deep breath and was able to look at Robert again. With both hands, Robert reached out and took hers. His hands were warm and as comforting as the feel of soft leather against her skin. His familiar smile mimicked his warmth with a genuine kindness that made her want to cringe with guilt.

"I must beg for your apology, my Lord, for the horrific way that I've acted." Julie struggled to meet his eyes. "I fear I've embarrassed you, Devonshire, and all of Greystone in one fell swoop." Her teeth sunk into the fullness of her bottom lip as she struggled to hold her wayward emotions together.

Robert's smile flickered slightly at her words, and his bright blue eyes looked her over openly as if seeing her for the very first time. A sad, almost resigned look crossed his tanned face. As if she were a spooky horse or a wayward child, Robert reached out with one calloused hand, gripping her chin with a tenderness that Juliet found herself leaning against.

"I am not embarrassed. You, me, even William, we are all humans, we will make," Robert hesitated for a moment, pensive, "Miscalculations." he finished with another soft smile. He tipped her head up a little so that she was forced to meet his gaze with her watery one. "I will stand with you through this, Juliet. But I will not marry you."

The simple, sure statement almost undid Juliet's entirely. Her knees quaked, and for a moment her stomach considered emptying itself all over the beautiful upholstery that surrounded them. Breathing hard through her nose, it was no use. Much to her horror the tears spilled over her eyes and fell in scalding streams down her cheeks.

"Oh, no, Juliet," Robert's voice was pained now, and he was pale under his tan. "Please don't cry." He frantically wiped at one cheek, brushing aside some of her tears as she tried to push down the overwhelming urge to break out in full-body sobs.

She had never felt such shame, such horror at her impulsive actions. Even with Lady Catherine's announcement that she would be married to Lord William, she felt out of control and alone.

And besides all that, she hated crying. The whole thing, the noises, the splotchy skin, and of course, the salt of the tears as they ran into her lips. And most of all, she hated crying in front of people.

Robert had been the source of her hopes, her dreams since her stepfather had agreed to the match. And now she has destroyed that possibility.

While she didn't love the man, she had loved the idea of what love would be like, what a real family would be like with Marian as her sister, and the powerful and elegant Lady Catherine as a mother-in-law. It had been everything Juliet had ever craved.

And it was over.

Now she was crying to her ex-fiancé about the woe of it. Sniffling hard, Juliet took her hand from Robert, and quickly, roughly swiped the remaining tears from her face. She stepped back, putting distance between the blonde man and herself.

Robert didn't back down. He stood firm, and while she had knocked his hand free in her attempt to hide her tears, he laid a brotherly hand on her shoulder.

He tried a smile, "We both know I would make a horrible husband, Juliet." Juliet let out a watery chuckle. The man had been incredibly complicated during their short engagement, avoiding her and all wedding topics with an impressive amount of skill. She looked up at him. He was indeed one of the best people she had had the pleasure of meeting.

"You would've been a fine husband," Juliet said, a smile breaking out, "Even if you have horrible taste in wedding details." Robert staggered backward in mock injury, holding his chest as his smile widened into a full-fledged grin.

Juliet laughed, a genuine one from deep in the core of her body. Something she hadn't done for a very long time. Robert straightened, and with a grandiose gesture, he offered his arm to her.

"Friends, perhaps?" His hopeful expression sent a beacon of warmth into her chest. Juliet slid her hand through his elbow, and she looked up at the man who would've been her husband. She had lost that now; she knew that for sure. But maybe, she had gained a great friend. Her fingers gripped the fabric of his jacket tightly.

"Friends," Juliet said the word softly, her head bumping against his shoulder for a moment.

"Alright, then let's go find the rest of our party, my friend," Robert said, leading them both from the parlor and out into the sun laced gardens of Lakeview.

CHAPTER FOUR

William was hiding. He would never admit it, but it was the painful truth. It was too early for brandy and too late to go back to bed. Instead, he was hiding out at the immaculate stables that Nicholas kept at the country house.

The horses were good company, the staff didn't seem to notice him, and better yet, there were no beautiful, gentlewomen jumping out of dark corners and straight into his life. That last part was essential to him at the moment.

He leaned his elbows against the stall of an amiable beast, it's long, chestnut face gently butting up to his arms. The horse's velvet lips searched his body for treats or pets, as William sighed deeply.

"Of all the people of all the women in the world who had to be here this weekend. Why her? Why them?" William asked the mare. The horse pulled back to blow a grass scented breath in his face before abandoning him for a pile of hay.

"Even you don't want to listen to me." William drummed his fingers lightly against the worn wooden edge of the stall door. "I don't blame you. I've made a mess of this lot."

"Eh, it's not all bad," came a voice just down from him. Nicholas stood there, leaning one elbow against the stall, one foot crossed over the other, the picture of calm well-cultured dignity. William forced a smile for his friend.

Nicholas Euston was a third son, the youngest in his family. Yet somehow had always been the leader in their trio, going back as far as their days of torturing professors at school. This house, one of many his grandfather owned, was called Lakeview Manor. Nicholas, Robert, and William had been coming here for the summer as long as he could remember.

"I mean," Nicholas paused and brushed a bit of hay from his otherwise immaculate overcoat, "At least it's only marriage."

William let out a sharp, barking laugh. Nicholas and the hay munching horse were both startled at the harsh sound.

William shook his head at his friend. "Only marriage, you say." Pushing off the stall, he turned to face his friend. "Then perhaps you should marry her. This is the ideal situation for your kind of heroics, Nicholas. Save her reputation. Win over Greystone. The crowds would swoon over you for decades." Nicholas' lips curled up in a wistful smile.

William hesitated for a moment. "If that's not enough, you can count on my undying gratitude for saving me from a lifetime of regrets."

Nicholas's auburn brow furrowed, and he nodded. "I understand you are frustrated, William. I can't imagine what you're going through, especially after your father's death, but the fact is, this is how things are done." Nicholas walked closer to stand alongside his friend, one hip cocked.

He reached out his hand and clapped William on one shoulder. "She is a lovely girl. Very smart, shockingly pretty. You could've and may have done much worse on your own. In my opinion, she's practically done you a favor not having to go through the season again next year as a single man." Nicholas shuddered dramatically.

William raised one arched brow at Nicholas. They had made a vow, years ago, that they would each help keep the others away from the altar and out of the casket. At the moment, it seemed to William that Nicholas was failing on his half of the deal.

Robert received a pass, as William would never be able to make up for the utter lack of scruples he had demonstrated last night. Even if it had been dark, and the woman had been unnamed, William was now the man who had kissed his best friend's fiancée.

"There's no part of you that is a bit relieved to have broken your anti-marriage campaign?" Nicholas's voice was gentle, careful.

William shook his dark head, his thoughts muddled by the speed at which things were happening.

"I saw what arranged marriages do to families. Even if I can't escape this one, I'm not ready to be celebrating."

William's greatest fear was becoming the man his father had been, a sullen, angry older man who denied his son his love and his wife her affection. He had died alone, holed up in his crumbly mansion with only his money for companionship.

Not that most people knew that. Most assumed that William enjoyed being compared to his father, yet nothing could be further from the truth. Sighing, William plastered a smile on his face and began to meander down the stable aisle. Nicholas followed.

"Looks like you will be facing the fortune-hungry Mamas all alone, Nicholas. Please, accept my sincere apologies." Nicholas chuckled as they crossed the lush green grass of the Manor's stable yard.

"I'm serious, William. I know you didn't want to marry, but she's the daughter of an earl. She's highly educated, beautiful, kind, and while it sounds like you two had an uncomfortable first meeting, you must give the girl points for creativity.'"

Nicholas sighed, tilting his head back as a cooling summer breeze wafted over the pair. "And all that aside, I like the girl. She and Marian arrived early, so I've had time to get to know her." Nicholas hesitated for a moment, nervous.

"She's not your mother, just as you are not your father. From what I can tell, she wants another chance at a family. Come to think of it; you two aren't so unalike." His voice was sincere, but William looked down as he spoke, unable to meet his friend's eye.

"I'd like to speak to her myself. Alone. Not in bed preferably." Nicholas shot him a small smile at his attempt at humor.

William did have to admit that he could have done much worse while this was not in his plans. Everyone in the house seemed to adore the quiet beauty who hailed from Greystone.

"You are correct. She does seem like the perfect candidate for any gentlemen in the marriage mart. It is my qualifications that I feel are lacking. My father was a poor example of a husband or a father. Everyone tells me I'm just like him, and thus, the life of domesticity will be a poor fit for me as well. It's quite simple."

Nicholas made a face at him.

"So what are you going to do? Keep attending balls when it pleases you, flirting with society, and then going off to hide at Mansfield Park when things get too serious? You can't hide forever. You speak about changing the pattern in your family yet continue to follow exactly in your father's footprints."

William was startled at the seriousness in his usually lighthearted friends' voice.

"You and me, William, we didn't get the family experience growing up, not like Marian or Robert. I know how intimidating it can be."

William nodded silently. He had spent much of his youth alone, the child of two horrendously mismatched people who never attempted to make their relationship work. Marriage was a matter of money, titles, and heirs. Emotions had no part in the arrangement.

Nicholas, on the other hand, had been tragically orphaned before he left the nursery. With his brothers, both significantly older than him, Nicholas had spent much of his youth alone except for his doting grandfather, Arthur Euston, Duke of Cullor.

"But that doesn't mean you can just close up every time something comes your way. I know you didn't want this girl in your life, but maybe fate is setting you onto a new path. It would be cruel to cast that path aside. And even crueler to set her aside, even after her misunderstanding."

William slowed to a halt, the garden surrounding them in the last brilliant blooms of the summer. He let his eyes sweep the familiar yard at Lakeview. "Thank you, Nicholas. I will try to be more open-minded. And yes, I need to speak with her myself."

"Good, walk back to the manor with me," Nicholas requested, pushing his hands into his pant pockets. He turned to stroll back down the way he had come. It was time to talk to the woman who had turned his world upside down.

William walked; his mind filled with visions of his new, *almost* fiancée. Her sharp, fiery dark eyes entrapped him this morning while Lady Catherine had given him his life sentence. She had been dressed in a dark red, one of his favorite colors, and that dress had highlighted every inch of her incredible alabaster skin.

And while those full, soft lips had been kept a safe distance from his own, he had had to catch himself every time she spoke, to be sure that he was listening to what she was saying, not just staring at the way her mouth looked.

She had tried to free him from this mess, taking responsibility for her actions, even while facing down the ominous Lady Catherine. He had almost been moved to go to her at that moment, her pain and confusion so sharp.

William had fisted his hands, letting his short nails dig into his palms to stay still and away from the lovely woman who was trying to sort out the situation she had caused. It had shocked him to his core that he had been driven to comfort her; his chest had ached to watch her struggle to explain herself.

Yet, as soon as she had asked for Robert, he had fled like a coward. He knew that they needed to talk, but he had wanted her to summon him, as silly as it might sound, first. This rush of protective behavior, and now an embarrassing bout of jealousy, confused William to no end.

It had been a misunderstanding. Those kisses, the noises she made in her throat as he melted into her body, those were not for him.

He and Nicholas climbed up the smooth limestone steps of the terraced garden space and quickly found themself face to face with Marian and Juliet. The ladies were sitting together atop a small stone bench and immediately launched to their feet. Juliet immediately dropped into well-meaning curtsies at their approach, with a sour-faced Marian following suit shortly after.

William knew that Marian would never have given him such a formal greeting had her friend not done it first, which made him grin. That smile widened as they both straightened, and he realized how significant the height difference was between the two women.

Marian was a tiny slip of a human being, her beautifully delicate features a mask for the iron that bound her together. But again, William found his eyes drawn to Juliet the moment she rose from her curtsy. Juliet was slender, much taller than her friend, with gentle curves that filled out her red dress, her breasts pressed tightly against the bodice of her gown, and while her long, graceful looking arms crossed her torso, he remembered from the night before how she had felt pressed up against him.

He blinked rapidly, bringing himself back to the moment. Quickly trying to forget precisely how lovely it had felt to have those curving hips cradle him and how her long legs had wound around his body to pull him in closer.

"Ladies. How nice to see you," Nicholas greeted the pair, returning their curtsy with a quick bow of his own. William stood utterly still, wrangling in his emotions. Nicholas' eyes begged him to do something, anything.

"Nice day for a walk." He blurted the words out, desperate to fill the void of silence but immediately regretting the strange and nonsensical comment. It was cloudy, and the end of summer chill was fresh upon the breeze that blew around them.

Luckily, or perhaps not so much, for William, Marian was there to help cover his moment of lunacy. She had coughed gently into her hand at his statement but regained her composure quickly.

"Oh yes, a very nice day," She answered, face alight with humor. "Juliet was just telling me how she wanted to go on a walk before we enjoy our luncheon with the newest guest arrivals."

William caught a quick, subtle narrowing of Juliet's eyes before a non-committing smile curved her lips. "Erm, yes, of course. That is precisely what I was saying, my Lord," Juliet nodded.

William fought the urge to roll his eyes as he realized the plan being put into place.

Dryly, obediently, he asked, "Would you like to accompany me on a short stroll, Lady Juliet?"

"She'd be delighted," Marian said, urging her friend forward with a little shove. It struck a chord of laughter in William as he caught the pained look Juliet had sent to Marian.

***

Juliet was glaring at Marian as hard as she could manage. The tall, solemn-faced Marquess stood like a statue waiting for her response.

"Yes. *Delighted*." Juliet clenched her teeth in what she hoped would pass as a smile.

"Well, that settles that. Nicholas, escort me back upstairs please, I believe these two are past the point of a chaperone." Marian grinned widely as Nicholas stepped up beside her, and they continued their ascent to the manor. Juliet wished she could stick her tongue out at her friend.

Rolling her eyes at Marian's departing back, Juliet suddenly felt very exposed. She looked around them, but other than William, they were alone in the gardens. Not even a servant in sight. The midday light peering through the haze of English clouds illuminated Lakeview's rolling landscape.

The grass was still a dark, lush green gifted by a wet, rainy summer, but hues of orange and yellows had stolen onto the edges of the tall ash tree's leaves which filled the land with shade. Of course, the namesake of Lakeview was a vividly colored body of water occupying the rest of the view from the manor. While it was far too cold to swim in, Juliet had delighted in watching the graceful swans glide across the water.

Nicholas explained to Juliet, just out of view of the manor was a small pair of cottages where some of the staff made their home. While they were permitted to live in the small village just outside of the Duke's land, many chose to reside here as they had done for generations. Juliet understood their inclination. Life at Lakeview was refreshing to the soul.

Ignoring William's heavy gaze on her face, she sent one more pleading look after her friend, but Marian never looked back. Her sweet voice filling the air as Nicholas walked alongside the woman, hunched over a bit in order to hear what she was saying.

Although not as broad, Nick was nearly as tall as the Marquess, his body more racehorse to William's workhorse. But regardless, he dwarfed Marian's petite figure as they wound their way back to the upper gardens where Juliet knew Lady Catherine and a few guests would all be gathering.

Once alone, Juliet and William stared, each waiting for the other to begin. Juliet, who had never had a problem once expressing herself, suddenly found herself struck silent. Standing there in the grey glare of the day, Juliet felt like she almost had to squint up at William.

He was taller than she remembered, his square chin around her eye level. His body was strong, solid, with broad shoulders and a narrow, fit waist. He wore his height and weight with elegance, a man in control of his body.

Heavy, straight brows contributed to his sullen demeanor. Juliet vividly remembered those powerful lips against hers last night. Today they were flat, thinned as if tasting something bitter. Smooth, close-shaven, strong cheekbones and a slightly arched nose and hair that curled neatly at the nape of his neck.

She could never forget this face now. Seeing him in the shadows of the night had shocked her but also entranced her. After all, he was the first man she had ever kissed.

Finally, William gave a soft, breathy sigh through his nose and turned and walked a few steps off the path and into the pillowy green of the garden. Juliet hurried to catch up with his long strides, a little miffed that she was being left behind.

Reaching him as the man stopped at the edge of the large centerpiece fountain, Juliet glared up at him, her cheeks flushed from the cool breeze, and her simmering temper. "Excuse me, Lord William," Juliet said. When the man didn't move or even turn to address her, she got louder. "Excuse me."

William turned abruptly, and Juliet realized very quickly that she was no longer in charge of this conversation. His face looked as if it belonged here in the statue garden, carved from marble and utterly still. He stared at her as if one might stare at a bug in their path, with such heavy disapproval at its existence, or the fact it had bothered to get in his way.

Her stomach clenched again, and her flush disappeared, replaced by a pale, frightened expression. Swallowing hard, Juliet began the conversation she had been preparing since this morning, the one that she knew she owed him.

"My Lord, I want to apologize for last night." Juliet pulled her shoulders back, and although her chin quivered a little under his gaze, she did not shrink away. "I made a poor decision regarding my own future, and now it is going to change the course of yours."

"That's one way to put it," he said curtly.

"Please, let me speak." Juliet's voice was confident even as her stomach flipped over.

William's dark eyebrows shot up, the wind had loosened his carefully combed hair, and a few strands fell forward over his forehead. Juliet thought for a moment that this tiny imperfection made him all the more handsome. A bit more like the man she had met the night before. She pushed onwards.

"I understand that Lady Catherine will not budge on her decision, but I propose that we discuss this future predicament as if two friends, instead of two strangers. I feel that a certain level of commonality will only aid in our ability to find an amicable solution."

William Huntington, the Marquess of Mansfield Park, had no idea what to say. This lovely creature, who had climbed into his bed last night and started the beginnings of a sensational scandal, she was asking him to speak frankly with him. The whole idea was preposterous to him, but he kept that pressed deeply down. Better not to make her think she was being made into a joke.

In truth, the bastard in him was enjoying her apology, enjoying the chance to watch the emotions flit across her beautiful face as she struggled to find a way to talk to him. For as bold as she had been in a nightgown, this young woman was as uncertain and confused as he felt inside. It warmed his heart, and he could not help but tease her just a little.

"Lady Juliet, are you saying you'd like me to speak frankly? We have already shared a bed, even if it was an accident. Why not speak candidly about our situation?"

Juliet felt her whole face blush this time, and she cursed her alabaster skin that would betray her every reaction to his words. Sniffling, Juliet took a deep breath, filling her lungs.

"Perfect. Thank you, Lord William."

"On that note, let's begin with calling me just William." William took a step towards her. "I think we can do away with honorifics and formalities."

Juliet nodded; a few tendrils of her own dark hair were loose and swept across her face. Pressing them back with a huff, Juliet said, "And I'm simply Juliet."

"It's nice to meet you, *Juliet*. Again. Since we didn't get to make full introductions last night." To her surprise, William's face creased in a sensual smile, one that made her heart stutter as she stared up into his face.

"I mean to explain myself, William because I don't want you to have any of the wrong ideas about me." Juliet clenched her hands, willing herself to get the story out, tell him everything she could, and quickly. Looking down, uncomfortable at how ridiculous she knew her story would sound.

"I heard a rumor that Robert was looking to delay the wedding another year. He had business to attend to and had written to my stepfather about pushing the date. I knew that my stepfather would agree to it."

Not willing to risk a look at the man in front of her, Juliet rushed on. "I couldn't do that; I needed the wedding to go forward as planned."

A cold tingle dripped down William's spine. There was usually only one reason women were looking to expedite weddings, and that would be a whole new problem for him and his new potential wife. But her story went on, and he listened keenly.

"I knew that if I was discovered in Robert's rooms, or even in his arms," Juliet turned a brilliant shade of pink at these words, "I-I knew that Lady Catherine would insist upon the earlier wedding date to cover up any potential scandal."

Juliet raised her dark eyes to his; they were filled to the brim with longing and desperation. "I want you to understand, I am an honorable woman, and I would've made Robert an excellent wife."

William was struck silent again; this girl was always doing that to him. His brows were low as he stepped up to her, their bodies only inches apart.

"But do you do mean to marry me, Juliet?" he murmured. With the quiet of the garden surrounding him, his words seemed to echo around them, reverberating through her body. Searching his face, Juliet gave him the answer he was dreading the most.

"I have to." Juliet opened those full lips again, obviously looking to discuss the subject further, when William stepped back sharply, leaving her hand hanging mid-air.

"You have to?" William asked again, suspicion lacing his low voice. "What aren't you telling me, Juliet?" Again, a cloud of suspicion seemed to surround them. From his own time out in society, women typically only moved up wedding dates to validate the children that were born into that family. If Juliet were indeed pregnant, that would change things altogether. At least he believed it would.

Juliet had caught onto the implication, and she turned a pasty white under a flaming blush. She followed his retreat, stepped up against his body, her finger jabbing into the hard planes of his chest.

"I made a grave error in judgment last night, but please understand that my integrity remains intact. And now that we have gotten a chance to get to know each other more, you don't have to worry about anything like last night ever happening again."

Her dark eyes glared into his with disdain, even as the heat from his body seemed to surround her. The soft scent of sandalwood and shaving cream invaded her nostrils as she boldly held her body against his, her anger heating her blood.

William almost smiled at her response, not just at the relief that he would not be parenting another man's child, but at the reappearance of the passionate woman who had charged into his life last night. The demure, soft-spoken lady from this morning made him nervous.

A voice rang out from above. Lady Catherine's was calling her name. Dropping a quick curtsy, Juliet began to walk back up to the main house to appease Lady Catherine's request from above.

"Goodbye, William," she said quietly over her shoulder.

He did not answer but instead stared at the elegant length of her neck as she made her way back up to the main party. That had not gone to plan at all, and now he feared he had made things even worse.

CHAPTER FIVE

When Juliet made her way up to the bright, sun-filled porch, Lady Catherine was waiting for her. With surprising strength, the older woman quickly gripped Juliet by the elbow and marched her right into a small circle of women, all of whom were sipping drinks and whispering amongst themselves. These must be the latest arrivals for Nicholas' summer ball.

"This is the young lady I was just telling you about," Lady Catherine said loudly, presenting Juliet to the group.

Juliet smiled kindly, looking from face to face and seeing several she briefly recognized from parties this past summer. She had only been out in society for part of the year, and it had not gone very smoothly. It was doubtful that any of these women would remember her, even with her prominent family.

To her surprise, one woman, a lady in her thirties with a rather flashy yellow hat across her silver and blonde curls, immediately leaned in.

"Well, of course we know Lady Juliet. She made quite the splash this spring, even if she was only in town for a few weeks."

Juliet looked at her, surprised. She didn't remember much other than the overwhelming nature of the seasons' biggest parties and events.

"My name is Eloise Jones. We met at Lord Hasselten's house the first weekend of the season." She held her hand out for a brief, kind embrace.

Juliet flushed, taking the soft hand that was held out to her. Stuttering, Juliet tried to bring up any memory of the smiling face. "I'm very sorry, my Lady, I have a poor memory," Juliet got out. Immediately Eloise waved her comments aside.

"Oh, don't be silly. I have a son a few years younger than you; the poor boy couldn't keep his eyes off you or his mouth shut about you for weeks. I'm sure he would've asked you to dance a hundred times over if he had had the chance."

Juliet blushed prettily as the ladies around them chuckled. Introductions were quickly made to the rest, and while Eloise seemed to be the leader, several others looked at Juliet with envy and rapt curiosity.

A few of the younger ladies in their group eyed her with a sharp edge of competition, and their mothers looked on eagerly, waiting for any signs of gossip or knowledge to lock away. Juliet couldn't help but wonder if Lady Catherine had already disclosed that she might be marrying the Marquess, not her own son.

While they hadn't officially announced her marriage to Robert yet, Juliet was sure that some people had to have come to that conclusion.

Juliet had loved her brief stay in town. It had been her mother and Stepfather who had sent her home to Greystone after only a few weeks. Marshall, her stepfather, claimed that it was too stressful for her mother to endure all of the societal pressures of having a daughter out in society.

Juliet had followed orders but suspected that it may have been more due to her questioning the absence of staff and items that had always been present in the Greystone townhome in London.

As if thinking the same thing, Lady Catherine suddenly broke into the casual small talk. "Oh, William," she called out to the man who was stalking by, "Come here for a moment, please."

Juliet groaned silently, forcing a smile as the stone-faced man dutifully approached. Steps away, Juliet was surprised to see that his face suddenly lit up into a wide, charming smile turning his silver eyes molten.

Stopping just short of their little party. Deliberately forcing herself to stare straight ahead, Juliet got a firsthand look at the immediate change on every female's face at his arrival.

For the young, single females and their mothers, the eyed William like he was a prized stud on display. And instead of shrinking away, the man seemed to be reveling in the attention, which only confused Juliet more.

Was he the passionate, hot-blooded man she had happened upon just last night, the polished, stern-faced aristocrat, or the charming young man who was about to cause at least one female in their group to swoon any moment? The man fascinated her.

After a moment of silence, Eloise broke the transfixed ladies by reaching out to pat the sleeve of William. His charming smile never faltered as he spoke, "Lady Eloise, lovely to see you again."

Eloise narrowed her eyes, "Now, William, don't you try to flatter your way into my heart. Mr. Jones will simply not be able to handle the competition. Nor will my poor heart." Chuckling, Juliet could see Lady Catherine cover a smile with her hand.

"I've heard that you may be a taken man," Eloise gushed, her eyes stealing away to glance at Juliet. For a moment, Juliet swore the moment winked at her.

Then every eye turned to William for affirmation, the air humming with anticipation of his answer. A glance up at the man beside her sent heat straight to her belly. He was looking at her, breathing deeply, the smile fading from his face.

It made her feel like she was the only other person on the entire planet. Her eyes widened as she almost stepped back at the intensity of his stare. Immediately his eyes softened, and with something close to affection, William's hand gently reached out to take hers. Bringing it to his lips with excruciating patience, he brushed his lips across her knuckles. Heat, sharp and tangy, raced down Juliet's spine.

His lips quirked. He knew what he was doing.

Finally, pulling his gaze from her, Juliet felt like she had been released from a spell. It shocked her that mere seconds had passed when it had felt like centuries should have.

"Not taken yet, but I believe that will be changing soon," William said, looking straight at Eloise with one brow lifted. Juliet dared to raise her eyes back to the group. Every one of them pinning Juliet with a collection of murderous and jealous stares.

Biting into her bottom lip, she worried it gently with her teeth, resisting the urge to pick up her hand and look at it. Could she still see the path that his lips had taken? It felt like a fire dragged across the surface of her skin when he had kissed her so deliberately in front of these ladies.

Her breath left her suddenly. If he was kissing her hand here, he must have decided to go forward with the relationship. Whatever that relationship may be, no man would risk the wagging tongues unless he were serious. Juliet was overwhelmed with relief, and she still felt a nagging pull in the back of her mind at his earlier words.

Perhaps he did mean to follow through with the marriage, as Lady Catherine had strongly advised him. But that didn't change the fact that Juliet had no idea where she stood with the Marquess of Mansfield Park.

When Juliet dared to look back at him, William was looking at her again, this time with confusion written across his features. Blinking, Juliet turned back to the group to accept the congratulations and happy wishes from the ladies all around her.

William leaned close to Lady Catherine, her head nodding as he whispered something quickly in her ear, and then giving a hasty bow, the Marquess made his escape to the main house. Juliet sorely wished to follow him, if not to avoid the fake well wishes that surrounded her, but to simply remain close to him. She felt like there was so much more that needed to be said.

It was hours before Juliet was able to beg off from the lady's luncheon and escape to her room. She felt like she might collapse straight into bed, but the moment she sat down, Amelia bustled straight up to her. "Messages for you, my Lady."

Sighing, Juliet flopped into a plush chair, taking the folded notes from Amelia with a deep sigh. The first was a short quick message from Marian asking her to see her in her rooms later in the day. But the second, it jolted Juliet out of her chair and across the room in seconds.

Grabbing Amelia by her shoulders, Juliet shoved the note in her face. "What are we going to do?" Amelia shushed her gently, as if she was a small child again, before picking up the note to read it herself.

To her credit, Amelia's face didn't give away the surprise that Juliet knew she shared. Folding the note back up, she reached up and took one of Juliet's hands in hers, squeezing tightly, Amelia comforted her mistress.

"It's going to be okay, my dear Lady," Juliet tried to smile, but her lips only quivered instead. "I've got to speak with the butler; please don't panic yet. At least until I return." Amelia finished, putting the folded paper in her apron pocket and hurrying out of the bedroom.

Amelia stared after her maid; one hand plastered to her mouth. Before she lost her nerve, she dashed out after her, but instead of heading down the hall to the main stairs, she turned and made her way to the guest rooms Marian was staying in.

"You're never going to believe this," Juliet said, quickly shutting the door behind her and turning to her friend.

***

William had marched straight from his conversation with Lady Catherine and her bevy of ladies straight to the study for a much-needed drink. He prayed to God that Robert was in there. There were some serious accusations that he needed to answer for. Not to mention countless apologies that William needed to make to his friend.

Walking in, he was relieved to find not only Robert but also Nicholas sitting in the room. Each man looked up as William entered.

"Ah, you made it out of the wolves' den," Nicholas slapped his shoulder in welcome.

"No thanks to you," William retorted, peeling his jacket off and flinging it over the back of a nearby chair before falling dramatically across the unoccupied sofa. Chuckling, Nicholas propped himself directly across, and Robert came to stand nonchalantly behind.

William looked over and noticed both men's faces, as different as night and day in appearance, both had the same impatient expression. It was one of anticipation and expectation.

William slung his legs over and immediately leaned forward on his elbows, his hands rubbing across his face. "Robert. Robert, I need to tell you how incredibly sorry I am about everything with Juliet. I mean it. I didn't know who she was."

Robert's blonde hair, curling in the humid air, caught the light as he ducked his head. When he raised his eyes, a shadow of a smile on his face, yet his expression held a sadness that threatened to crush William.

"I know you would never purposefully hurt me, William. There is no need for any more apologies, except for perhaps from me to you."

William looked at him quizzically, and Nicholas turned to look over his shoulder, confused as well. "After all," he continued, his voice growing rich with suppressed humor, "if I hadn't been walking along with Mother, who knows what would've happened. And maybe far before that, if I hadn't ignored the poor woman, we wouldn't be in this situation either." Robert shrugged his broad shoulders, the overcoat he wore protesting the exaggerated movement.

William sighed, looking down at his hands and watching as his knuckles slowly loosened, relaxed. He wanted to be angry, and he wanted to growl and shout about the situation. Maybe run to the stable for a hard, fast ride on one of the horses. Or better yet, a quick, brutal boxing match with Robert to settle the score. Anything to take away the writhing, nagging pull in his gut.

Or at least he thought that is what he wanted. His mind was full of the way Juliet had looked up at him, those unbelievably thick lashes fluttering as she had stood tall and proud as those harpies glared at the beautiful newcomer.

Her quiet solidarity had won him over faster than any of her words ever had. It was her strength at that moment that stole just the smallest corner of his heart. He may have been distant and a bit severe lately, but it was because of the mantle that had always been placed upon his shoulders.

William didn't want to be the cold, cruel-hearted villain in Juliet's story. That had been the role his father had played in his wife's life. In the deepest part of his heart, he wanted to be the hero. And it was that idea that scared him more than anything else.

He needed a drink—a strong one.

"You can't blame yourself for things far outside of your control. Shall we call it a draw then? I'd like to get back to the way things were before."

Nicholas and Robert looked at each other, exchanging worried glances, and then slowly turned back to William. William realized how he must sound.

"Or rather, back to things being as normal as they can be, seeing as I may be getting married in a few weeks." William corrected himself.

He felt the collective sigh from his friends, and a part of him was offended that they thought he would try to negate his part of the deal. While he might be upset at the nature of things, he would never leave a woman, especially this one, out for the crows of society to pick at and torture.

Nicholas stood and walked to the bar cart, his lean frame blocking the view as he poured them all drinks, his hands a whirl as he orchestrated a small draught for himself and Robert. He made William's last and presented it grandly, more than twice as much amber-colored bourbon in the glass.

"For you, a double." William looked at Nicholas, his expression baffled.

"You might need it. After all, this is the part where you tell us everything that happened." Robert grinned at him; white teeth bared as he took a sip of his drink.

"Start at the beginning, old man; we want to hear exactly how you came to meet Lady Juliet." Nicholas pressed the glass firmly into William's hand and quickly retook his seat.

Both men stared expectantly at William, Nicholas's foot bobbed in the air, counting the seconds that passed, and William considered what damage sharing this story might cause. And what damage not telling them might do as well.

Expertly swirling the drink, William watched the deep brown spirit tease the lip of the glass. William thought back to last night and the passionate, proud creature who had come hurtling into his life. To his surprise, his chest warmed, and it felt like suddenly he was too big for his skin. Sitting back, letting his body sink into the heavily pillowed chair, William began his story.

By the end, both Nicholas and Robert were guffawing, each holding their torso's as if the good humor might burst from them with force. William rolled his eyes, rubbing his hand across his temples, but he was secretly glad the story had amused them. It meant that it was in actuality as ridiculous to hear as it had been to live through.

Robert wiped his leaking eyes on his sleeve, taking several heaving breaths. "You know, the worst part is that Mother only came to get me up because she had heard Marian sneak out. She fully believed we were on our way to discover her in your room, not Lady Juliet." He began to laugh again, one arm across his belly as if the laughter were slowly killing him.

William rolled his eyes. He had wondered why Lady Catherine had been stalking the household at night, and now it made perfect sense. Even though it was Nicholas' family house, she had a way of assuming control, and she would've seen it as a dastardly offense had her own daughter scandalized on her watch.

Nicholas was slowly recovering from his latest laughing fit and set his glass down on the table in front of them. Smiling easily at his brooding friend, Nicholas had to ask. "So, William, which is it? Did she ruin you? Or did you ruin her? Based on your story, I'm not truly sure."

William narrowed his eyes. "Well, clearly it is my own reputation that is in danger here," he said coyly, "Lady Juliet is all but a stranger to society. She may have gotten away with this had it not been for the clever timing of Lady Catherine. Or you know if she had gotten the rooms correct." He winked at his friends. Robert rubbed the back of his neck, his ears a bright red.

Nicholas held up his hand, halting William's speech. "She's only a stranger to you, and maybe Robert. I met and danced with the lady several times this past summer. Just like *you* told me to Robert."

Robert rolled his eyes, throwing back what was left of his bourbon with a grimace. "And you were only supposed to be dancing with her to make sure no one else was dancing with her. I asked you to make sure that no one else made a pass at my fiancée."

"A lot of good that did. I may have danced with your finacée all summer, but it was William that welcomed her into his bed." Nicholas's smooth voice prodded Robert, obviously looking to tease the usually quiet tempered man into about.

William eased his glass down onto the table behind him, sharp eyes watching to see what came from this barb.

The words flew like arrows across the room, and William saw the moment they hit home with Robert. Maybe he had forgiven William for his part in the mistaken identity last night, but the hulking man did not enjoy being made a joke of. And Nicholas knew it. William could feel the charged air between the two as they stared each other down.

Robert was typically slow to anger, but today wasn't exactly an ordinary day. And while Nicholas thrived on their verbal and sometimes physical bouts, William always had to be ready to put a stop to it. Nick had the unfortunate habit of starting things he couldn't finish, at least alone.

William had lost count of the times he or Robert had been dragged into a brawl of some kind because of Nicholas' sharp tongue and penance for public displays.

Whistling softly, as if to himself, William rose to his feet, picked up his glass, as well as Roberts, and walked to the bar cart. Frustrated, he let the heavy class clank as he selected the decanter. By the time he handed Robert back his glass, Nicholas had sat back, his catty grin back in place.

His reputation, they all knew, was mostly unknown as well. While he'd been out in society for the past few years, he had made it a strict point of any conversation that he was not interested in matching-making mothers and their daughters, no matter how pretty, no matter how wealthy.

He had seen his own parents' horrible, arranged marriage and had no interest in that type of life. From his perspective, the moment that he'd been born a boy and fit to inherit the title, his parents had dropped him at boarding school and gone their separate lives until the Marquess' death several years ago.

Even at the old Marquess' funeral, his mother, Lady Claire Huntington of Mansfield Park, hadn't shed a single tear for her husband. Sitting tall, her still handsome face turned up from the casket in a defiant, clenched stare. When they had crossed paths there, for the first time in years, she had curtseyed and uttered the chipped words, "My lord, Marquess," before billowing by him in a flurry of black fabric.

They had not spoken since, but his steward kept him updated on his mother's travels. She had recently acquired an apartment in Italy and seemed content there. William couldn't help but be glad she was both happy and far away. She had never had a kind word for her only child anyway.

His throat suddenly felt dry, and he coughed a bit to clear it. There was one final thing William had to know. His cheeks heated simply thinking about saying it aloud.

"Please forgive me, but there is one thing I must know before I proceed with this wedding ordeal." He looked down at his thighs, already feeling guilty for what he knew he had to ask.

"There's no chance that she was pushing the wedding forward this year in order to cover up a past indiscretion?" William leaned forward, inclining his head in a way that he hoped his friends would understand. Robert immediately did, and the tanned man actually blushed, hard. Shaking his head, he caught William's eyes.

"None whatsoever. Lady Juliet is as pious and proper as they come, and those are my sister's words. She would never lie to me," Robert continued, "In fact, I think that she is most eager to get out from under Pinecrest's roof. I've only met the man once, but he doesn't strike me as the fatherly type."

William settled a bit, thinking of the desperate look on Juliet's face when she had tried to make him understand. Now he understood a bit more, but at the same time, at least her family cared enough to make the match to Robert, that had to show some level of care.

William had never even felt that degree of warmth from his parents. His father had passed away without so much as a note, other than an intricately worded will deeding everything in the family estate to his heir and only child. Those final wishes had conveyed more about the man than William had ever known while he was alive. He supposed he should be grateful for that, but it didn't compare to having a flesh and blood family who cared for you.

Juliet's apology may make sense now, but he wasn't so sure it let her totally off the hook from her indiscretion.

The three of them stayed in the study a bit longer, drawing out the time before Nicholas would be called back to handle some crisis of the social variety. The ball was only days away, and he had been. They laughed, reminisced, and by the time William slipped back out, he was feeling infinitely better about the situation.

Was he getting married in a few weeks? Yes, it did appear that way. But at least he, or rather she had had the gall to at least pick a partner with a similar upbringing and far enough bloodlines that their children had a chance to be accepted members of society. And honestly, the more he thought about it, the more he was sure he could marry this girl and then plan to keep his distance.

Having a beautiful woman on his arm would defer more obnoxious women in his life, and it would satisfy a strange desire to see himself as a true Marquess. He knew without asking that his father would have wanted him to marry a lovely lady to have on his arm, to demonstrate once and for all that Mansfield Park was superior to all others.

In a long line of powerful men, William could not think of a single Huntington husband who had done right by his spouse. His family's history was rife with mistresses, absentee wives, and lonely childhoods. William's thoughts tumbled over each other as he wandered his way across the Lakeview Manor. Perhaps, it was better to marry her before she knew that. And then allow her to drift safely away, just as his mother had.

Finally making it back to his room, he yanked off his cravat, undid a few buttons, and collapsed into the first seating element he came to. Smiling to himself, William finally felt good about things with Juliet. He would marry someone that would make his title proud, he would be free to society's eyes, and he was sure Juliet would be more than happy to oblige his plan to be as distant as possible. After all, according to Robert, she was only desperate to get out of her house, not into his.

***

Juliet was dressing for dinner, her thoughts consumed with the confusing man she had all but agreed to marry. Not by words, obviously, but by choices. Getting the note from Lady Catherine earlier today had only made her future surer. She would not be Lord Robert's wife, but more than likely Williams. And if not his, then probably no one.

As of this week, with the crowd that had slowly been arriving at Lakeview, there would be talk. Already most of the manor was alive with the buzzing of gossip. How had a wealthy but largely unknown girl from Greystone snagged the biggest catch in all of England? Everyone wanted to know.

Juliet lifted her arms as Amelia gently pulled her evening gown over her body. The pale rose number was a miracle of sewing and fabric, reminding Juliet of the delicate colors of the inside of the conch shells her father would bring home from his trips.

The dress was truly one of her favorites. When the dressmaker had brought it early this spring, along with numerous new frocks, to Greystone in preparation for her first season, Juliet had coveted it above all the rest, wanting it to be perseved for a special evening.

She hadn't even had to say anything to Amelia; the woman had simply sensed how important tonight was. Juliet knew that dinner, and every evening to follow at Lakeview until the Summer ball, she would be under close examination doubly so if whispers of her shocking entanglement with Lord William made the rounds.

Juliet fixed an errant slip of lace before flattening her hands against her body, sliding them down and admiring the fine garment. While her stepfather had never been a giving man, he had made sure that she and her mother were outfitted in the most elegant fashions in London whenever in public. In his eyes, the family's appearance was somewhere just below godliness and far above integrity in his priorities. Or at least that's how Juliet imagined it.

"You are a Lady of Greystone, and you will present yourself with every elegance possible," Marshall had snapped at his stepdaughter. "Or you will find yourself without a title to hide behind."

Juliet looked down. She could remember every line on his powdered, pinched face, every inch of his sneer, and the black hatred that had filled both his eyes and her own. He was a miserable human. She pitied him as much as she despised him.

Amelia held up two necklace options for her, each gold with a twinkling of diamonds and precious stones intermixed. While Juliet barely paid any attention to the selection she made, she was thinking how grateful she was that this would be the last summer she would ever be under the thumb of that monster of a stepfather.

Her marriage meant a future, a real future, and no matter the circumstances under which she found her husband, she couldn't wait. It had been the motivation behind her begging for a traditional season in town, and now it would be the reason she would win over William if that were even possible.

Their walkabout this morning had turned into an uncomfortable exchange of curt words, and Juliet had returned to the manor feeling less than optimistic that the man had emotions, let alone ones that resulted in love.

Juliet had to remind herself that love can grow and that mutual respect and understanding were most important. It didn't hurt that the man kissed like the devil himself, and she had found herself thinking back to last night's embrace more than a few times during the day. Her cheeks flushed as she fingered the necklace's metal links, so cool against her suddenly hot fair skin.

Stepping back at long last, Amelia beamed at her mistress, her kind eyes watery as she stroked one pink sleeve with tenderness.

"Oh, my lady, you look lovely. That marquess is a lucky man indeed." Juliet's jaw fell open as she looked down at her treasured maid. "Even if he doesn't know it yet." Amelia finished her compliment with a lusty wink.

When Juliet looked in the mirror again, her blush graced her cheekbones, a perfect match to the flowing gown that hugged her slender waist while emphasizing the fullness of her breasts.

Some might have been shocked by her low-cut bodice, as it did boast a wide neckline of exposed, delicate skin, but Juliet loved it. Her mother had always requested her to cover her voluptuous attributes, saying that she brought too much attention when they were out together.

But here, away from Greystone, Juliet knew that the truth was her mother wasn't ready to compete with her daughter in looks. Perhaps, Juliet wondered why her mother rarely bothered to attend events with her, instead enlisting various aunts and companions to accompany her.

Yet this dress made her feel daring and wild. More like the girl who had charged into a man's bedroom bound and determined to seduce him into a marriage. Less like Marshall Pinecrest's hidden away bonus child.

Pursing her lips, Juliet raised her chin high like the lady she was. Nodding to Amelia she made her way to the hallway and prepared to join the small party of Lakeview's guests for dinner.

CHAPTER SIX

William was standing with Marian and Robert, listening to Marian recall the story of when she had once locked him out of the Devonshire house and forced him to sleep in the barn. All because William had dipped her vibrant blonde curls in black ink.

He was laughing, head tilted back to the vaulted ceilings of Lakeview's two-story foyer. It felt good, the laughter. After the year he had had every moment of laughter, a tiny bit of darkness crumbled from his heart.

When he looked back at Robert to serve the Wains siblings up an embarrassing story of his own, he noticed that both Robert and Marian were staring behind him, their nearly identical blue eyes opened wide. Marian wore a smug smile as she jerked her chin a bit, encouraging him to look as well.

William glanced around. The entire room seemed to have quieted, and most were staring at the main staircase directly behind him. Twisting around, he looked for the source of everyone's attention.

Of course, it was her, William though, chastising himself. Juliet was halfway down the auburn carpeted staircase, one long-fingered, delicate hand placed on the railing, the other holding her pink skirts away from her descending feet. With each movement, the silken garment she wore shimmered, ivory, rose. Her dark hair was swept off her neck, and a coy smile played on her quirked lips.

She was enchanting, a vision in silk, and he couldn't fill his eyes with enough of her. She had been beautiful in a simple nightgown but seeing her wrapped in this gown made his heart skip a beat. Juliet was making a habit of stunning him, and he would be damned if he ever admitted it, but it was enjoyable.

As if sensing William's appraisal, she boldly met his eyes, as if daring him to keep looking. As it turns out, he did. After a moment, he tried valiantly not to stare more at the lovely sweep of her body or the breasts that begged to spill over the top of her bodice. It was useless to try, but he was a gentleman.

Or he was meant to be. Clearing his throat loudly and pointedly at Robert, who was suddenly looking more disappointed about his lack of wedding plans, William whispered. "I do believe that's my cue. Excuse me." Cutting across the tiled room, William hid a smile, listening to more than a few men being brought back to earth by saucy remarks and wary looking wives.

Reaching the bottom stair just as Juliet did, William held out his hand with a small flourish. Just for a moment, he saw her smug mask slip, and the shy, unsure girl underneath peeked out. His heart softened, and he offered her a hand to descend the last step, carefully tucking her hand into the crook of his elbow as they began to cross the marble floor together.

***

Grateful that only a few guests had arrived two days before the official ball, Juliet didn't know what to do next. She had planned on leaning on Marian throughout the night, as they had planned this afternoon, but it had been William, not Marian, who met her on the stair. It had been William who Juliet couldn't keep her eyes off of. As soon as she turned and began to walk down, she had seen him.

He was standing beside Marian and Robert like a somber shadow, his dark suit molded to his frame like a second skin. And when he had turned, a grin on his handsome face, she had seen a hint of the carefree man under the marquess' costume. Her knees had gone weak, her belly tight as she watched him come for her across the room, a predator to her flight filled prey.

As the gilded back across the foyer, he suddenly leaned down his lips just a breath from her ear to whisper to her. "You look lovely tonight, Juliet."

A shiver flew down her spine, warming her entire body as it went. She turned to look up at the man towering beside her, his clean-shaven face a picture of aristocratic power, and his silver eyes glowing darkly, staring at her with open appreciation. Juliet let her gaze slide slowly over his handsome face, from the long straight nose to the full lips that were pulled back a little in a pouting half-smile.

He knew she was studying him, and it was as if he was enjoying it. She swallowed hard, suddenly wishing it were just them at this dinner, instead of the loud, chatty crowd that surrounded them. But at least in a crowd, Juliet would be distracted from the seductive man beside her.

Pulling her eyes from his face, she managed in a tight voice. "Thank you. You do as well." And he did. His perfectly tailored jacket fit his form perfectly. Under her clenching fingers, Juliet could feel the swell of muscles as they crossed the space.

Perhaps he was a nobleman, but he didn't sit idle behind a desk all the time. In the back of her mind, she pictured the wind tossing his dark hair about his face as he rode a white horse across a rich green pasture.

"Hello? Juliet, did you hear me?" Marian's voice crashed into her daydream.

Juliet's mouth fell open, and she stared back and forth between Robert, Marian, and William before realizing that she had been caught openly fantasizing about the man beside her. Forcing an awkward laugh, Juliet attempted to cover it up with a smile. She was sure her cheeks were aflame.

"I'm sorry, Marian, could you repeat the question?" she said sweetly, her eyes begging her friend for mercy. She received none though, Marian covered her mouth quickly, obviously covering up her laughter. Smoothing a hair over her carefully coiffed hair, Marian gathered herself before looking back to Juliet.

"No question Juliet, I just wanted to remark how lovely your dress is tonight. That shade of rose is perfect for you." Marian said. Juliet tried to bury the nervous chuckle that desperately wanted to bubble-free of her chest.

Grateful the conversation was gaining less embarrassing momentum, Juliet immediately questioned Robert on stories of his youth with Marian, especially hoping to tease out any good tales where Marian had embarrassed herself similarly. If she was planning on spending more time around William, Juliet needed to prepare adequately with stories to hold over her giggling friend's head.

Robert was immediately aware of her meaning and quickly jumped to her rescue. His arms flailed about wildly as he regaled them with tales of the outrageous and tiny Marian who had mercilessly tortured her brother, Nicholas, and William any chance she got. Marian played along with them, her affection for both her brother and William evident in every retort and laugh.

Watching them, Juliet was captivated. She had always longed for a sibling. Even after her mother had married Marshall, she had prayed that perhaps another child would mend her family's broken relationship. But no sibling had come, and her family stayed as damaged as it had been since the day her father had died.

Glancing coyly up at William as he watched the siblings immersed in their story, Juliet's stomach clenched. Perhaps this was her chance to have a real family. Sure, they had not gotten off to the best start, but she could not deny the man was magnetic, drawing her to him as if his every word were vital to her very survival.

She had had girlhood crushes before. Being trapped alone at Greystone may have limited her exposure to the outside world, but she knew what it felt like to have her heart skip a beat or flush when a handsome boy would look her way.

This feeling, this was not that. Juliet felt like her body craved him as if being close to him would cure the ache that had settled into her soul after their midnight kisses.

It was true that she did not know the marquess well, but her body claimed otherwise. Begging for her to release her hold on the reins and let her sinful thoughts run rampant, with no concerns for the dangerous ramifications.

Juliet hoped that her lustful thoughts weren't written as plainly across her face as she felt them across her body. She took several long, deep breaths. She skimmed her hand across her waist, to her hip, closing her eyes gently as even the touch of her own hand tightened her breasts and caused her to bite her lip, holding in a soft gasp of pleasure.

Was this what being tucked in, close to this man did to her? Juliet's rebellious mind flew. What would it possibly be like to be back in his arms? To celebrate these rushing feelings, this heat that threatened to overwhelm her careful facade.

Marian and Robert were waving now, seeing another guest they had not greeted yet. The siblings marched off jauntily, the bright hair weaving through the small assembly and disappearing from Juliet's view. Unsure of what to do, Juliet swallowed hard and snuck a look at her escort.

There was no way he had heard her pitiful, restrained noises just a minute ago. Was there?

Amber eyes met silver as Juliet's mind went blank. He knew her thoughts. He had to. It was the only reason he would be staring at her like this, like an overly polite starving man at the dining table, waiting to feast, to devour.

His jaw was twitching, teeth clenched, he tried to smile at her, but it came out a snarl. The soft growling noise was sending heat coursing through her body straight to the place between her thighs.

"We should walk," William had barely spoken before his hand covered her own against his sleeve, and they moved through the foyer and into one of the manor's many rooms. The dark paneled wood walls seemed muted as Juliet's eyes glazed over.

She continued to hold her lip between her teeth, worrying over the marquess' sudden change of scene and mood.

"Are you alright?" Juliet finally asked, her voice small in the darkened room. They were alone. This chamber was traditionally the Duke's office, and save a few opportunistic scones the servants had lit, they were the only two souls inside.

That didn't stop William from prowling the room like a great black cat, surveying the room as if someone may be hiding in wait, his overcoat's tails flaring out behind. Her words stopped him, though, and as he turned to her, she took an involuntary step back.

"Am I alright?" His voice was like velvet against her skin. He walked gracefully to her, sliding one of his hands through his dark hair as he approached. Juliet locked her knees, forcing her face to remain serene, calm, even as he brought his body right up against her own. Breast to breast, belly to belly. *Breathe*, she chanted to herself, *just breathe*.

"The answer is no. No, I am not alright. I was going to spend the whole of the night ignoring you, punishing you for that trick you played on me last night."

Juliet opened her mouth, but William put a finger over her lips, pressing them closed again with the firm, calloused skin. She glared at him over his fingers but stayed quiet.

"But then I saw you, in that dress, with that smile, and most of all, biting this poor, bottom lip." He let his fingers whisper a stroke against her bottom lip, and Juliet's body quaked in response. Her knees threatened to buckle.

"Now I can't stop thinking about it. Nor can I stop wondering what you could possibly be thinking about that causes you so much distress."

Juliet tore her mind away from his fingers, slowly let her eyes crawl up his chest, past the thick column of his neck, and finally to stare straight into his wide, dark granite eyes. There was no way to deny it. "I was thinking about you kissing me. About you--"

With a groan of half vindication, half anguish, William cut off her words with his mouth. "Thank god," he murmured before capturing her lips in his.

The kiss was hard, forceful, his strong hands holding each side of her face as his mouth conquered hers. Juliet moaned softly, letting her lips slide open. His hot tongue swept in to explore her mouth with the vigor of a desperate man.

This was almost too much. Juliet felt her legs give as her thighs quivered; the desire to wrap herself around him, to press herself against the hard length of his body overwhelmed her. As if sensing her dilemma, William caught her around her waist, taking handfuls of her body as he searched her body for what he craved.

Juliet realized her hands were knotted into his hair when he pulled back, holding him to her. A sensual smile curved his lips as he took a step between her legs, practically carrying her as he moved them closer to the parlor walls.

Reaching off to one side, William grabbed for the parlor door, which had been slightly ajar. Slowly, and with great purpose, William shut the door silently, his eyes never leaving hers.

Juliet blushed but didn't release him. His body was folded into hers, his muscular thigh separating each of hers, his hands rubbing slowly, hypnotizing circles on her lower back.

"How did it compare?" William asked quietly, his nose caressing the side of her face as he pressed her body back against the wall. Juliet briefly registered the pinpricks of pain through the fog of desire as her body was pinned between two hundred pounds of powerful man and the harsh paneled wall.

"The kiss?" Juliet choked out. How could he ever ask her such a thing? Ladies never spoke about male performance, let alone to the man responsible. But then his lips followed, leaving a blazing trail of kisses up the side of her neck to her ears, where he breathed gently, waiting for her answer.

"Yes, the kiss," came his rumbling reply. Juliet swallowed, frantically trying to string the words together while her mind was filled with delicious and very forbidden thoughts about the man wrapped around her.

"Well. All things considered, I think it was wonderful for a *first* attempt." Juliet responded, dragging her fingers enticingly across his nape. These feelings, this rush, this heat. It made her bold.

William snorted. "For a first attempt?" His teeth mouthed her ear, but Juliet could hear the laughter in his voice. Trying to ground herself back in the real world, Juliet smiled as well.

"Yes, for a first attempt. Although I believe I would be agreeable if you wanted to give it one more try before dinner."

"Oh, would you. How kind." William drew back, his incredible eyes sparkling as he surveyed her. When he stayed like that for more than a few moments, looking lost in the moment, Juliet began to feel uncomfortable. Here she was pressed up against the wall for this man, suddenly keenly aware how sinfully wanton she had been, begging him for more kisses.

"But...erm...perhaps we should just get back to dinner? They will be missing us soon." Shame slid into her voice, choking her words.

He frowned, clearly worried he had done something wrong. "But I don't want to go to dinner," William said, his deep voice rumbling in his chest. The vibrations from his words and the implications of them set Juliet's finally quieting heart back to racing.

"You're not hungry?" Juliet said, looking at him through her lashes. Barely believing the voice that slipped out was her own.

"I didn't say that," William said, a hungry smile on his lips as his bold gaze was swept across her exposed collarbones, down to her breasts as they were pushed up between their bodies.

Juliet sighed into his gaze; her body felt sluggish, heavy, except for the sharp points of her nipples, which rubbed against the lace of her corset.

With a careful, practiced motion, William ran his fingers from the curve of her waist, gliding over the valley of her waist and straight to the line of fabric over her bust. His hand lingered there, holding both of them on the edge of a blade.

On one side lay what was left of their control. The other was a blur of passion, hot lips, and pleasure Juliet had never experienced.

William was waiting. Patiently, as if he had nothing better to do but to wait on her decision. Juliet could feel the heat of his body and knew that his calm expression was hiding a dark, powerful hunger, ready to strike. Her control over him at this moment made her mind sharp, focused. She could feel every inch of his body against her own, except where she wanted it, needed it the most.

Licking her lips slowly, Juliet gripped his shoulders as if to push him away, his eyes following every move of her tongue. His expression dropped just a little, but his body shifted back respectfully as if to release her when she used her grip on his body to raise her generous hips to cradle his.

Pressing her heat against the burning core of his body, Juliet couldn't help but sink her teeth into her bottom lip again. She could feel all of him, from the broad shoulders to the hard, eager length of him throbbing against her. It was addicting. Now that she had felt him, how was she to let him go?

With a soft moan, William dropped his head to the side of her neck, his heavy breath warming her skin as he panted with her. Juliet felt a smugness settle over her body, two could play this seduction game, and while she had made the first move last night, it was turning out to be quite the volley.

"You are killing me," William murmured against her skin, but he did move his hips just slightly against her, dragging a soft moan from her lips. Even with the fabric between them, Juliet ached for him. Somehow moving against that hard body eased just a little of her need.

"I assure you, you feel very much alive from this end," Juliet responded breathlessly, continuing to run her fingers across the planes of his upper back, feeling the thick muscle under his formal coat.

"Ha, very funny. Bad joke," William spoke into her neck, his words muffled as if his lips didn't want to lift off of her body to form the words properly. He pulled back to look at her, his tousled hair making him look younger, and a bit wild, but no less handsome.

"What now?" Juliet whispered every fiber in her being, waiting with harsh awareness of all the places they were woven together and all the places they were not. William groaned loudly, his shoulders sagging under her hands.

With an unhappy expression on his face, William began to set her down when a sharp rap of knuckles on wood startled them apart. William dropped Juliet the rest of the distance to the ground and stepped away as quickly as possible, his feet stumbling slightly as the door swung open to reveal Nicholas.

The lanky man immediately made a face; his left eyebrow arched to his hairline as he stared at the two of them. Juliet knew that even while they were separated, her dress, hair, and face had been displaced by William's embrace.

"Really? You two are begging to be caught. Again!" Nicholas put his hand on a narrow hip, glaring at the both of them.

"It's not what you think." Juliet began, her hands hurriedly straightening her gown back in place.

"Oh yeah? It is not you two sneaking off with the best intentions to get to know each other better, then spiraling into a fit of repressed passion?" Nicholas looked between the two of them as they looked guiltily back. "You must've forgotten; I am both of your friends, so know both of your stories."

William coughed lightly into a fist. His pallor was a bit more crimson than Juliet had ever seen it.

"Well. Perhaps you are closer to mark than I expected," Juliet said coolly, smoothing a shaking hand over her hair. Thank goodness all the pins that Amelia had tirelessly placed seemed to have held.

"And also, as your friend, I highly recommend both of you get yourselves back to the foyer so we can pretend that I've been with two the entire time."

"Thank you, Nicholas." Juliet moved to his side, tucking her hand into his arm; she sent a broad smile back to William. He had leaned back against a sofa and was decidedly looking everywhere but at her. Seeing her smiling back at him, holding Nicholas back from their exit, William stood to straighten his jacket.

"No," Nicholas said, pointing an accusing finger at William, "I've told everyone I had promised Juliet a quick tour of the manor's library, which is coincidentally down this hall as well. But you, you get to stay here and cool off." Nicholas nodded pointedly at William, who sat quickly, crossing his leg and sending a disgruntled look at his friend.

Juliet covered her mouth at the inappropriate remark, suddenly feeling very exposed by Nicholas' keen eyes. When she turned to look up at the tall man, she was worried he would be upset at her. However, as soon as they left the room, an easy smile graced his face.

"I'm sorry for all that, Juliet. You have to understand that I never, and I mean never, have had this many opportunities to torture William. So, I have to take advantage of every single one I can."

"Oh, Nicholas, isn't that rude? And you never know what might be coming back your way."

That's the best part. Someone has to be having some fun at these things." Nicholas eyed Juliet carefully, making her blush. "Well, someone besides the two of you." Juliet snorted, covering her suddenly hot face with a hand.

"You are out of control, Nicholas."

"Again, kettle, meet pot." Nicholas grinned at her, wiggling his eyebrows as they entered the foyer. Thankfully, it was as if William and Juliet had never left the room. General hubbub surrounded them; merriment and drinks were in high demand.

Across the room, Juliet and Nicholas both spotted Marian, who held a glass of champagne in one hand, while staring intensely at both of them. Quickly they looked at each other, then down at their clothes; nothing was out of place. Nicholas cleared his throat and leaned down to speak directly into her ear.

"I cannot be responsible for what I'll do if Marian comes at me over this. I was not built for interrogation."

Juliet laughed, the sound ringing from her body. "I understand."

Nicholas winked at her one more time, brushing his lips across her knuckles quickly before stealing a glance at Marian. Seeing her come this way, he suddenly saw someone on the other side of the room who needed to speak with him. Mumbling a hasty goodbye, he disappeared, leaving Juliet with a grin on her face.

Dinner was a quiet event. Juliet was able to procure a seat by Marian, who was still eyeing her suspiciously and was lucky enough to have Lady Eloise seated on the other. The older woman left Juliet alone about the curiosity of whether she was or was not engaged with William.

She proved to be a fantastic dinner guest, her throaty voice dominating much of the conversation on their end of the table. It turned out that she completely besotted with her husband. Together they had one son, Andrew, who was now almost seventeen. They were well acquainted with William's family as their townhome in London directly abutted the Mansfield Park dwelling. It was clear that young Andrew was William's biggest fan, even though Juliet wasn't sure that William knew that at this point.

Marian was unusually quiet during Eloise's chatter, and Juliet let her hand drop to her friends' knees to give her a comforting squeeze. The friendly other woman regaled them of stories from London and the insanity, it seemed, of raising a vivacious son.

Marian had spent years engaged to the man she claimed was the love of her life, a Mr. Theodore Conning. As the youngest son of a Viscount, he had decided to take on a commission and choose the soldier's life, promising that as soon as he was an officer, they would be able to begin their life together.

Marian had waited patiently, totally devoted to her beloved soldier while he was abroad. Only to find that when he returned to England, he had another woman on his arm and his ring on her finger. Marian had been devastated.

She had met Juliet just last winter at the theater when her family and Juliet had shared a box. Marian was scrounging up gossip for her blossoming friend group, and Juliet had been invited by her mother to make a rare appearance away from Greystone.

They had bonded between ballads, instantly friends as Marian fought through her heartbreak, and Juliet tried to drag herself through a society still fixated on her mother's antics from years ago.

Juliet could tell that Eloise meant no harm in her stories, but there were still moments like this one that she could tell her friend was overwhelmed. She was now two and twenty, and Juliet knew that she wished to contribute a family story of her own, as the other women in the vicinity were doing, but she had nothing yet to offer.

Juliet assured her that someday a man would sweep her off her feet and give her the love she deserved. But Marian remained unconvinced, always claiming that love was never guaranteed and that she had missed her chance.

Staring at Marian's twitching fingertips on the bright white table linens, Juliet felt such deep sadness for her friend. Sure, her engagement had gotten a bit turned around this week, but she still had a fiancé waiting to marry her. Marian didn't know what her future held, and while the Devonshire estate would never leave her destitute, it was different from what she had dreamed of for herself.

When they had first gotten to know each other, Juliet had begged Marian to join her this spring for all the most significant events and all the most prominent parties that season. Robert had been hiding somewhere in the West Indies, William had been dutifully mourning his father, but Nicholas had stepped up and been a top-notch escort for both ladies. Juliet had immediately adored the slim, charismatic man who had known the Devonshire family for over ten years.

After dinner, the ladies found their way to the parlor, and the males seemed to flock elsewhere for their late-night drink. Juliet hung back, hoping to run across William. Seeing the empty hall and deep male voices inside disappointed her. She had missed her chance for tonight.

Turning to make her escape to her chambers, she bumped straight into a wall made of dark wool. The now-familiar scent of sandalwood washed over her senses. Her hands flew up to catch herself, and easily a pair of large hands caught them. Suddenly those silvery blue eyes were just inches from her own. Swallowing hard, Juliet meant to step back, but the firm, gentle grip of his hands on her wrists encouraged her to stay where she was.

Her eyes searching his stony face, Juliet wet her lips. "I meant to ask you earlier. Did you speak with Robert? About everything?" She said, going straight into the subject. William seemed surprised at the question, and she noticed a jump in the pulse of his throat.

"I did," he answered, and Juliet felt the words rumble beneath her chest where they were still loosely entangled. She didn't know how to go on, how much it meant to her that she hadn't ruined his friendship with her stupidity. Her eyes watered, stupidly tearing up at the stresses that the past day had brought out. All of which were her fault.

A hand slipped from her wrist, and she felt gloved fingers under her chin, forcing her to look into his face again. William's face had softened, and the small crease around his eyes deepened as he gave her small, secretive smile.

"Robert and I have been through much worse than ruining his future bride's scandalous plans," he said.

That got a chuckle from her, and she smiled up at him. They were so very close now. She was mere inches from his lips, and it would be nothing to press her mouth against his. For a minute, those silver eyes went dark again, and everything in her body went tight in response.

Other parts of her body were aware of the change in the atmosphere too. She could feel a warm, tingling pressure in her stomach as it traveled south, making her breath short in her lungs and her fingers tight against his chest.

His Adam's Apple bobbed as he breathed in sharply through his nose. A small shake of Williams' head began to pull away slowly. Juliet didn't break his gaze until he had stepped back from her, and when she did, she felt the need to rub her hands against her body. The air was chilly against her overheated body and mind.

Giving a slight bow, William went to move around her. As he passed her, though, it was his hands that betrayed him, as his fingers brushed softly over her arm as he passed. Juliet turned slightly to watch him walk away, her mind filled with the feel of him against her body.

At the entry to the library, William turned and looked over his shoulder to her. An earnest, open expression on his face. "It's going to be okay, Juliet." Then he ducked in, leaving a befuddled Juliet starring after him.

She prayed he was right.

CHAPTER SEVEN

The first thing on Juliet's mind the next day was the Marquess of Mansfield Park. She felt consumed by him as images raced across her mind, distracting her.

Covering her now hot face with a pillow, Juliet wallowed in her risqué thoughts. When she had thought up the plan to sneak into Robert's room and seduce her then-fiancé, she had known it would be tricky. She never guessed it would end with her being entangled with another man. Let alone the intoxicating Marquess of Mansfield Park.

He was everything that intimidated her about the ton. Yes, handsome, *painfully handsome*, but more than that. He was educated, cultured, and experienced. In more ways than one, she was sure.

His cutting looks and stony expression had conflicted entirely with the warm, passionate man who she had conned into kissing her in her nightgown that first night. But still, she didn't know which mood made the man.

Was he the tall and broody nobleman who kept her at a distance and was worried about scandalizing her reputation? Or was he the fiery, seductive man who had pressed her against the walls of the Duke's parlor?

Juliet let her fingers trail down her arm, remembering how it had felt to be entwined around William's body. She had enjoyed touching him just as much as being touched by him, and she couldn't help but wonder when she'd get the chance again.

Perhaps this relationship wasn't such a doomed match. Physically they seemed to be very well matched, and Juliet was more than happy to continue her education into what William wanted from marriage.

As for the emotional side, Juliet could only pray that it would come in time. Marian had mentioned the chaotic upbringing that William had experienced, that his parents had never got along, not even for the sake of their son.

Juliet understood William's hesitation about marriage. But in her heart, she knew that she craved being a part of a family. Juliet straightened her shoulders and sat up in bed.

The bottom line is that regardless of being kicked out of Greystone due to the scandal or married hastily to William, anything would be better than living another year under her stepfather's painfully strict rule.

Even thinking of him now chilled her to the bone. Her father had been a good, kind man devoted to championing Greystone's historic heart through the dynamic industry changes of the early nineteenth century. His death haunted her every time she looked out over Greystone's crumbling estate or the pain of watching another man steer the family straight into ruin.

Juliet wanted a chance to start over. There had been plenty of interest from the eligible bachelors of the ton when she had come out in society this spring at age nineteen. Still, after attending only a few weeks of events and parties, her step-father had decided that Juliet had had enough of town life for the summer.

They had immediately retreated to Greystone, and again, Juliet had been seconded to the country's solitary life. Far from any chance of securing her future husband. Letters to Marian had been the only solstice. That and riding horses, which always brought her great pleasure. Her father had been a quality horseman, and she had grown up astride some of the most excellent horses in all of England.

Although Marshall had let the stables fall to the wayside since his marriage to Juliet's mother, there were always one or two nice riding horses on the property. Juliet's favorite was her father's treasured stud, Winsome, who, even in his teenage years, was always ready for a gallop along the tree-lined paths that crisscrossed Greystone's vast property.

Juliet missed the enormous chestnut stallion, one of the only creatures on the property who welcomed her presence. Her mother and Marshall were often gone, attending parties in town, or vanishing to visit friends for long periods.

Earlier this month, when Marian had written saying that she had convinced Nicholas to host a monumental end of summer ball at Lakeview, Juliet had jumped at the chance to attend. Her mother had been surprisingly supportive in not only Juliet attending but arriving early to help with final preparations.

Nicholas had been raised by his grandfather, the Duke, as Arthur Euston preferred to be called. The Lakeview property was largely empty, especially now with his two older brothers, the heir and a spare, living elsewhere.

The past week had been a riot. The young women were working every day with the Lakeview staff to polish, preen, and prepare for the ball and the events leading up. Juliet went to bed exhausted but happier than she had been in years.

Depending on the guest's proximity to the country manor, many would arrive and stay on-site until the ball itself. Nicholas proved that he was a charming, contentious host, happy to jump in and lend a hand. Still, he was a bachelor and was quick to find Juliet or Marian when faced with a particularly difficult decision like linen colors or floral arrangements.

Juliet guessed that his staff had welcomed the pair of women who had come in charging, arriving just two weeks before the ball was set to begin and brimming with ideas. Marian had come alive in this task, her laughter infectious as the women sampled the wide variety of dessert items with Cook and becoming a gentle but firm leader in their little party planning crew that developed.

Juliet was glad Marian took the lead; her friend hadn't been herself since her heartbreak last year. It seemed like here, in the lush English countryside, Marian was finding some peace in her efforts.

Juliet and Marian spent days pouring over party details and late nights discussing the gossip that came out of the ton. Slowly more guests began to arrive, starting with Lady Catherine.

Marian's mother and youngest sister had been in London prepping their townhouse for the change in season. Laura, the youngest Devonshire daughter, had gotten a cold; she opted to stay at the townhouse and continue recovering. At only thirteen, Laura wouldn't have been able to dance or attend much of the ball anyway.

Marian had told Juliet that she imagined her younger sister was glad to be left alone. The girl much-preferred books and walks around the London museums than she did ballgowns and stiff dinner conversation. Lady Catherine was dutifully horrified at her youngest's preferences but doted on her last child every chance she got.

During one of their planning sessions, Marian had let it slip to Juliet that she had heard Robert discussing the possibility of delaying his wedding a year with his father. Juliet knew that Robert was overwhelmed by the onset of so many responsibilities, but she couldn't budge for her own reasons.

Another year unmarried meant another year listening to her mother and Marshall demeans her and another year of witnessing Greystone's purposeful decline. It would crush her.

Marian had jumped at the chance to help her friend. Robert just needed a little encouragement, they decided. Marian had written to him, demanding he celebrate the end of the summer event. No excuses, she had written.

He had arrived shortly after, skillfully managing to avoid Juliet and spending most of his days with Nicholas. They routinely disappeared to the stables or into the woods to scout for potential hunting spots. When Juliet, at her wit's end, had finally gathered her wits about her and decided to act, it had turned into a mess.

And now she was hopelessly entangled with William Huntington. Who would've guessed when she left Greystone that all of this would transpire? Not her, that much was certain.

She had to admit that while Robert was quite good-looking, he had not made her body and mind go wild the way William had. Even when she had kissed William that first night, thinking he was Robert, she had been delighted to find herself powerfully attracted to the man.

When William had thrown back the curtains to reveal himself in the moonlight, dark, deliciously rumpled, a small part of her had whispered, *that makes sense* in her head.

Shaking her head against her pillow, Juliet forced herself to climb from the bed. Although it was barely dawn, she was drawn to her window.

Her father had been a morning person, always out to supervise and handle the horses that were his love. She used to crawl out of bed in the dewy mornings to join in. Now it was ingrained in her. Juliet's favorite part of the day was the quiet mornings she spent on her own, unhindered by societal agendas or her mother's quarreling.

Today, the air's coolness created a beautiful and mysterious mist that seemed to rise to encompass all that passed through it. Juliet had selected this chamber for many reasons, but primarily because she was so close to the main staircase, so she could continue her habits while here with Nicholas and Marian.

Now that there were a few more quests, she felt hesitant. Would she wake anyone? After waffling a bit, Juliet strode over to her wardrobe, where Amelia had left out a deep navy riding habit for her the night before.

After years in the Greystone service, Juliet knew Amelia would not be up this early, and she didn't mind. It was nice to have a moment with her thoughts. It was easy to dress, and she left her riding boots off until she had tiptoed her way down the carpeted stairs, remembering how just the night before she had descended these stairs feeling like a wayward princess. She shook her head. How different life already seemed.

William had looked breathtaking when he arrived at the bottom stair, taking her hand in his, lending her his strength as they walked through the crowd of staring eyes. Together she had felt like they could conquer anything.

Slipping through the kitchen and down the still misty path to the stables, she met up with Edmund, the head groom at Lakeview. After her arrival, Juliet had gone to Edmund, begging for a mount to ride during her stay.

The short, plump faced man had taken his hat off at her first arrival, bowing low while he listened to her request as well as an explanation of her riding abilities. The next morning, he had greeted her with a slender, older grey speckled mare named Rosalie, who was pretty, but not the forward, eager ride Juliet preferred.

Juliet had not pressed the issue, but as she returned the horse she borrowed each day, Edmund offered her another ride with another with a bit more blood. Now, over a week into her stay at Lakeview, she knew when she arrived in the stables, there would be a lovely charger waiting for her to jump astride. Not that she minded a ladylike stroll through the gardens with Rosalie, but there was nothing like a strong gallop in the early morning air to clear your mind.

Stepping into the stable, she spotted Edmund hurrying down the hall. Juliet immediately smiled at the man, her fondness for him radiating into the dimly lit morning. Edmund gave a shy smile but immediately set his face downward in a scowl.

"My lady, I had an idea earlier, but I've changed my mind," he muttered, slapping his cap against his thighs as he looked up at her anxiously—Juliet's brows lowering as she tried to make sense of what he was saying.

"What idea is that, Edmund?" She asked sweetly. Edmund's ruddy cheeks glowed at her casual use of his name.

"A new horse got here yesterday. He's a real beaut," Edmund said, his voice flustered.

"A new one for Nicholas? I'd love to see him." Juliet was eager. Walking past the sputtering man, she patted the man kindly on the shoulder.

Another groom, a slender youth who worked for Edmund, led a leggy, dark dappled grey mount from his stall. Juliet's mouth formed an "oh," as she stared at the beautiful creature as it stood posing in the stable aisle, blowing softly out of its quivering nostrils.

"My lady, wait, please," Edmund shouted, flapping his hands at the youth holding the horse, ushering him away. "This one is no good for you. I'll get you out a different one. A better one," he promised, now wringing his hands in front of his prominent belly, a deep blush continuing to tint his cheeks.

"What's wrong with this one, *sir*," Juliet replied, purposefully using the word to soothe the worked up stable manager.

Edmund froze for a moment, not expecting her question. Juliet stepped quickly around him, approaching the grey, she removed her gloves and held her bare fingers out to the horse's muzzle. With incredible softness, the horse snuffled into her, his warm breath making a colossal grin break out on her face.

Looking over her shoulder at Edmund, she beamed. "He seems like a perfect option, Edmund. I appreciate you selecting him for me." Seeing that Edmund was still battling his decision-making skills, and the gentle affection the lady was showing him.

Juliet looked at the red-haired boy holding the horse's lead. "What is his name?"

Not meeting her eyes, the groom quietly answered her, "He is called Sterling, my Lady."

"Sterling," Juliet repeated, stroking the muscular shoulder of the horse. One large, intelligent brown eye observed her curiously, the bit jangling as the stallion mouthed the metal. Smiling to herself, she turned to face the saddle. "Could you give me a leg up?"

The young man holding the horse was blushing red from his hairline to his neck, but he nodded at the usual, casual behavior of an Earl's daughter.

Bending down, he knitted his fingers beneath her boots to give her a soft boost into the saddle. She was seated fully astride today, versus the sidesaddle which she rode in often, Juliet settled into the worn leather, as comfortable there as anywhere else in this world. Looking down, the young groom held the bridle for her until she had slipped her gloves back on.

Edmund was still huffing about the aisle, looking unsure at the idea of putting a favorite guest of his master on the large stallion.

But to his credit, he didn't stop her. As she nodded to the young groom and Sterling stepped forward, Edmund grabbed for her stirrup. She halted, gazing down into the worried face below her, "Be careful, my lady, this is quite a lot of horse."

Juliet nodded solemnly and squeezed her legs around the grey's belly, getting a feel for his energetic movement. She didn't look back. If she had, she would've seen Edmund go grumbling after his young staff member, cursing his job, his wife, and generally his world for having to deal with a stubborn noblewoman who rode around like men.

The stallion was not a casual rider's mount, that is for sure, and Juliet could tell why Edmund may have been concerned that the horse would be too much for her to handle. But luckily, Sterling rode very similarly to Winsome, her favorite horse at Greystone.

Quickly Juliet sorted out the stallion, and they set off across some of the beautiful terrains that surrounded Lakeview. Juliet knew that a short ride to the north was Devonshire's expansive property where Marian and Robert had grown up under the careful eye of their mother, Lady Catherine, and doting father, Lord Robert, the elder.

The opposite way, perhaps a day's ride south of London's city limits, would be Mansfield Park, William's prominent family estate. Marian had told her that there hadn't been anybody in residence since the old Marquess' death.

William had kept the family townhouse in London, and he, Robert, and Nicholas commonly ventured off on their own adventures, procuring apartments or houses as they needed. Marian had confided that she believed William avoided the mansion because his childhood there had been so tumultuous. Juliet nodded to herself at the beat of Sterling's hoofbeats.

If her stepfather agreed to the change in groom, would she be the new lady of Mansfield Park in only a few short weeks? A marchioness? The thought was both terrifying and electrifying. Mostly because of the intriguing man who would become her partner.

William was nothing if not a temptation and a puzzle. But Juliet was convinced that she wouldn't spend her entire morning ride dwelling on the tall, dark, and handsome man who she had dragged into her life.

Leaning forward, she let her gloved hands run down Sterling's sleek neck. The muscles under her hands bunched eagerly, and she laughed out loud, her voice echoing across the empty fields.

"I know, love, let's stretch those legs," Juliet said to the powerful animal as he bunched his legs under them. With a squeeze of her calves and a softening of the reins, they were off, the grey stallion's robust and steady stride carrying them quickly through the shimmering dew topped gold grasses.

Ducking under a far-reaching branch, Juliet was thankful she had left her hat in her room. Today was a day for wild gallops and free hair, she thought to herself, feeling the ends of her hair dance across her face in the breeze.

Juliet leaned back as they galloped into the darkened riding path; it was lined with sweet, scented conifer boughs, guiding the pair of them further and further from Lakeview manor.

This bridle path was Juliet's favorite; she had ridden so far. Lakeview had been in Nicholas' family for generations, and Juliet savored the feeling of ancient tranquility. A comfortable silence enfolded them as the trees embraced her.

Giddy laughter peeled from her as she mentally shoved William from her mind, letting the cool, damp air fill her body with a sense of peace and happiness. By the time she pulled up Sterling, both were out of breath but vibrating with the sheer joy of the moment.

Juliet murmured sweet words to the horse as the two of them made the turn to begin their path back to the stable. Finally, William, and his wickedly distracting body, was the furthest thing from her mind, and she made a mental note to leave some apples in Sterling's stall as a thank you.

"If you keep talking so sweet to him, he won't want to go to work anymore," came a deep voice from her left.

Sterling and his rider both spooked hard, the big horse swinging around to face the source of the sound. Juliet was sputtering mad as she scrambled to stay astride, and by the time she gathered up her reins, she opened her mouth to give her critic a scathing retort.

Except there, sitting aside a deep brown mare, was William himself. Sterling whinnied softly at the mare, but the mare pinned her small, well-formed ears against her skull and looked at Sterling with white-rimmed eyes. Sterling immediately backed off, dejectedly dropping his head to chomp on his bit as Juliet stared open-mouthed at the other rider.

William smiled at her, the picture of comfort in his loose, open-necked white shirt, blown wide by the wind. While he had to be cold in the morning air, Juliet couldn't help but admire both the strikingly handsome picture he made with all that dark hair and olive skin, as well as the gentle, confident way he sat on his horse.

"He won't want to work anymore?" Juliet finally said, her throat tight as she dragged her eyes away from the attractive man. "In my experience, most men need extensive sweet talk to produce anything close to work." She was goading him but couldn't help it.

Alone here in the light mist, Juliet felt that same overwhelming need to be close to him, to know him.

To her surprise and pleasure, he threw back his head and laughed, the rich sound seeming to bounce off the trees and fields around them. There was real humor shining in his face; his eyes crinkled in laughter as he looked at her.

"You make a valid point, Juliet. And Sterling looks quite content to serve his lady," William said, kneeing his mare forward towards them.

"You know him?" Juliet said curiously, butting Sterling forward with her heels. He quickly matched steps with the brown mare, his tail swishing contentedly as the pair marched along.

"My Uncle up North bred him and sent him down to Nicholas since he knew I'd be here. He has some very desirable bloodlines I'd like to have at Mansfield." William looked over at Juliet. She could feel his eyes approving of her relaxed pose and gentle grip on the reins. "Although maybe he missed his calling as a Lady's horse."

Juliet smiled and patted the horse's neck. "He's a lovely creature, but not just any lady's horse." William scanned her position in the saddle, his face pensive.

"At least not yet. I've been riding since before I could walk; it's a little different," She said quickly, blushing as she realized how arrogant she must've sounded. William was silent for a minute, but there was a smile on his face.

"Just when I think I've got you figured out, Juliet, you go and confuse me again," he murmured, but the tone was joking. Juliet smiled sadly.

"I promise there's a lot more to me than a desperate girl throwing herself in your bed. Or onto your lap," she said, her eyes trying to find his as a bright blush brightened her face. When they did, she continued. "I hope to prove that to you someday."

William grinned, his white teeth flashing against the dusting of dark stubble on his cheeks. "We shall see," he said, suddenly leaning over to smack Sterling's rump and launching his keen mare into a fast gallop.

Sterling was immediately offended, and with only a little encouragement from Juliet, the horse went sprinting after the first pair. Juliet couldn't help but laugh. The feel of the galloping horse and the smiling, joyful expression on William's face did nothing but brighten her spirits.

Bent low over Sterling's thrusting neck, the two pairs came galloping into one of Lakeview's fields, Sterling just behind William and his mare. Pulling up her mount, Juliet mumbled soothing nonsense to the big horse as he calmed to a jaunty walk.

William's mare wasn't as pleased to be pulled up, and she popped up repeatedly on her back end, her front hooves pawing at the air as she protested the end to their race. Juliet watched, appreciating as William moved effortlessly with her, speaking to the excited animal in low, soothing tones.

Finally, on all four legs, he maneuvered her over to join Juliet for the final stretch to the stable yard.

They strode along in silence, an air of pure contentment swallowing both of them. The sun was slowly crawling into the sky, and Juliet turned her face to the sky to watch as the last of the mist seemed to disappear around them. Breathing deeply, she tried to soak in as much of this moment as she could. With the ball tomorrow, there was going to be no more time for relaxing.

Turning to William, Juliet meant to thank him for the race and tease him for cheating. However, as soon as she opened her mouth, she heard a strange voice come across the fields. At first, Juliet looked around for birds, as if there was a cawing flock flying overhead. Then suddenly, she saw Amelia, hurrying towards them, calling her name over and over.

Stomach clenching tight, she knew that the appearance of her horse scared maid would only mean one thing. Slowly Juliet turned to William as they stopped in front of the stables. Amelia stopped a short distance away, her face pale, her fear keeping her from coming any further.

"My Lady, they are-," Amelia gasped, halting as she noticed William's curious gaze. She didn't need to finish her announcement. Juliet looked glumly at the new carriage parked alongside the Devonshire rig behind the stables. Swallowing hard, Juliet pushed off, landing on the ground beside Sterling's flank.

No sooner had her boots hit the pebbled path before she heard the voice she had been dreading. Amelia grew silent, and her flushed face pulled tight. She sent a bobbing curtsy William's way before quickly retreating to the manor, peeking over her shoulder several times as she made her way up the smooth hill.

"I should've known you'd be here among the animals." Marshall Pinecrest, the Earl of Greystone, emerged from the stable aisle. His slitted brown eyes crawled over her as his lips wrinkled in distaste. Juliet briefly saw stable manager Edmund appear behind him, the smaller man appearing apologetic, as his eyes darted from Juliet to her stepfather and back again.

Juliet registered William swinging off his mare behind her in the back of her mind, but she was consumed with the man walking across the driveway. He was dressed for riding, but she knew it was a farce.

His beautiful new boots, polished to a mirror shine, had never seen a day in the saddle, nor had his pristine buff breeches. He looked pompous in her opinion, but it was evident that he found himself appealing, and her mother readily agreed.

Squaring her feet, Juliet prepared for the moment she had been fearing since Lady Catherine had left the note in her chambers saying she had invited Juliet's parents last minute to join them for the ball, where they could approve of her new fiancé in person.

Since then, she had been praying that they wouldn't come. But here he was. Juliet was sure that her mother was hidden away inside the manor somewhere, far from conflict.

Painting her face with as much dislike as she could, Juliet faced down the man who had ruined her father's legacy. "Hello, Marshall," Juliet said quietly, hoping that whatever conflict that was about to happen would be minor compared to their past spats. She didn't want William to witness the ugliest part of her so soon after they had shared such a lovely moment.

"That's all you have to say, Juliet?" Marshall said to her, his whining voice cutting across the open air. He was only feet from her now when he stopped, his face pinched. Juliet glanced over at him, taking on his dust-free clothing, understanding that they must've arrived sometime in the night for him to be up and dressed in fresh clothing.

"We should talk inside" Juliet felt Sterling's velvet muzzle butt lightly against her shoulder.

"Don't you dare tell me what to do. Not after everything you've done." Marshall's word dripped in loathing. Juliet felt her temper rise.

"Everything I have done? You came all this way to put *me* on trial?"

"You have made a mockery of Greystone," Marshall growled at her. "You made a mockery of your mother and me." Juliet focused hard on the familiar ridges of leather still gripped in her hand. Her breath was even and quiet, her reactions practiced to perfection. She never wanted him to know how much his words hurt her. Choosing her own carefully, she looked up, meeting his muddy brown eyes head-on.

"I'm sorry I hurt Mama," Juliet said softly, trying to keep this already embarrassing conversation between the two of them. "Perhaps we can go inside and talk to her."

Juliet could easily see the stable staff and some of the gardeners seeming to linger nearby in an effort to overhear what was being said. However, she whispered words that only sparked more outrage.

"Well, apparently, we need to hurry along that conversation. First one man, then the other? Your mother and I have no idea whose bed we will find you in tomorrow." Marshall's judgemental eyes were crawling over her form.

Juliet squeezed the reins she still held, the leather biting into her gloved hands, trying to keep her emotions in check. She didn't trust herself to open her mouth right now, too afraid to cry in front of this monster her mother had brought into her life.

"I think you have been misinformed, sir," came the deep voice behind her. Fluttering her eyes up, Juliet realized that William was now standing beside her; the look on his face was murderous.

Even in his flowy shirt, power radiated from every pore of his being. Juliet took great pleasure at the moment that Marshall stepped backward, his face blanching as he took in the dominating man now standing beside his stepdaughter.

"Lady Juliet and I were just returning from a ride together, and I can assure you, the only bed she's been sleeping in is her own," William said, his eyes cutting into Marshall like silver daggers. "I would know, as it is my offer of marriage that lies on the table."

There was stunned silence, but this time, it buzzed with the ferociously that flowed between the two men. Acting as if it were the most normal thing in the world, William reached over and gently took Sterling's reins from her hands.

"Edmund, Red, would you mind?" handing over their horses to the grooms who quickly walked the horses inside, their eyes cast downwards.

Her chest warmed instantly as the dark-haired man stepped closer to her and somehow seemed to tower over Marshall. Not only in proper height, but in the way that he held himself. Marshall watched with a keen eye, taking in the proximity of the Marquess to Juliet, as well as the beginnings of breakfast chatter behind him at the manor. It would be swarming with the guests soon, and there would be no way to explain publicly berating his stepdaughter.

William extended a hand, "I'm William Huntington, Marquess of Mansfield Park. I take it you are Marshall Pinecrest."

Juliet noted that a sheen of sweat had appeared on her stepfather's blonde brow. Giving a slight, jerky bow, and like a dog afraid to turn his back, Marshall never dropped his gaze from William.

"Nice to meet you, Mr. Huntington," he said, his jaw clenched and tight, "We have much to talk about."

William looked down at Juliet, and she knew he was taking in her pale face, clenched fists, and defensive posture. "Yes," he said, "It seems we do. Have your man talk to mine. Perhaps I can make time later this afternoon."

Juliet fought the urge to step closer to him. Even from where she stood, she could feel the warmth of his protection enveloping her. As if sensing this, William gently reached down and gripped Juliet's fist, drawing it up and tucking it into his arm. Her eyes were wide as he again gave a small bow to Marshall before simply striding off across the drive and up to the yards to the side of the manor. He never looked back, and Juliet followed his lead.

They had made it up the smooth hillside and were approaching the side entrance to the manor when the weight of the situation caught up with her, and she sagged against his arm.

"I am so sorry, William, I didn't think they would come here," Juliet said, her eyes filling with embarrassing tears as she stared at the damp earth underneath her boots.

William was shaking his head and turning to her, and she could feel his gloved hand slide across her cheek. Surprised, Juliet jerked her face upwards, staring at him as he cupped her cheek.

For the first time, she realized that he hadn't been angry at her; he was angry *for* her. Her heart skipped a beat. It had been so long since she felt protected, but here, with him, Juliet knew she was safe.

"Is that-," he started, before swallowing and starting again, "Is that how he always is?"

Embarrassment colored her cheeks, but she held that magnetic, kind gaze. "Always."

Those silvery eyes turned sharp again, and while she couldn't stop staring at the carefully concealed danger that lurked within them. For the first time since she met him, she realized that William Huntington, Marquess of Mansfield Park, might be a dangerous man.

"It's going to be okay," William whispered, and suddenly he pressed warm lips to her forehead, lingering there when her hands gripped his wrists, holding him fast. Juliet knew that there were plenty of people around them, all watching the couple closely. Juliet savored the sliver of affection, letting it settle in her heart, a warm, healing memory.

In the next instant, he released her, giving a quick smile goodbye before he disappeared around the backside of the manor. Standing there shocked, Juliet slowly let her hand creep to her face where she traced the warm outline of where he had caressed her face.

He had held her while she had quaked in fear and still looked at her like she was something precious. Juliet ducked into the house. She had to find Marian and tell her about what had happened.

CHAPTER EIGHT

Luckily, Marshall and her mother, Elizabeth, had disappeared into their private suite. Juliet threw herself into preparations for tomorrow's ball, trying very hard to ignore the fact that the man she hated most in the world was again in control of her life. Pulling herself out of her dreary thoughts, she sorted through the delicate summer flowers that staff had been bringing her all morning.

Nicholas suddenly appeared in the kitchen area, followed by Marian, who was flushed and sputtering as they entered.

"Nicholas, you can't come marching in here the day before and ask for these changes!" Marian was saying, her small frame standing firm against the much taller man.

Nicholas reached over and snagged a piece of fruit off the table in front of Juliet. He winked at her before turning back to Marian's outraged face.

"But Grandfather prefers the blue, and the chicken," He said earnestly, but Juliet could see the humorous pull of his lips as he toyed with Marian's temper. Chomping into the fruit, Nicholas smiled widely before leaning forward and, with a quick snap of the finger, pressed Marian's slack jaw closed again.

Juliet snorted as Nicholas waltzed from the room, cool as a cucumber, leaving a trail of chaos behind him. It didn't take much to imagine them together. Nicholas was a hard one to read. His interest in women, in marriage, seemed to change by the hour, if not sooner. And Marian, she wanted something different now than she had stolen away to meet her Mr. Conning. But even still, the tension between them was palatable.

Selecting a slender white bloom, Juliet cleared her throat loudly, in case her friend didn't realize she was still standing there frozen in a fury. Marian jolted out of her trance and stomped to the table where Juliet stood arranging.

Grabbing a large bough of blue flowers, Marian began to stuff them haphazardly into various vases. Without hesitation, Juliet reached out and grabbed her friend's arm before she massacred any more centerpieces.

"You shouldn't let him get to you so," Juliet said, "And please stop helping me." Laughing, Juliet quickly took the offending florals out of Marian's hands before drawing her friend close.

"Everything is going to be perfect. You and I both know this." Juliet felt her voice humming with positivity. She couldn't help it. After spending her morning with William, she felt that her body was overflowing with thoughts of happiness, of a new start.

Marian quirked an eyebrow at her; she had already heard the Marshall and William story, and while she had listened with rapt attention during Juliet's story, she was still concerned. Tugging her hands gently loose, Marian pulled a chair free of the table and plopped down in the most ladylike way possible.

Propping her elbows on her knees, she went silent, a far-off expression on her face. For several minutes, Juliet savored the quiet. Sorting and arranging the centerpieces for tomorrow's ball, waiting for her friend to say something.

Marian looked worn down, and it worried Juliet. She had thrown herself completely into this event, and while Juliet was sure it would be a hit, that didn't make it any less stressful. Setting one last blossom, Juliet went around and dropped to her knees at Marian's feet.

To her surprise, her friend's sweet face crumpled, and for a moment, Juliet thought Marian might start crying. Then quick as lightning, Marian braced herself, the strict training of her upbringing preventing her from giving in to the overwhelming feelings.

"I just want to do a nice job for him," Marian said brokenly, "But he's so impossible." Juliet's hand reached out and gripped Marian's slim arm as it draped across her knees.

"You've done such a great job, Marian," Juliet said earnestly, "Just imagine what kind of party this would be had you not taken control." She smiled at Marian, biting her tongue. "Can you imagine Cook and the staff all chasing Nick around the countryside, trying to get his opinion on tablecloths?" That pulled a laugh from Marian, and immediately, Juliet felt better.

She hated seeing her friend stressed, and it was evident that since last winter, she had been fostering a bit of a crush on Nicholas, but it was impossible to act on. Or at least that is what Marian had told her when Juliet gently prompted the question weeks ago via letter.

Juliet knew that Marian felt she had missed her chance to find a husband in the traditional method. Juliet feared that the woman had all but given up on love altogether. Maybe she wasn't a fresh-faced girl in her first season, but Marian was sweet, loving, and beautiful. She deserved every happiness.

Juliet wasn't sure if she and Nicholas were a true match or if they just enjoyed torturing each other in place of having to find something more serious to occupy their futures. But regardless, it made them both happy. For now, at least.

"Ugh," Marian moaned before sliding her hands up and over her delicate cheekbones as if she could wipe away the frustration as she wiped away the trail of tears. "You're right. Of course."

Juliet smiled. It wasn't often that she got to play advisor for her friend, and she found herself enjoying the opportunity to return the favor. Juliet stood and pulled Marian up from the chair.

"I've got to go, but I'll see you soon," Marian squeezed Juliet's hands quickly.

"Don't worry. I'll finish these right up." Juliet smiled at her friend. Marian went after Nicholas, her footsteps hurried.

Shaking her head, Juliet returned to the last of her centerpieces. They were a lovely assortment of flowers from the manor's elaborate gardens, as well as several Nicholas had brought down from his grandfather's greenhouse a short ride away. Juliet hadn't been in that part of the property yet, but based on the beauty of these flowers, she knew she wanted to see it someday.

Frowning, Juliet twirled a stem in between her long fingers, her expression darkening as she realized that her stay here at Lakeview Manor would be ending. Amelia had informed her that her mother and Marshall weren't planning on moving into town for two or three more weeks.

That meant that even if she bought a few days more here in Lakeview after the ball, that would be several weeks stuck at Greystone with her family. Her nose wrinkled; the thought was not appealing.

After being here with Marian, Nicholas, Robert, and even Lady Catherine, Juliet was accurately aware of how lonely she was at Greystone. Not because she didn't love the property, but because there was no one there for her. Not anymore.

With the Greystone townhouse under renovations in London, Juliet knew that Marshall would be a sullen, pouting presence at Greystone. The man was hateful and nasty on his good days and downright threatening on his bad. Juliet shivered just thinking of having to stay in such proximity to him long term. She hoped that Marshall would agree to William's offer, and they could put this scandal behind them and start fresh together.

But her traitorous mind couldn't help but wonder what would happen if Marshall didn't accept William's offer for her hand. Juliet truly would be all alone, with no prospects.

Taking a deep shuddering breath in, Juliet shook her head as if she could physically wipe the slate of worries in her mind clear. She would find love. Even if Marshall tried to stop her marriage to William, she would find a way to get the family she longed for.

A quick smile flitted across her face as she stared down the long kitchen table. It was covered with dozens of beautiful vases and flowers, each arranged to a perfect combination of soft blues and whites and bright yellow buds.

Dusting her hands against her dress, she gave the centerpieces a satisfied nod before turning to leave the kitchen area. At least if her family abandoned her for all her indiscretions, she might have a future in the business of floral arrangements. What a ridiculous week this had been.

***

To everyone's surprise, save Juliet, Marshall, and Elizabeth hadn't emerged from their suite, even for dinner. They had requested be brought to their room, saying they were weary from their travels. While Juliet had thanked God that they didn't have any interest in socializing with her or her friends, she dreaded when she finally had to speak with her mother.

When Juliet was young, they had been close. Together they shared such similar features, both tall and slim with too much dark brown hair and flashing amber shades in their eyes. But that is where their similarities ended. The bubbling, loving personality Juliet remembered was fading from existence. In its place was a frivolous, condescending countess who had little interest in her daughter's life.

Elizabeth had even requested Juliet's Aunt accompany her to all social events, claiming she didn't want to distract her attention from Marshall and the family business endeavors. Juliet assumed that the only business Marshall was into was the kind that involved extensive gambling.

But that didn't matter now. Juliet could finally see a way out of Greystone and into her new life, and she wasn't afraid of taking the next step, whatever that might be. She hoped that the next step included William.

The way that man devoured her with his eyes, his full lips quirking up in a half-smile as he tempted her body with those kisses. She could get used to being held, being loved like that.

That night at dinner, Juliet tucked in close to Eloise again, enormously enjoying the woman's candid nature and sweet stories of her youth. She was a vibrant note in every room she went into, and Juliet couldn't wait to meet her son, who would be arriving in the morning to attend the ball with his mother. Still a little young for these events, he was attending the early portion as a dear friend of the family. From what Juliet could make of it, the boy idolized William.

Eloise joked that her boy would probably be shadowing William, Robert, and Nicholas' the entire night. Juliet grinned, thinking of what it would be like for a young man to follow around some of the most significant titles in high society. He would likely get to meet plenty of lovely young women, and Juliet couldn't help but wonder if that had been part of the plan.

Shortly after the group broke from dinner, the guest of honor arrived via carriage. Juliet's chest squeezed as Nicholas ran through the main foyer and down the front steps to greet his grandfather. Easily in his late seventies, Arthur Euston, the Duke of Cullor, stepped down from his carriage and straight into his youngest grandchild's waiting arms.

Nicholas displayed no embarrassment at the open affection, heartily embracing the man who had raised him. Juliet guessed that the Duke had once been quite tall, like Nicholas, in his youth. Age had pressed him into a slight hunch. A long, black and silver cane also appeared in one hand, and as Nicholas stepped back, the Duke popped his cane to the stairs and climbed them handily.

Everyone in the party attempted to act nonchalantly as the Duke made his way into the manor. Juliet felt Marian pulling her towards the older man.

"What are you doing?" Juliet whispered at her, but Marian only shook her blonde head and continued to drag her towards the incoming men.

As one, they dropped into a slight curtsey, which the elderly Duke returned with a slight bow. When he straightened to his usual drooping height again, a bright smile creased his face as he held his hands out to Marian.

"Lady Marian, my dear girl, have you changed your mind and come to make me the happiest man in the world after all?" Marian's twinkling laugh was genuine, and she drew the man's hands to her lips where she gave them each an affection kiss.

"My Lord, you cannot go on like this. What will people think of your proposals?" Marian teased back.

"To hell with those stuffy aristocrats," the Duke said grumpily, handing off his hat to the waiting staff. "You have no idea the relief it is to have Nicholas and his brothers standing in for me nowadays. Instead of wrangling spoiled, powder-haired children, I get to travel the world, read my books, torture my grandchildren." He waggled his bushy grey eyebrows at the ladies, and both laughed.

Julie instantly adored him. His jovial nature and no-nonsense way of speaking were not what she had expected. He had seen great tragedy in his many years, the death of his oldest son and daughter-in-law, Nicholas' parents, had nearly undone him, but he was not the type to let something keep him down.

"And who is this lovely creature?" The Duke thundered, releasing Marian's hands in order to step towards Juliet. Although she was prepared for his appraisal, she didn't receive one. His soft, foggy blue eyes held hers for only a moment before he gallantly dipped down to kiss her hand.

Marian spoke for Juliet, "My Lord, may I introduce Lady Juliet Sonders of Greystone, my dearest friend."

"Greystone, eh?" The Duke stroked his chin for a moment. "It is a pleasure. Your father was a great man, Lady Juliet."

Juliet bowed her head in surprise at the compliment, "I'm happy you think so. I'm sure he'd be delighted to visit with you while he is here-."

The Duke cut her off, his tone suddenly sharp, "No, my lady, your father, not that silly creature Pinecrest. We worked together many years ago. Terribly sorry about what happened to him."

Stunned into silence, Juliet merely nodded. She hadn't known any association between her father and the Duke before this conversation. Giving her a look, Marian stepped in, chatting another moment before she made their excuses to go back to the card table.

"Are you okay? You're white as a ghost." Marian said softly, her slender hand gripping Juliet's arm as if she were afraid the taller woman might faint.

"I'm fine, Marian," Juliet said, forcing her cheeks to smile at her friend's concerned face.

Even though the very mention of her father had her insides quaking, she was aware of how curiously the group was looking at them. Their small party had grown, and Juliet did not plan on giving them the satisfaction of breaking down in front of anyone. She would not prove to anyone that she was the same flighty, irrational woman that her mother was.

"What a delightful man." Juliet inclined her head towards the Duke, who was now making his way down the hall, happily berating his guests, cane tapping lightly against the polished marble.

"Oh, he's something else, that's for sure," Marian laughed, looking hard at Juliet. Tonight wasn't the moment to stew in old heartaches.

Shaking her head lightly, Juliet pulled at Marian, dragging her playfully across the room and back to their game. Out of the corner of her eye, she felt the simmering presence of William's eyes on her body. Biting her lip, she forced her eyes to her cards. The man was positively distracting.

The rest of the night passed in a blur of chatter, introductions, and laughter. Juliet was surprised to find herself enjoying the activities. Whereas this summer she had feared any questioning guest and every smiling face suitor, she felt at ease here with her friends behind her.

Not to mention that she had thoroughly enjoyed looking up to find William periodically checking in on her. His dark brows were low over those incredible eyes that seemed the spark every time he caught her staring back. More than a few times, he had acted like he would move towards her, only to stiffen and retreat again.

Juliet couldn't help the heat that flushed through her whole body in those moments. How could he make her feel like this when they were separated across the room by a dozen other people? She could feel the path of his eyes every time, the way they took in her face first and then slowly slid down her person, over every curve, every breath. Every time he smiled or pursed his lips, Juliet wondered how they would feel against her skin.

By the end of the evening, Juliet was overheated and feeling more than a little like a spectacle. There was no way their little stare down had remained a secret, and while she didn't regret a moment of it, she desperately wished to find a cool place in her bedroom to bury her head until the ball tomorrow.

She didn't want to face that room again, or any room with William in it until she got a hold of herself and her rebellious body. The man was positively sinful with those knowing looks.

Leaning back against her door, Juliet quickly noticed the room was still being put back together after her scramble to get dressed for dinner hours before. Amelia was no doubt a bit overwhelmed, seeing as Marian had told Juliet that her mother's maid hadn't been feeling well and had not joined the couple at Lakeview. That left Amelia to care for both Elizabeth and Juliet on her own. Juliet was certain her mother wasn't as lenient as she was.

Juliet was fairly independent with her nighttime ritual. She was more than happy to slither out of her cerulean dress, petticoats, and underthings on her own. However, she was struggling with the final stays of her nightgown, one arm stretched over her shoulder and the other below, attempting to tighten the last ribbon down her back.

Thankfully, Amelia's quick knock sounded at the door, just as Juliet found herself getting even more twisted in the mirror.

"Come in," Juliet called, turning to the side before continuing her quest to find the errant strip of ribbon. "Thank goodness you are here. I have again made a mess of things."

Juliet lowered her head, her freed hair sliding forward to hide her face, waiting for Amelia's hands to find the ties and quickly set her free of her tangle. Eyes on her toes, she sighed in gratitude as she felt the ribbons tighten gently against her shoulder blades. Tossing her long mane of hair over her shoulder, she smiled and looked into the reflection to thank Amelia.

But the person in the reflection wasn't her short, smiling maid, but a very real, ominous-looking William. Gasping, Juliet turned and leaped back, bumping into her wardrobe as she covered her chest with one hand.

"William," she whispered, shock apparent in the way her voice seemed to cling onto every syllable in his name. Juliet's whole body flushed. Not only was her nightgown was impossibly sheer, but the hungry way William was looking at her.

The fact both horrified and thrilled her, as she found herself falling deeply into those silver eyes. Tonight, as they stared at each other, those eyes were molten, sliding over her skin like freshly cured metal.

Oh goodness, what would Lady Catherine think? Juliet scolded herself silently. This man had probably seen her more in her sleeping garments than ball gowns.

"Lady Juliet," William said, oddly formal as he straightened away from her. His form swayed forward and back as if his body and mind were on different paths. Juliet noticed that he was clenching and unclenching his hands. "I didn't mean to intrude. I assumed you were still awake from dinner and came to say a quick goodnight."

There was something so disarming about this full-grown man standing in her bedroom, clearly uncomfortable, that warmed her heart towards him even more.

Juliet smiled, trying to draw him out of his brooding. "I-I just thought you were my maid returning from my family's suite. I didn't assume anything." William remained completely still as if turning to marble where he stood.

Juliet shrugged, her voice teasing, "Between the two of us, I'm the one more likely to be invading people's bedrooms." That one worked, and Juliet's smile grew as she saw the Marquess' eyebrow quirk, the lines around his eyes crinkled in the smallest tell of laughter.

Finally, the slightest half-smile lifted his full lips, and she crossed her arms slowly, somehow needing to hold herself a little lest he sees how much it pleased her that she had broken down his walls.

"That is true, Juliet, but I would never have brought that up myself," William took a step closer, "I'm much too much of a gentleman." His face remained serious, but the tone of his voice was vibrating with rich humor.

Juliet let her head fall back to stare up at him, the man who might be her husband. He was astonishing. She struggled not to reach up and touch him, just to remind herself that he was real, that this kind of masculine beauty not only existed but was interested in her.

"In that case, you're welcome," Juliet cooed, plying to bring out even more humor. His face softened now, relaxing and shedding years off his cool demeanor.

His sensual voice was barely above a whisper now, "Just to be clear. I am thanking you for your invasion of my privacy, for your corruption of every aspect of bachelor life that I had. Is that what you meant?"

Juliet faltered for a moment, unsure and confused at his line of questioning. She had hoped that perhaps they would have come to some sort of understanding in the past two days. But just when Juliet was about to begin frantically apologizing, William's handsome face broke into a smirk, his eyes darkening further as he took another step to her. This time they were only a breath apart, and Juliet could feel her heartbeat quicken as her body thrummed with a sharp awareness of his intentions.

Slowly, with excruciating carefulness, William reached out and placed one of his bare hands on her waist. The sheer fabric was no barrier, and Juliet could feel the rough warmth of his skin as if it were gripping her skin itself.

He closed the distance between them, letting his body settle just against hers. Her chin rested on the level with his collarbone, her breasts pressed lightly against his ribs, sending sharp tingles straight to her core. Her breath caught at the rush of heat, and she closed her eyes, savoring the feeling of him against her.

This warmth wasn't frantic like the first night she'd felt him against her body. Juliet knew with every ounce of her being that it was something special. From the tips of her toes to her parted lips, she fit to him. Reaching one hand up, she tenderly slid her hand against his chest, gripping the fabric of his dinner jacket with her fingers. She couldn't decide if she was meant to push him away or pull him to her, but the rough texture of the coat grounded her in a way her body was desperate to have.

She wasn't alone in her feelings, either. She could feel the way his chest heaved, the wool of his coat rubbing deliciously over her sensitive body. Just in front of her eyes, his Adam's apple bobbed as he swallowed several times.

Finally giving into the moment, Juliet let her head relax, tucking her chin to his chest, nestling against him, and letting out a gusty sigh. His scent rushed over her body and straight into her memories. He smelled like sandalwood and cigar smoke. She had never smelled anything so good in all her life.

"You're going to want to stop that."

"Why?" Juliet nuzzled into his cravat, letting the silken fabric caress her face.

"Because I know for a fact that I only have a few minutes I can be in here."

Juliet pulled back, looking at him, confused. "What do you mean?"

Shockingly William seemed to flush under his sun-kissed face.

"My valet, Simon, offered to run interference with your Ms. Amelia so that I could have a few moments with you." Juliet's eyebrows flew upward. He was arranging to spend alone time with her.

Her body flashed hot, the tingling growing sharp and aching between her thighs. Eagerly, she leaned back, flirtatiously running her fingers across the planes of his chest. "Really?"

"Certainly, my Lady." William had to grind out the words. His jaw clenched as Juliet eased her hands up and over his shoulders, fitting herself perfectly against his powerful body. From her breasts to her thighs, she wound around him like a long-awaited skeleton key, smooth edges to his hard, opening the door to more than she could ever imagine.

"Do you always inspire such devotion from your employees?" Juliet was teasing him, attempting to distract herself from the way his hands had begun to draw delicate patterns over the back of her linen nightgown. It was getting difficult for Juliet to focus on anything other than how her body reveled in his adoration.

"Well, of course. I'm a very likable employer." William's eyes were glassy as he stared down at her. Juliet was barely listening at this point, his voice just another caress.

"I hadn't heard that. How nice." Juliet's mind had gone fuzzy, and her hips were moving on their own accord, dancing gently between his two hands as he played with the gossamer fabric that separated them.

"I'm not that nice. And I can promise you he will be quite upset with me shortly."

Juliet raised an eyebrow at him, focusing on his lips. "What do you mean? But you just said-"

"He's going to have to buy myself a few extra minutes. That's why he's going to be upset." William said before swiftly scoping her up in his arms.

Moving to the bed, he laid her down delicately, his gaze devouring her even as he reached up to untie his cravat and throwing it to the side. Cursing under his breath at the restricting garment.

His shirt now gaped at the neck, showing off the thick column of his throat as he leaned over her body, his eyes hungrily taking her in. Juliet felt her heart and body pound as one, the heat in his gaze, threatening to burn her up entirely.

Crossing the large mattress, William settled himself into the bed, and he sent his fingers twirling across her belly, making her twitch with desire.

"I won't do anything you don't want." His voice was low, below a whisper, and yet upon hearing it, every part of Juliet seemed to crack open. She gasped then pushed up a little onto her elbows so she could capture his lips.

The kiss was gentle, reverent at first, making Juliet's chest ache at the sweetness. Then slowly, it turned fiery, dangerous, his tongue sweeping in to claim her mouth, drawing her into a sensual dance of dominance.

Juliet learned quickly that he wanted her to push back, using her sharp teeth to nip at his full bottom lip. He rewarded her responsiveness with a deep moan.

Breathing hard, Juliet let him press her back into the mattress, his delicately searching hands growing bold, finding first one breast, then the other with his skilled fingers. He circled the precious mounds first, then spiraled in until he could gently tug at her tightly peaked nipples.

Juliet had to break their kiss then, biting her lip hard as she fought the urge to groan. The sensations, the pressure, it was overwhelming, and at the very center of it all was William. He remained fully dressed, save the long-forgotten cravat, and when she reached for his shirt, her hands were brushed away.

"No, darling, not tonight," His voice was unmoving.

Juliet almost pouted but briefly had a flash of what would happen if someone, most likely Amelia, discovered them again wrapped up in each other. William had the right answer, even if every part of her body cried out in disappointment.

Juliet sat back into the pillows hard, closing her eyes as she tried to rein in her arousal, her disappointment. "Well, drat." His eyes twinkled in quiet laughter.

"Drat, indeed. Although I strongly believe that there are other things we could do to occupy the remainder of our brief visit this evening." Juliet opened her eyes to find him lazily looking her over, a possessive edge curling his lips. She was quickly learning to love that look.

"And what is that?"

"Something wonderful. But perhaps a first for you," William murmured, dropping kisses against the still clothed shoulder next to his.

"Whatever it is, I want to try it," Juliet was eager, her body thrumming with pleasure. "Please, William."

Dropping to her lips, his own just a breath away, William said, "You don't have to ask me twice.' He kissed her hard, urging her leg closest to him to bend at the knee. Immediately his hand fell to her inner thigh, his fingers stroking first the fabric before skimming lightly underneath.

Finally feeling his strong, sure fingers against her, it almost undid her. Her body clenched and tightening as she tried to turn towards him on the bed.

"Easy Juliet, easy." William soothed her with soft, quick kisses as his fingers traced sweet words into the skin of her inner thighs. Juliet moaned breathlessly; her hands grabbed for William as her entire world focused on the feelings he was provoking in her.

Carefully William's skillful hands made it to the apex of her thighs, and this time it was him who broke their kiss, panting softly into her bare shoulder as his fingers found their target.

"You are so ready, so hot here," William's growl rumbled through her body. Juliet's hands splayed across his chest, feeling the heat of his skin through his thin shirtsleeves.

Juliet's hips shot off the ground at the first glide of his fingers against her burning core. Gasping again, Juliet tightened her hold on him, her pelvis rocking against his teasing motions.

"Are you alright?" William asked, his voice tight.

"Yes. Please, William, do something." Juliet choked out, her hips moving desperately against the faint touches from his hand, the sweep of his fingers gentle against her swollen lips. Craving more pressure, more of everything.

William groaned at her eagerness, using a trousered leg over her thigh to pin her writhing body. His fingers slipped deeper, filling her carefully, slowly, drawing out a whimper from Juliet as she tried to process the pleasure that was rolling over her body from her most intimate place.

William was breathing harshly, "My God, you are beautiful." Drawing his hand back, he began a gentle, aching rhythm. Pulling away to rub and tease Juliet before letting his hand rush back and serve her the pleasure she now begged quietly for.

She gasped when he added another finger, stretching her further as something started to break away inside of her. The scattered stabs of passion beginning to overwhelm her, Juliet arched her body up so that she could grind herself against his hand.

"William," Juliet whispered. His fingers were pulling her towards the edge. She twisted in her sheets; the forgotten nightgown caught up behind her waist.

"I'm here. Let go," His breath hot against her ear.

Juliet leaned back, her body bowing against his as he kissed her deeply, holding her tight to his body as he thrust his fingers into her body one last time before she exploded around him. Squinting her eyes shut, Juliet felt like it would never end, the mind-melting, clenching pleasure that gripped her in a vice.

William swallowed her shout in his mouth, his hand slipping from the heat of her core to soothingly rub circles along her naked hip as she came down from her high. Instinctively Juliet curled into the side of his body, her heart racing as he murmured nonsense against her hair.

"That was indeed a first," Juliet said breathlessly after a minute. She felt William smile against her body. With a regretful sigh, he started to straighten, to untangle himself from her mussed bedding.

"I'm sorry, but I need to go." William's voice was rough, apologetic.

"But…what about you? Don't you…" Juliet began, unsure of what to do about his needs. William shifted his legs away from her, but not before she saw the telltale ridge of male flesh begging at the crotch of his trousers. It was evident that he hadn't enjoyed the same completion she had, and she wanted to remedy that.

"Don't worry about me," William said over his shoulder, his eyes smoldering as he took in her delightfully rumpled appearance. Juliet curled her legs underneath herself, coming to lean her upper body against his back as he sat on the edge of the bed.

"It looks a bit painful," She whispered. His rumbling chuckle made her smile.

"Well, it is a little painful. But that's not for you to worry about." William stood, straightening his clothes and settling his pant legs in a less obvious way around his swollen body. Cracking his neck first to one side, then the other, Robert turned to look at her; his smile was predatory.

"When I finally have you, Juliet, I will take all the time in the world. It is worth waiting for that," William said softly, coming around to her side of the bed. Silently, he swept her now loose hair to the side and began to tie the stays at the back of her nightgown.

"Well, erm, thank you, William," Juliet whispered to him, her body still quivering in pleasure, the aftershocks making her want to beg him to stay. William made a face at her, shaking his head.

"I think I owe you a thank you, not the other way around." William moved across the room towards the door. Over his shoulder, his flinty eyes found hers. "I hope you have sweet dreams. I know I will." He opened the doors and vanished into the hall, leaving her in a cloud of pleasure and giddy relaxation.

For a moment, Juliet wondered if she had just dreamt up that whole interaction, but as she straightened, she felt the tightness of her nightgown down her back. He had indeed fixed her ribbons before embracing her. What an odd combination of tasks, Juliet thought to herself with a slightly hysterical chuckle.

Sprawling across her covers, Juliet couldn't stop the smile from taking over her face. What an incredible feeling. It had been everything she had ever dreamed, and it wasn't even the best part. Or at least according to the maids and governesses that she'd eavesdropped on growing up.

Amelia suddenly burst into the room, sending Juliet straight back up as she attempted to put on an at-ease, relaxed pose. When she saw it was just her maid, Juliet let her shoulders droop and walked over to flop in the most unladylike way onto her bed covers. Amelia immediately bustled over to her and leaned across her body to grip her cheeks.

"I just saw Lord William," She said casually, "And for once, he wasn't wearing that dark stare he seems to find so comfortable. Perhaps…" Amelia stopped, tapping her lip with one finger, "Perhaps, he has found a lady who pulled him out of his self-induced reclusion and, dares I say it, let him enjoy his life?"

"You saw him in the hall?"

"I did. Oh dear, look at you pink up so prettily, that man must have a similar effect on you as well?" Amelia smoothed back some hair from her face, her motherly gesture as natural as if Juliet had been her own.

"You know his valet thinks so as well. Kind man he is, that Simon." Juliet grinned at Amelia, seeing the older woman flush a bit when she talked about the balding, kind-faced Simon. *Interesting development there*, Juliet thought to herself.

"Your stepfather cannot deny you this match. Not just for the implications for Greystone, but also because no one could deny you this happiness. Everyone spoke last night of how you two with your dark looks and flashing eyes would surely be the hit couple of the ton for years to come." Amelia stood up, hands on her plump hips as she gave Juliet a brilliant grin.

"Amelia, you know I don't care if the ton approves of us, but I won't lie," Juliet said, rolling onto her side and watching as Amelia straightened up a few things around the room. "There is something so magnetic about him."

Amelia laughed, "Magnetic indeed, the two of you can barely keep your eyes off of each other." Juliet blushed. She knew that their staring would've been quite apparent. Except now, they had progressed to the point where it was now their hands that they could barely keep to themselves. But she wasn't ready to share that bit with Amelia. Not yet, at least.

Watching her maid pick up the last of the laundry, Juliet spotted a familiar white cravat at the edge of her nightstand. William's that had been cast off during their embrace.

Her heart pounding, she quickly jumped off her bed, snatched the fabric, and vaulted back into the covers. When Amelia turned to look at her curiously, Juliet casually pulled her hair over one shoulder and began to braid it, acting as if nothing had happened, her heart pounding. Meanwhile, the cravat was shoved under the covers by her knees.

"I will say that Lord William seems to have some unusual preferences." Amelia stacked the laundry into a pile. "When I saw him go marching by this evening, he yelled out for Simon to find him a bath, an icy one, he said."

Juliet snorted, the laughter bubbling up in her chest. Clenching her lips shut to stay silent, Juliet painted on a look of calculated interest and attempted to avoid Amelia's eyes.

"Isn't that interesting, Juliet?" Amelia said, her voice low, suspicious. She turned to her mistress and raised a brow. The moment Amelia left the room, Juliet burst out laughing. She hoped poor William had found his bath.

CHAPTER NINE

The next morning dawned soft and beautiful, the dewy grass just on the edge of being frosted, creating a dulled effect in the rapidly fading foliage. Juliet breathed in the refreshing air in gulps, using it to wake up her blurry mind.

She had tossed and turned so much of the night that she was having a hard time clearing it. She blamed William's body first. Then his lips. Then his hands.

How could a man be blessed with so many devious abilities, she wondered? Maybe she had been the instigator in the beginning, but William had been in complete control last night, and it had left her buzzing.

Nearing the stables, she heard hoofbeats against the cobbled stone aisle and immediately smiled. She hadn't been able to ride the day before. Marian had sent her on too many errands for her to slip out and escape.

But even Marian was sleeping in today to prepare for the long night and most likely morning events. Juliet was not sure how she would make it all night, but she did know that she only had a few days left here at Lakeview, and she wanted to take advantage of it.

Turning the corner, Juliet stopped, staring in surprise at William standing there in the middle of the aisle. One hand on his bay mares' reins, the other holding a persistent looking Sterling's bridle.

The stallion had his nose poked out and desperately tried to brush his muzzle over the mare's shoulders. Neither the mare nor William looked excited for the possibility of the stud's affection. Laughing, William was leaning against the grey, holding the horseback from his pestering.

Juliet hurried to the trio, grinning at both the horse's interest in the mare but also at William's valiant attempt to separate the two. Taking Sterling's reins from his hand, Juliet questioned William, "What are you doing here?" It came out more aggressive than she meant it.

"Good morning to you too, Juliet," William said, ignoring her saucy question.

Feeling unsure of how to act around this man, now that he had seen her at her most vulnerable, Juliet shuffled her boots nervously.

William put his hands up in defense. "Whoa there, my Lady, I just thought I'd join you for your morning ride. If you'd rather me not, I'm more than happy to go my own way."

"Really?" Juliet said, her gloved hand finding Sterling's neck and gently stroking it as she looked from William down to her riding boots.

"Yes, really," William said back, and to her joy, she noticed that he was giving her a wide smile. "So, my lady, what will it be?"

A bubble of happiness rose in Juliet's chest as she stared into William's face, his cheeks slightly pink in the cool air. Biting her bottom lip, she remembered exactly how he had looked holding her against him, kissing her, bringing her such pleasure the night before. She couldn't resist the chance to spend more time with him.

"I'd love a riding companion."

William gave a toothy grin, "Let's get moving then. I want to show you the path down by the lake."

William led his mare out to where he'd left a stool out in the courtyard. He braced one foot against it, hitching himself up onto the mare's broad back. William's mount was every inch the size and depth of Sterling, but her features were more refined, more delicate.

Juliet followed suit, launching herself up on to Sterling. Struck by a bout of nerves, Juliet took an extra minute to situate her dove grey skirts over the saddle. When she looked up, William sat waiting on his mare, the picture of aristocratic relaxation in his navy jacket, white cravat, and brown breeches. Heart skipping, she picked up her reins and urged Sterling towards them.

"What's her name?" Juliet asked as the pair of horses plodded off into the grassy fields just beyond the Lakeview gardens.

"Athena," William answered, patting his mare's dark brown neck as she strode powerfully over the smooth ground, her thick black tail blowing lightly.

"She's lovely," Juliet said, "My Father would've loved her movement." William looked back at her, and she realized how good it felt to talk about him, even in passing.

"Well then, he and I would have plenty to talk about. We share a common interest in females," Williams said coolly, winking at her as his deep voice washed over her, as soothing as the gentle sway of Sterling's march. Juliet smiled softly at his gentle flirtation. "She's going to be one of my broodmares. Hers is one of my favorite bloodlines."

"You keep horses?" Juliet said, curiosity brightening her voice as Sterling took a few jogging steps towards the leading pair.

"Mansfield Park has a fantastic stable set up, but mostly my Uncles manages that part of my family's business now. He's two day's rides from here. But when he sees one that is extra special," William pointed between Athena and Sterling, "He always sends them my way."

Comfortable silence descended over them as the sun continued to burn the delicate dewdrops off the grass around them. When the two horses grew close to each other, William leaned over to brush a gentle, sweet kiss across her lips.

It sent butterflies to her chest and a bolt of fire to her still sensitive core. William's sharp eyes took it all in, his jaw clenching as he settled back on his horse.

Thankfully, William was feeling chatty, his deep voice carrying across the fields on their ride as he told stories about learning to ride as a child, and his devilish pony named Peppermint, who still lived at Mansfield Park.

"I grew up in the stables with my father. He had horses in this blood and always told me I did as well," Juliet said softly, "The past few years, I haven't been able to ride as much, but I've greatly enjoyed being here. My hack at home was my father's favorite stud, a dark chestnut who I adore, but" Juliet paused, "I don't get as much time to myself as I used to." She finished lamely.

William shot her a sad smile, his face looking sympathetic as they continued on a short way in quiet companionship. The only sounds around them were the gentle hoofbeats on the path and the faint creaking of their leather saddles.

Juliet was in heaven. She leaned back, opening her eyes to stare up at the vast blue skies above them. Breathing in the calm, Juliet tried to soak up every moment so that she might be able to remember what it felt like to feel this comfortable, this at peace.

William seemed to be in the same place mentally, his body swaying calmy with every step Athena took his shoulders relaxed, and a serene smile on his lips. Juliet had not been to this part of the property yet; the woods-filled scenery was lovely, but nothing like the view that they stepped into a few minutes later.

The small lake was surrounded by dark, lush green forest, its smooth waters impeccably clear sans a few mottled brown ducks swimming alongside one large swan. The water was a shade of cerulean blue that Juliet was not sure any other water body in England could compare to it. When they reached a soft bed of sandy ground, William quickly swung off Athena and came to hold Sterling so she could do the same.

Her boots hit the soil with a muffled noise, and immediately she patted Sterling before moving towards the water. Standing on a smooth rock at the water's edge, Juliet reached curious fingers into the lake, delighted to find the water as clear as glass and still warm from the hot English summer.

She turned to William, grinning, "Does everyone know about this place?"

William was a short distance off, his back to her, looking out into the lake. Giving her a teasing glance over his shoulder, he laughed before answering, "No, not everyone. Most people believe that Lakeview is named for the other lake. The one just beyond the manor's gardens. But this one is the best swimming lake in all of England. In my humble opinion."

His roguish smile stole her heart as he strode back to her. "Robert and I would always beg for Nicholas to take us here when we visited. His grandfather, the Duke, was always an easy mark. He would let us hide out here for days. We could fish, sing, make campfires, swim, anything a group of boys could dream up for fun."

"You can sing?" Juliet asked, hopeful.

"Absolutely not. That was part of the fun," William said.

Juliet laughed. "So, it was a special place for the three of you to act like children you truly were. I can understand the desire to break the mold."

William swiveled in place, his face thoughtful, before pointing across the narrowest portion of the lake. "Right over, there was the best camping space, right at the foot of the old ruins."

Juliet followed his finger point and grinned to herself, thinking of a young version of Nicholas, Robert, and him out here causing problems, being carefree.

"After a day or two, the Duke would always happen to drop by, just in case we had failed on our fishing endeavors and might need a little sustenance from the kitchens." William shook his head, laughter on his face. "Some of the best times in my life happened around this lake."

"Nicholas and his grandfather seem like a matched set," she said quietly, eyes wandering the lakeshores and taking in the beautiful space.

"He's fortunate to have him," William said, his voice distant, "I don't think he knew how much so until we were already in school and he almost lost him," Juliet stilled, feeling the pain that accompanied those words. "My family was less than supportive. As a boy, the Duke, Lady Catherine, even Robert's father took me in treated me like family. Someday I hope to be able to pay them back." He finished quietly, focused on the water in front of them.

Juliet's chest ached for him. Marian had told her a little about how William had grown up alone, his parents in an ever-evolving feud. Marian claimed that even as a child, William had been painfully aware that he was an unfortunate side effect of an arranged marriage, and that was part of why he was determined not to marry.

Walking towards him, Juliet reached out to touch the tightly woven wool fabric of his overcoat. Acting as if she were brushing a bit of leaf or dust from it while she took the opportunity to tuck herself into his warmth.

"It's taken me a long time to understand, but I believe that you can choose who your family is," Juliet murmured, not meeting his eyes. "Or at least I hope so." She finished, smiling up at him in the bright morning sunlight.

He was staring at her. The pain and memories in his eyes were fading as something else filled them, darkening them as his breathing increased. Juliet couldn't make herself step back, her belly flip-flopping over as she tilted up her head to his.

"I believe so, too," William whispered softly, only a moment before his lips were on hers, the tenderness there almost making her want to weep. Her hands reached out and found his arms, squeezing the hard muscle that she found flexing underneath his riding jacket.

Opening her mouth in a soft sigh, he angled his mouth over hers, and she felt just a trace of the silken heat of his tongue caress her lips before he pulled back slowly.

She wished he would kiss her again. To feel that gentle power, the passion that he kept so carefully hidden under his mask of seriousness, was addictive. Juliet sunk her teeth into her bottom lip as she looked up at him through her lashes.

William pulled her against him again, his arms tight around her waist. She tucked her head against him; his hands traced a slow, winding path down her back, beginning at her neck and trailing to end dangerously low on her body, just above her hips, before starting again. Soon, Juliet felt restless and aching from his attention, shifting her body against his as her heart beat quickly.

"You have ruined me, my Lady. I could think of nothing else but you last night. And the night before that," William's voice said softly into her hair, and Juliet turned to rub her forehead against the narrow slip of skin exposed by his collar. With a disappointed moan, William gently set her back from him, those flinty eyes not missing anything as he took in her flushed face, kiss-swollen lips, and misty eyes.

"I thought about you too," Juliet said quickly, then blushed. William ran his thumb along the curve of her jaw.

"Only good things, I hope," he teased.

"You could say that." William chuckled as Juliet nibbled her lip. "Has my stepfather approached you? If I know anything about Marshall, I know that he will resist conflict, and I'm guessing he sees you as conflict. His perfect little picture of marrying his bonus child off to a shipping family didn't work out the way he planned. He will be disappointed."

"Frankly, I don't care what he is. As long as he promises to never speak to you again, then I think he and I will get along famously."

Juliet laughed softly, feeling something sink into her skin, like warmth, but more permanent, final. Was this what it felt like to be protected, to have someone watching out for you?

"We should get back," Juliet finally said, not wanting to at all but knowing that the longer they stayed out here, the more chances they would have to need to explain their absence back at the manor.

William nodded and, taking her elbow, steered her towards Sterling. Placing her hands upon the saddle's seat, she lifted one heel, and without a moment's hesitation, William bent, gripped her boot, and boosted her onto the stallion's broad back.

She fiddled with the reins as he quickly sprang on Athena's saddle, and together, they began to walk back. They took a shorter route now, and it only allowed one horse passage at a time, the branches much less groomed at this point in the estate roughly brushing against her legs and pulling at her riding habit as they marched home.

William had his serious, brooding mask pulled back over his handsome face when they arrived at the stable. Edmund practically pranced up to her to take Sterling and give her a wide smile. Juliet had to admit that she would miss him when she returned to Greystone.

William was delayed, fiddling with something on his saddle, and not turning to face Juliet. She felt a bit uncomfortable and unsure of herself, especially after their moment of shared vulnerability. She sensed he was, too, just based on the tightness of his shoulders and jawline. He needed a minute, and she was happy to give it to him.

"Good day, my Lord," Juliet said gently and began the trek back to her room. She was about halfway across the yard when William jogged up behind her, his boots crunching the pebble of the driveaway under his feet. Turning, she gave him a bemused look.

He caught his breath quickly and tried a strained smile, his expression dulled in the shadow of the great manor. "Your dress tonight, what color is it?"

"It's yellow. My dress is yellow." She said back, her heart again fluttering to life as he bowed to her. With a turn of his booted heel, William again disappeared back around the corner. Juliet stared after him for probably too long, worried he might pop back out again and have another question for her.

Finally satisfied that he was staying put where he was, Juliet turned and hurried up the slope.

The preparations for the ball were already beginning, and she was sure that tonight was going to be a night to remember.

***

Juliet had been waiting for her mother to make an appearance. She had always been taught to never intrude on her mother's life. Elizabeth had preached that like the conversation at the dinner table children were to speak only when spoken to and seen only when needed. At least that's how she had been since Marshall came crashing into their lives.

By the time the curt two knock request came to Juliet's door, both she and Amelia were feeling quite anxious. Without waiting for a reply, Lady Elizabeth waltzed into the room dressed casually in a stunning, pale blue day dress. As always, Juliet was struck quiet by her mother's severe beauty.

Juliet suspected that there might be some grey streaks hidden in her dark hair, that she must have her inky locks dyed over, but she would never ask her mother that. Marrying a much younger man only seemed to make her vainer and more careful with her appearance.

And now, even just to visit her daughter, she wore a fully painted up face, her eyes darkened with kohl and lips tinted a deep red smile as she made her way over to Juliet's small sitting space.

"My dear Juliet," she said as Juliet rose to her feet, giving her mother's powdered cheeks each a soft kiss.

Juliet gestured behind her mother, urging her to sit, and she sent up a prayer that this conversation could be over as soon as possible. Gritting her teeth, the two women faced each other, both offering phony smiles across the widening silence.

Thankfully, Amelia blazed into the suite, quickly dropping tea and some iced biscuits between them before making her retreat to the small, attached maid's room. Without a word, Juliet poured them both some tea before offering her mother the delicate cup and saucer.

"You wanted to speak to me?" Juliet began, attempting to prompt her mother into beginning what she was sure would be a lecture. Elizabeth moved to the edge of her chair, smoothing the fabric over her knees and skillfully avoiding her daughter's gaze. Clearing her throat, she seemed very focused on a speck of dust upon her skirts.

"Mother. Please," Juliet finally ground out, focusing on not rolling her eyes at the avoidance Elizabeth was demonstrating.

"What were you thinking?" Elizabeth cut in harshly, her lovely face pale and drawn as she looked at her daughter. "Can you imagine how we felt getting a letter from Lady Catherine? A letter that essentially stated that you had thrown the very advantageous marriage we had procured for you in our faces and gone off and scandalized yourself with your fiancé's best friend."

Elizabeth took a breath; nostrils were flared, and she seemed to be dragging the air into her lungs by force.

Juliet, on the other hand, was breathing deeply, feeling the warm air fill her. Focusing on her breathing almost made it possible to ignore the disappointed tones in her mother's voice.

It was precisely the conversation she had been hearing in her mind for days. That she could prepare for and steel her emotions against, she could appreciate her mother's flair for drama; it was, after all, quite impressive. She also knew that Lady Catherine would never have stated the situation like that to Marian.

"I hope you're proud of yourself. Marshall was devastated, as you again thwart any chance of the two of you have any kind of relationship." Elizabeth sniffed hard. "He was feeling so good about your opportunity with the Wains family. Devonshire, my dear, you threw away Devonshire."

Juliet had also known that this would come up. Reaching across the cool empty air between, Juliet placed her teacup back on the tray. Quieting her heart and her emotions, Juliet leaned forward to find her mother's flickering gaze.

"Mama. To begin, Robert proposed to *me*, and while I am glad you approved of him, Marshall didn't make any arrangements other than to approve the match after the fact." Elizabeth's red lips parted, but Juliet held up a hand to stop her, "And as for my actions with William. I don't need to explain anything to you, but I will tell you that it was my own fault. None should fall to Robert or William."

Elizabeth back snapped straight. "Also, Mama, I'm fine, thank you for asking. As it turns out, I quite like my new suitor, and I believe he would make a better match for me than Robert ever would have been. Not to mention I wasn't aware that the Greystone family wasn't strong enough to stand on its own. If Greystone needs the Wains, or even the Mansfield Park estate to remain relevant, then I'm more afraid than ever for its future."

The silence grew again between the two of them, heavy and thick. Juliet kept her back as straight as steel as she stared down at her mother. She waited for the wave of guilt and shame that usually washed over her every time the two of them had any disagreement.

Strangely enough, Juliet like that. If anything, she felt strong. The lingering warmth of William's support, his protection and care ran hot beneath her skin. She didn't owe this woman an apology, the same woman who, when she had heard her only child may have been caught in a scandalous situation, immediately thought the worst of her.

"Well then," Elizabeth murmured to herself, rising from her chair and sucking her cheeks in disappointment at her only child. "Since you've got everything sorted, I'll see myself out."

"Goodbye, Mother." The words were rough on Juliet's tongue, but her eyes were dry and clear.

Juliet rose but stayed where she was, letting the older woman do precisely what she had stated, and when that door closed, Juliet sat down hard. Amelia slowly opened the door between their rooms, and seeing that Elizabeth was gone, she quickly went to Juliet's side and while she made quick work of cleaning up their tea trays.

Juliet suspected Amelia was simply providing a source of conversation if she needed to get something off of her chest. But again, Juliet didn't feel guilt remained at bay. Her mother had said her piece, and Juliet had owned her own mistakes in the best way she knew how.

What she said was true. She had made a mistake, but maybe, just maybe, this misstep would be one of the best things that had ever happened to her. Thinking back to William's kiss this morning gave her strength, conviction.

"How much time before I need to start getting ready?" Juliet said tartly, giving a tight-lipped smile to her maid.

"Plenty of time for a quick lay-down, which I highly suggest you take." Amelia moved to the bed and fluffed a few pillows in a meaningful way. "I heard from Cook and Lady Marian's maid Betty that the last event Nicholas hosted here at Lakeview ended up going straight until breakfast time. They served kippers and eggs to a hundred guests."

Amelia shook her head, laughing at the incredulous lifestyle choices of the ton, but had a small smile on her face as Juliet passed her, climbing into the bed, uncaring that her dress would be wrinkled since she would be changing as soon as she woke up.

"You're right Amelia, I'll be here if you need me," Juliet said, her eyes already feeling heavy and gritted under her lashes. Amelia was right, and she needed every bit of rest she could get if she wanted to help Marian with the party and maybe squeeze in a few dances of her own. She was asleep in moments, a smile curving her face.

***

Hours later found Juliet was sitting as still as she could while Amelia wrestled her hair into submission. Juliet's dark mahogany hair was naturally wavy, but these tight curls were a different matter entirely, and while Juliet had to admit she loved the final appearance, she wondered if Amelia would ever attempt it for her again. It was a lot of hair to manage, and Juliet almost regretted asking her to do it.

Even with her face red and a bit sweaty, Amelia appeared more than up for the task. Behind them, Juliet could see her effervescent yellow gown hanging from the arched doorway. Juliet rubbed her hands together, excited to get the evening started. Most of all, she was excited to see William.

"Don't move," came the mumbled voice above her, as Amelia plucked another hairpin from the collection she had between her lips.

Pursing her lips, Juliet held in a laugh, trying to be perfectly still, channeling her best impression of William and his grave, still face. Which only made her want to smile more.

With a relieved sigh, Amelia seemed to sag in relief as she set the last pin in place, the weight of Juliet's hair curled and swept backward, baring her neck and the long planes of her face. Not to mention the yellow made her dark hair seem exotic and lush against her fair skin. Or at least that's what the dressmaker had claimed.

Nevertheless, yellow was one of her favorite colors to wear in the summer. When they got back to town, Juliet knew that the colors would be more subdued, so this was her last chance to wear the shade she enjoyed so thoroughly.

A knock turned both of their heads, and while Juliet briefly considered that it might be her mother again, Amelia quickly moved across the room to open the wide cream-colored door. Juliet was tucked into the vanity and couldn't see who Amelia was speaking with.

When she heard the door close again, Juliet peeked around. Amelia was gently sliding a tray onto the little table. Upon it seemed to spring a beautiful combination of bright, happy yellow, yellow roses, surrounded by baby's breath and soft blues of cornflower.

While the majority of the stems were wrapped neatly into a tall, white vase, on the tray beside lay a small bundle intricately tied with lace. Picking it up, Juliet realized that there were several small hairpins along the backside. Instantly she knew, William had sent her flowers for her room and flowers for her hair, made to match her dress for tonight.

The consideration and thoughtfulness of the action robbed her of speech for a minute, so she slowly swirled the hairpiece between her fingers, taking special note that he had included one perfectly formed cornflower in the center of the yellow.

Amelia was watching, her hands planted on her hips as she examined the florals. "My, my, I believe your Marquess is a bit besotted with you," she announced, "Don't you think, my Lady?"

Juliet smiled, leaning to let her pert nose dip in to smell the beautiful bouquet on the table, feeling the soft flutter of petals against her skin and imaging what must have possessed William to send something so affectionate.

"My Lord William, indeed," Juliet whispered against the petal.

CHAPTER TEN

Lakeview had been transformed this past week. There was not a chair out of place or a speck of dust upon each staff member's perfectly starched uniform. Juliet sighed in pleasure at the aroma of Marian's carefully chosen impressive dinner menu wafting through the rooms, mixing with the bright florals that graced the main ballroom.

It was something to be proud of, and she hoped that Marian would be pleased when she finally had a minute to sit and enjoy the atmosphere she had worked so hard to present to Nicholas' friends and neighbors. And even beyond that, the Duke himself had been so pleased to see his old residence decked out in summer finery.

He had gripped Nicholas' forearm and shaken his head over and over. Finally saying, "I hadn't had a night like this since before your parents left us, Nick. Thank you, my boy," his voice got a little higher, tighter, "I'm so glad you decided to do this."

Then he had smiled at Marian and Juliet before slowly making his way from the ballroom again, his wrinkled hand reaching out as he paused to let his fingers drape over the hanging floral garland.

Marian had had to leave the room to compose herself, and even Nicholas had looked a little teary at his treasured grandparent's joy. Juliet had quickly made an excuse and now found herself in one of the many open parlors, just out of sight of the guests. She waited here, watching as the streams of them passed the Duke and Nicholas, greeting the hosts.

Juliet smiled. The manor had always been beautiful; its elaborate detailed walls, tall, brightly lit gilded rooms left every guest in awe, their eyes sweeping the home. Marian made sure that while the interior would be lovely, it was the back gardens that would be perfectly lit up and available for strolling and enjoying the fountains and artwork placed amongst the flowers in this farewell to the summer.

"You should be proud. Everything turned out lovely," came a familiar, rumbling voice just behind sent shivers down her spine. Without turning, Juliet ducked her chin, a smile upon her full, pink lips.

"I did very little, but I'm happy to be a part of something so magnificent," Juliet whispered back, turning her head to be sure that he could see his gift softly interwoven into her curls. A splash of color against her shining brunette.

For a minute, there was silence, then she could feel the tender brush as fingers touched the small white and blue flower bouquet in her hair's swept up style. A very soft, warm laugh followed.

Juliet's smile grew, and she could tell he was pleased. Juliet felt one hand on the small of her waist with unmistakable ease, searing her to the bone, even though her layers of fabric. She turned only her head, widening her dark almond eyes as she stared at the perfect male specimen who stood behind her.

His eveningwear fit him like a second skin, and while the silken white cravat at his neck may have appeared feminine on some, it only served to make him less human and more godlike in his omnipotent appearance.

She remembered the way he had thrown his other, desperate to be freed from it so that he could focus more completely on her pleasure. Her body hummed. From the thick dark hair combed back from his face to the tips of his polished black boots, he was lust-worthy.

Her stomach was clenching as she found herself holding her breath, waiting on his next action. His legs were pressing into the skirt's folds at her back.

With a breathy sigh of his own, he leaned close to her ear, "You are magnificent," he rumbled against her back, his breath grazing her bare skin, "Never let anyone tell you otherwise." Then with a toe-curling slow move, he dropped his head and pressed a tender kiss to the bare, ivory skin of her shoulder. Just the tip of his tongue slipped out to taste her flesh.

Heat shot through her body, making her heart pound and her chest tingle with a sharp awareness of those burning lips. Of where else she wished they tasted.

Before she could stop herself, she let out a slight moan, only halting the noise by again biting her bottom lip, hard enough to bring herself back to the real world. She longed to reach over her shoulder and run her fingers into that thick black hair, to hold his lips to her body.

They were in a parlor of Lakeview and could be discovered at any moment. While a midnight case of mistaken identity was something, this was quite another. She must've stiffened against him.

Understanding that the moment had passed, William pulled away, stepping back from her and letting his lingering hand fall from her waist. Without a word or a second look, he turned and walked back out of the room, leaving Juliet standing there, breathless and more than a little disorientated.

The first part of the night passed in a blur after that moment. Juliet's head was crammed full of names, titles, locations of all the different people who had shown up for Lakeview's summer finale. Juliet felt their curious eyes on her, the whispers that followed. She was the daughter of an Earl. For her title alone, she would've drawn interest. But now, with rumors of her impending union with a Marquess, there would be no other topic on many guest's lips.

Once when she met William's eyes across the extensive buffet, those silver eyes had smiled at her, full of joy at seeing her enjoyment. She knew that this winter wouldn't be the same, not with these friends by her side or this man in her life.

Maybe she'd only met William a few days ago, but every moment with him left her begging for the next. Now Juliet didn't want to let him go.

During a quiet set, she had noticed her mother waltzing around the ballroom in her stepfather's arms, a brilliant blue and green dress flowing around her slim body like waves of the ocean.

For a moment, Juliet truly wished her happiness; the look on her face when she stared into Marshall's did seem authentically happy. Above all, Juliet wanted happiness for her mother. She simply wished she hadn't found it in this young, title-hungry peacock. The opposite of everything her father had been.

She pushed that thought from her mind, reminding herself that she was a safe distance from them tonight. Juliet doubted her mother would approach her about William or Robert again.

As the music changed, Juliet suddenly realized she had promised this next dance to a friend of the Duke's she had just met, Lord Henry Faber. He was a long-time business associate of the Dukes, whom she had only met at the beginning of the night.

Hurrying down the dance floor, Juliet immediately spotted him, his bright cobalt evening coat making him stand out in the crowd. He, too, had been looking for her, eagerly waving as she approached, her yellow dress blazing a golden path through the deepening crowd.

"Lady Juliet," Lord Faber murmured, bowing dramatically low over her hand. Juliet stood tall, letting the man complete the motion, even as she felt the prickling of stares at her back. She was the daughter of an Earl, and she was allowed to dance with whomever she'd like.

"Lord Faber," Juliet said, speaking over the musicians who were picking up the pace for the next dance, a lively waltz. She quickly scanned the vicinity but didn't see William.

"May I have this dance?" Lord Faber asked, smiling widely at her before taking her waist and hand in his own and drawing them down the final steps to Lakeview's dance floor.

There he turned to her, and she only had a moment to get a good look at the man before he began to steer them around the room. He was a middle-aged man, a bachelor, she had discovered, and his blonde and red mixed hair was a bit thin on top but very full over his puffy lips where a thick mustache grew.

He was a seeming jovial person, keeping up a steady stream of chatter while Juliet focused very hard on keeping her body tight and a bit off from his body. She didn't want to accidentally brush against this rather prominent belly as it dropped between them.

Juliet surprised herself by having a lovely time. Faber was a great dancer, his conversation pleasant, teasing her about the sheer number of flowers in the room, and his hands stayed precisely where they belonged. None of those things had gone according to plan in her first foray into society last winter, so these successes alone left Juliet feeling giddy and pleased.

Feeling a powerful gaze pull on her body, Juliet searched the crowd. There, off to one side, William stood, surrounded by a small group of men who were all sipping champagne and conversing in low tones. He, on the other hand, had assumed his favorite position as a resident marble statue, and his handsome face seemed frozen in place even as his eyes were glued to her frame.

"Oh, Lady Juliet," Lord Faber whispered after seeing the direction of her looks, "Never mind the Marquess of Mansfield Park, that man has a stare that could turn us all to ice." He shivered dramatically, squeezing the hand that held her, drawing her attention back to the dance.

Juliet brought her attention back to the man she was dancing with. She wondered if standing up straight, whether she would be taller than him, and it, or the champagne consumed earlier, sparked a bubble of laughter in her.

Juliet thought he had to have been a blonde in his youth, seeing as his thick mustache was still a bushy reddish blonde. It quivered as he subtly tightened his hold on her, thinking that her giggle must've been a girlish flirtation.

Cocking her head to the side, she pinned him with a teasing look, letting her eyes flash at him, "My apologies, sir, I didn't mean to lose my focus."

"Not at all, you are a lovely dancer. I just wanted to warn you against that one," Lord Faber said, carrying them swiftly across the blue and white marbled floors. Juliet felt her stomach sink. She knew precisely what man Lord Faber was talking about.

"What do you mean?" Juliet said, her voice barely audible amongst the thick noise of the audience.

"I just mean to say that Lord William is known to be quite the ladies' man. Or he would be if he didn't just string women along. You should have seen the trail of ladies left wilting in his wake the past few years," Lord Faber said, anger and what Juliet thought might be a bit of jealousy seeping into the tone of his voice.

Juliet involuntarily loosened her hold on his sweaty hand, finding more space between the two of them. The song suddenly felt too long, and Juliet was ready for it to be over.

Lord Faber noticed and looked back at her. His face held an expression of pity, or perhaps disappointment as he pursed his lips, mustache twitching as he did.

He leaned in to whisper, "It's okay, Lady Juliet, your father, has already spoken to me about the impossibility of your current situation." Her stomach clenched. What could he be talking about, she frantically thought.

Lord Faber smiled at her, gripping her hand harder again. "I'm sure everything will work out advantageously for both of us."

"Advantageous? Us?" Juliet felt dizzy. The brightly lit room blurred as she tried to absorb his words. Especially that word, advantageous. It seemed to haunt her, floating through her mind as she stared at her dance partner in horror. Lord Faber was blissfully unaware of her mood change and continued to spin her gently across the floors.

Juliet felt more and more nauseous with every step. She halted, stomach rolling, trying to get her wits about her. Pulling her hand from his sweaty one to press it against her thumping heart, Juliet now frantically looked for William, fear making her mind race. But it was Lord Faber that was gripping her waist, his scrunched face looking into hers, worried and flushed from their dance. She felt herself sway.

Thankfully, within a moment, she felt familiar firm, strong arms close around her waist, the ones she had been looking for. And the voice she wanted to hear most in the world filled her ears. Soothing. Comforting.

"It's okay, Faber, I've got her," William uttered, his legs never stopping as he quickly helped her off the dance floor and through the crowd of people beyond. Her legs seemed to follow his lead, but her mind still swirled in fear and confusion. Within seconds, they burst into the back balcony, the autumn air washing over Juliet liked waves on the shore. Filling her lungs, she slowly found her bearings.

When she was able to focus again, she realized they were standing at the balcony's edge. The fresh air calmed her racing heart and mind, almost as much as the gentle hand William kept at her back. Feeling self-conscious, Juliet touched her hair, her dress, her chest before looking up into William's stony face, her teeth worrying her bottom lip as she tried to figure out what to say.

"I'm sorry," was all she could think of to say aloud. Had she just fainted on the dance floor in the arms of the Duke's neighbor? It was something governesses had been warning against for decades. With a wretch, she realized that somehow William had made his way across the dance floor to capture her in his arms before she crashed onto the marble tile. Instantly saving her and Lord Faber from an incredible embarrassment.

"And thank you," she finished, dropping her voice low as she tried her best to remedy the impossible situation she had put the two of them in again. Gratitude for his rescue filled her person as she leaned against the balcony wall, her yellow dress a dull gold in the firelight of the porch.

William moved slowly, his brows low over concerned, dark eyes, so that the other pairs out enjoying the fresh air couldn't see her. One large, calloused hand warmly tipped her chin up to his appraisal.

"You have nothing to apologize for. Are you okay?" he said, his voice rich and concerned. Shaking her head, she felt the tears that she hated threatening to come spilling down her cheeks.

His hand tightened, but as they were in clear view of everyone else, he restrained himself from touching her anywhere else.

"Shhhhh," he whispered, positioning his body between her and the curious eyes that gazed out from the other side of the balcony. William's trademark serious expression fading into one of concern. "Tell me what happened, Juliet."

Juliet tried to breathe in, but one traitorous tear slowly slid down her cheek where William's thumb tenderly brushed it aside.

"Marshall is not going to approve of your offer. That's why he hadn't reached out yet," she finally choked out, William's face growing darker at every word, "Lord Faber claims that they've already spoken about how advantageous the marriage will be. But I know he must mean Marshall; there is no way Lord Faber has anything to offer me. Before the season, Marshall had threatened to set me up with some of his associates this spring, but I never believed it would happen. How can he do that? Especially now."

Juliet knew she was rambling, but she couldn't stop, her body shivering slightly.

"You're sure that's what he meant? Do you remember the words exactly?" William questioned darkly.

When Juliet nodded, he cursed loudly enough to disturb at least one of the couples alongside them. Juliet would have laughed had she not been replaying the conversation over again in her mind.

"I'm sure. He said that I should be wary of you too," Juliet swallowed hard, "Lord Faber said that you were a womanizer. I don't understand." She looked up into his face, clouded with anger. William snorted at her words.

"Wary, yes, maybe. Womanizer, not particularly." William tilted her chin up again, "Frankly, you ladies terrify me. Hence the brooding."

Juliet gave him a watery laugh. William smirked at her, but she could tell that his thoughts were off, galloping a hundred miles an hour away from here. There was quiet as Juliet leaned quietly into William's hand, waiting for him to sort out his path forward.

Finally, those magnificent eyes settled back on hers, serious, bold, and begging. "Tell me one more time. What did he say?"

Juliet straightened on the wall, taking a deep breath, "He said, Marshall had spoken to him about my situation," William sighed as she continued to relay the conversation, "And that he knew he would find a way that it would work out for both of us."

"Juliet, do you-," William seemed to pause, clear his throat even as Juliet's heart skipped a beat at his words. She would never have expected a real proposal from this man, but again, this was not the usual situation in any way or type, "Do you believe your stepfather would pledge you to this man? Even against your will."

Blinking, Juliet looked up at him. "Of course, he would. He is a monster," her anger at the man who had destroyed Greystone shining through her words.

"And you don't want that?" William's voice was soft.

Juliet raised her eyebrows, "Am I the one who just almost fainted, or was that you? Of course, I don't want that. How can I make that any clearer?"

Suddenly and without any fear of consequence, William pulled her tight to his body. She could feel his heartbeat rhythmically pounding beneath her cheek. Turning to push her face into his body, she felt the pace rapidly picking up as she curled into his warmth.

Juliet sighed deeply, loving the slow burn that seemed to grow from his body to hers, leaving a series of tingles rushing down her spine. Ignoring the stares of the other guests, William gently set her from himself with a soft laugh.

"This has been some finale."

Juliet groaned, sagging against his hands, "Don't remind me. I'm never going to another ball again."

"Someday, I would like to ask you to dance, at a ball, like a real gentleman. One that you deserve," William said, his fingers sliding down her cheek in a soft caress, "But I'm afraid that tonight won't be that night." He swallowed, his face looking sharp and pained in the shadowy firelight of the outdoor torches.

"I may have an idea why Marshall and Faber are in business. I don't think that we are getting the full story." William murmured thoughtfully, his thumb running over the back of her hand as he spoke.

"I have to go now," he said, "But please don't worry, we will see each other soon." Juliet felt his gentle kiss across her forehead. In a whisper of fabric and moonlight, William had disappeared off the balcony and out of her sight.

She stayed where she was, heart racing, but her hands were steady as she gripped the edge of the banister. The man could make an exit, but she wished that he would stop and try a simple goodbye at some point.

It was evident that Marshall had other plans for her future, but she was tired of playing by another man's rules. And based on what William had said, he had an idea, and she wanted, no, she needed to stay faithful to his ability to come through with it.

She waited for what felt like forever before walking back inside, her chin up, her eyes level. To her amusement, very few people seemed to have even noticed her disappearance. Even Lord Faber, whose eyes immediately crawled over her form, kept his distance as she sought Marian.

She found her sitting in a plush out cove in the main hall, seated beside the Duke, who had a champagne glass in each hand and who was finishing up an entertaining story, based on the laughter all around his small group of observers.

"Juliet!" the Duke cried out, waving one champagne in greeting, "Ah, the lovely Juliet, come here, please." The small crowd parted and let her in; appreciative glances from the gentlemen there stroked her ego a tiny bit but did nothing to detract her from her mission.

She curtsied low to the Duke, murmuring her greetings as he smiled and set one glass of champagne down. He patted the seat next to him with his white-gloved hand. Instantly Marian hurried down, and the crowd seemed to disperse.

Looking at her seriously as she sat beside him, the Duke settled himself on his cushioned side of the settee. Taking her hand in his, he kissed her knuckles, sighing as his warm blue eyes looked into hers.

"It is such a pleasure to get to know you, my dear. I worked for your father for several years before his untimely death," the Duke spoke quietly, his unfocused eyes staring off somewhere behind Juliet's shoulder. "Such a tragic thing, his death," his voice was tremulous, almost breaking over the words, "There are many, many days I wish that I had been with him that day, as I had planned."

Juliet's head shot up, catching the Duke's unfocused gaze; she could feel her body thrumming with surprise.

"You were supposed to be with my father that day?" Juliet said, her teeth clamped shut, her eyes looking from side to side. But the only person paying any attention was Marian, and she was mostly out of hearing range anyway.

"Yes, we were late at court in London, testifying about some unhappy business with a local trading company. Samuel had begged for the use of one of my carriages to get home early," the Duke leaned into Juliet, a soft smile on his creased face, "He was badly missing his young daughter and wife and wanted to be home as soon as he could."

The elderly man settled back, tapping his toe once on the floor as he mulled his thoughts over. Juliet felt like she couldn't breathe, waiting on his next words, desperate to hear anything he might have to say.

"He was so enamored with you, I wish I could find the words to describe it," the Duke said, his voice strained and full of emotion. Juliet herself was having problems speaking at this point, but she reached out to grip his slender forearm, squeezing gently.

"Thank you," she whispered, so grateful to any piece of her father's life that this man could fill in for her.

"It was my honor, Lady Juliet," the older man's eyes cleared, and the eyes that he fixed her with were sharp with the wit and intelligence born of a lifetime as an aristocratic businessman. "If you ever need anything, you only need to ask. I owe your father more than I can ever repay."

Juliet let her head fall in a small nod of appreciation, unable to force any words past her lips. First, the news that her stepfather was discussing her scandalous mistake with suitors, he found advantageous, and now, with news of how her father had died while attempting to get home to see his family. It was just too much.

Standing up, Juliet turned and quickly leaned forward to give the Duke a soft kiss on his wrinkled cheek. He was an honorable man, and he had always been so. If her father had associated with the Duke, it only deepened Juliet's belief that her father, too, had been a great man.

And every story she heard, every scene she pictured, helped to fill in those gaps that she wished so desperately she had been able to live through. Hearing them from the lips of his friends, though, was a second-best option.

It must have been close to midnight, but the party was still in full swing. Juliet wound her way across the room and through the crowd, murmuring apologies and greetings as she found her way upstairs. Amelia was waiting, and one look at her mistress, and she remained silent, helping to peel the layers off of her slim body.

With not a word said, Juliet, let her hair down, fingering the beautiful floral hairpiece one more time before setting it down on her bedside table. The tiny flowers were wilting, and Juliet sympathized. She was asleep before Amelia blew out the last candle.

***

The next morning Juliet woke up late, and on top of that, she didn't feel much like going for a ride today knowing that William had gone. It was a grey, overcast day, which many household members seemed grateful for as they poured themselves out of bed at long last. Many begging forgiveness for assorted headaches and stomachaches from a long party the night before.

By midday, Juliet listened to Marian, Nicholas, and even Robert rave over the night's activities, laughing at elements and reliving the best parts. She had nodded along to the stories, truly glad her friends had had such a lovely time.

She hadn't had time to tell Marian about the possibility behind Lord Faber's veiled statement or Williams' untimely departure yet, but that could wait. For now, they were enjoying the good moments.

At one point in the conversation, a young staff member appeared at Juliet's elbow, handing her a tray with a folded letter upon it. Taking it, she raised an eyebrow at the fact that each of her friends had immediately gone silent, staring at her, waiting with her for whatever this news was. Wetting her lips, Juliet slowly slid the letter open to see a brief note in long, swirling cursive letters.

She read it once, paused, and scrunched her brow before rereading it. Then looking up at her friends, she grinned. Juliet tossed the letter at Marian, who deftly caught it and looked up at Juliet as she stood.

"Where are you going?" Marian shouted as her friend walked away. Both Robert and Nicholas cursed her, covering their ears with a groan.

"I've got an invitation I cannot refuse," Juliet shouted back at them over her shoulder as she headed off the side of the manor to the stables. There, waiting in full uniform, for the first time since she had met him, was Edmund.

Juliet gave a quick curtsy, acknowledging his formal attire, and in return, Edmund gave a deep bow. Then gesturing behind himself at the darkened barn aisle, Edmund smiled at the young woman. Standing there in the shadows stood Sterling, the gorgeous grey stallion with who she had bonded so thoroughly with.

Walking straight to him, Juliet took his heavy head in her arms, letting him press against her chest. Dropping her head atop his, she breathed in the stud's warmth and sweet hay-smelling scent. The first genuine smile of the day pulling at her lips.

Edmund was grinning now, looking between Juliet and the red-headed youth who always seemed to be down at the stables. Juliet didn't even realize she was crying until she pulled back from the horse's embrace and dropped a kiss on the swirling hair of his forehead.

"Thank you, Edmund, I'm sure you had a part in this," Juliet choked out, trying to blot at her tears in the most ladylike fashion one could while they held the reins of a horse in one hand.

Edmund tilted his head, holding up his two fingers and measuring out the sign for a small amount. Juliet laughed. So just a little bit of help. It was William she needed to thank. She couldn't wait to see him and do exactly that. A terrifying yet wonderful emotion bloomed in her chest. One she had never dared dream about.

"Do you think you can keep a secret?" Juliet said to Edmund, who immediately bowed his head and nodding enthusiastically.

"Of course, my lady," he said.

She leaned into Sterling's shoulder and held up a delicately booted foot. Edmund only took a second to read the situation before he bounded forward and expertly vaulted her onto the horses' broad back. Juliet found her seat on Sterling's broad back quickly, situating her skirts out behind her as she reached around to grip the two sides of the reins.

Turning the stallion towards the lush green garden, Juliet looked down at Edmund, who seemed positively tiny from this view, and she winked. To her joy and amusement, the stable manager winked back and then slapped Sterling's powerful hind end, sending him off into a smooth, balanced canter.

Juliet's laughter as her dress blew back behind her, its soft blue texture blending perfectly with the deep silver dapples of his coat as they crossed the backyard of the manor.

Above her, on the balcony, Marian leaned over, watching her friend canter happily across the yard and into the softly waving fields that would take her to the intricate riding paths beyond.

She smiled, so glad that her friend was finding this happiness, this joy. Marian looked down at the letter still in her hand, and a smile took over her expression, even as tears blurred the writing.

My dear Juliet,
You were right. We do choose our family, and Sterling has chosen you. Please understand that I will be checking on his health and well-being at Greystone in the near future.

I cannot wait to see you again.

Yours truly,
William

Marian held the letter to her chest. The level of understanding and love in those words were enough to make even her believe in second chances and in love.

She couldn't wait to watch the rest of her closest friends' love story unfold before them. Tears burned at the backs of her eyes, and Marian hurriedly wiped them away. Marian wondered if either William or Juliet knew how badly they needed each other.

CHAPTER ELEVEN

Several days later, Juliet stood in front of Lakeview, looking up at the vast manor, it's beautiful stone exterior glowing in the early morning sunlight, the heavy paned windows reflecting the warmth and brightness of what felt like a very dark day. Juliet sighed, squeezing Marian's hands one last time before turning to her carriage.

They had said goodbye a hundred times now, each attempt worse than the rest. Even Lady Catherine had made a rare appearance early in the morning, looked a little teary as she said her goodbyes. Juliet took one last look at the place she had only called home a short time but had fallen deeply in love with.

Or perhaps it was that she had fallen in love here, which is why it made leaving all the more challenging.

Robert approached, his footsteps quiet in the dewy grass as he gently raised her into Greystone's black and green carriage. Seeing her family's silver crest blazing on the side of the doors only saddened her further. Greystone may be her destination and the home of her family, but her family was here, behind her, in Lakeview. Or at least, almost all of them. There was still one exceptional man missing.

Robert didn't release her hand, so she turned to him, her deep navy traveling dress filling up the small space in the carriage. "I hope we part as friends, Lady Juliet," he said, his blue eyes hopeful as he observed her.

Smiling broadly, Juliet gave him the only answer she could think of, "There's nothing I would like more."

Robert turned as if to leave but changed his mind. Quickly pulling her hand a little, he forced her to lean forward towards his face. Her heart leaped in surprise, but the man only leaned to one side by her ear, where he laughed for a moment.

"He will come for you," Robert whispered, his voice gentle as a summer breeze against her neck. Leaning back, he dropped her hand and nodded to her as he closed the carriage door. Juliet returned his nod, her lips tight as she valiantly tried to act like she was as sure as he was. William had ridden out the night of the ball, and no one, not even Lady Catherine, had received word from him yet.

"Off you go," Robert called to the drivers, and in a moment, Juliet was off, craning her head to watch as her friends disappeared as she was carried down the long driveway and out into the English countryside.

The grasses around her glowed a burnished gold, and the trees above were turning the color of scarlet and bronze. Fall was here, and while the parties were waning and events would be more spread out, she had such high hopes that this winter would be better than any before it.

Leaning her head back against the pillowed carriage walls, Juliet closed her eyes and tried to plan her return to Lakeview, or perhaps she could visit the Wains family home for the holidays. After the past week, she was sure that it would be better than any time spent glaring across the table at her stepfather or her mother. They also left early the morning after the ball, and without a word to her or Amelia.

While it was nothing new, something stung especially hard at this exit. Perhaps it was because she now knew that her stepfather had outed her to the rest of the peerage. While at one point, she had hoped that her midnight venture might spark a prompt marriage, she also had been empowered by the act of making her own life decisions. With William gone, and her stepfather already speaking to other possible matches, Juliet felt more out of control than ever.

Luckily, she knew that her parents would only be at Greystone with her for a few weeks. Marshall preferred the bustle of city life with its access to the clubs and gambling that he loved so dearly.

Juliet would remain behind at Greystone estate; she had already decided. As much as she loved the theater and seeing the city lit up for the holiday season, it would not be worth the emotional destruction that spending more time with Marshall and her mother inflicted upon her heart.

Her chest ached sharply, not just as the idea of the holidays alone, but suddenly the act of leaving her friends reminded her of the void she often felt. The one that she attempted to fill with books and letters. But in the end, she knew that she was alone, and she hated it. A single tear slid down her face, which she ignored, enjoying the hot path it wove down her face.

Suddenly a loud and piercing whinny broke her sorrowful thoughts, surprising a small laugh out of her as she leaned back out through the window.

If she stretched her arm, she could just barely stroke the silken nose of Sterling, who was gamely trotting behind the carriage, his sharp black lined ears twitching back and forth as he took in their surroundings.

"Shhhhh," Juliet murmured, "I guess I'm not as alone as I thought." The idea comforted her, not just in the horse himself, but in the belief that William had promised he would come to check on him. Or really, on her.

Maybe she had only known him for a week, but Juliet was sure that William was not a man who broke his promises. When she leaned back to her seat, a smile pulled at her lips, and his promise pulled at her heart.

***

William was not a patient man. He already felt like he had been in the deary, frostbitten city of London for too long. But that night at Nick's ball, he had had a bit of an epiphany, especially hearing that it was Lord Henry Faber who Marshall Pinecrest wanted to pursue as a match for Juliet.

The minute he had seen Juliet pale and grow quiet in the older man's arms, he had known something was wrong. It had brought him an inexplicable joy to sweep her away from him and out into the fresh air.

He told himself that he had done it to help her from fainting, but he had spent the entirety of the night snarling at every man who even dared look at her. She had been a goddess wrapped in bright gold, dark swirling hair, and features exotic against the glistening satin. He hadn't been able to keep his eyes off of her.

At the first chance, he had jumped to whisk her away to where she would only be his. Even though hearing about her conniving stepfather had angered him, he had to admit that having her in his arms, for any reason, had given him life these last few days of traveling.

Adjusting his trousers impatiently, he grew frustrated in the stiff, high backed chair he had been seated in. He had been waiting for almost an hour if his pocket watch was to be trusted. William had come to the Blue Fiver society club in the heart of London to meet with one of its elusive owners, a Mr. Bohart.

William's people had done as much digging as they could into Juliet's stepfather and Lord Faber. After turning up only minute details, William had shifted his mind to finding someone who would know more.

William knew that Montgomery Bohart was the current operating owner of the Blue Fiver and that he prided himself on keeping an elite, exclusive establishment. Moreso than anyone William could think of, Bohart had the force and influence to maintain the high level of standards that the club had been founded upon.

Only the most powerful gentlemen were members here. New guests were allowed in only on a trial basis and only through a direct invitation of a good standing member. His source had conveyed to William that the club catered exclusively to the highbrow society of London year around. William had always assumed his father had been a member but hadn't pursued it since his passing.

William also knew that Marshall Pinecrest, Juliet's sour-faced stepfather, was a well-known patron of the club, both for entertainment and gambling accessibility. William needed to gain an advantage on the cruel man, and he was ready to go as far as necessary to make that happen

The door slammed open, and William flew to his feet, swallowing a curse of surprise and straightening his overcoat as he went. Dressed in a fashionably dark suit, the man who charged into the room aimlessly wove his hands through dark auburn curls.

William couldn't tell if the action meant to tame them or enflame them, but regardless the hair framed his face in a wild, almost savage way. A petite man with silver hair and an impressive mustache followed quietly behind, his arms filled with a collection of books and papers, which he dumped unceremoniously onto the desk between William and the redhead.

"Mr. Bohart, I assume," William began, extending a hand to the man across his vast wooden desk. The man didn't move. Not even an eyebrow twitched as he stared down the Marquess.

"You assume correctly," Bohart said, a gravelly voice giving no hint to his actual emotion, "And I can assume that you are the man who has been harassing my staff for a meeting," he emphasized the last words as if they were particularly offensive.

William frowned, dropping his hand to his side as the other man placed both hands on the desk, leaning towards him, a dark glint in his deep navy eyes.

For a moment, William felt his hackles rise. This man was the definition of intimidating; his perfectly tailored suit stretched tight over what seemed like unnaturally broad human shoulders.

But it was his face, which would probably be considered attractive to some, that gave William pause. There were several scars, one crossing an eyebrow, the other the edge of his jaw. And there was the matter of the dark airs that seemed to swirl around the man as if he himself was draped in shadow.

William knew Bohart was looking to intimidate him, but something was appealing about his demeanor in all truth. A sort of brutish charm.

The man seemed unconvinced to sit and discuss the matter, but after the silence filled every inch of the room, he finally dropped his mass into his desk chair and leaned back, folding his hands over his lap. Two could play this game, William thought, a thin smile on his face. William sat loudly with a sigh, crossing his leg over one knee and looking up expectantly at Bohart.

"I'm inquiring about one of your patrons, Mr. Bohart," William began, his voice polite, practically disinterested.

"Then I'm afraid that is the end of our meeting, Lord William," Mr. Bohart said, as he drummed his long fingers against a flat belly, his eyes still sparking at the intrusion into his private office.

"You mistake me, Mr. Bohart, with someone who will leave here without what I want," William ground out. Mr. Bohart's face twitched a little, in enjoyment or anger, William couldn't tell. The club owner's eyes slowly crawled over William. Even in his most casual clothing, William was sure he looked every inch the peer that he was.

"And what precisely is it that you want to know?" Bohart said, his deep voice less aggressive now. William had weighed his conversation carefully on his ride into town. The club owner must profit from Marshall and his friend's extensive use of the gambling tables, and William was no idiot. He knew far better than to put himself between this man and his money. William decided to share the idea that he had been mulling over since Juliet uttered Lord Faber's name.

"There is a well-known loan agent who has been frequenting a friend's home this summer. I believe it is because he has come to collect dues for loans and cash that traces back to this facility. He is causing quite a stir, and I'd like to know whether he is associated with you," William lifted his eyebrows, letting the story unravel in between the two men, "I never step where I do not belong, Mr. Bohart. Still, in this case, he has come too close for good measure." William took a breath.

Eyes narrowing, Bohart nodded a bit, wanting him to go on. "I knew that you would appreciate taking care of your own business, without the interference of my people," William finished before looking down and focusing on picking a thread off of his pant leg.

He wanted to let the story be digested before pushing the owner any further. William knew that the meeting could go one of two ways. One, the man was interested and might lend his assistance in the matter, or two, this mountain of a human would have him thrown out in the streets without a backward glance.

"You must be talking about Faber," Bohart said finally, breaking the thick tension between the two. He stood up, shuffling over to look out of his front windows at the bustling street below. "We requested that Faber no longer be available for the patrons of Fiver earlier this year after several similar issues arose. His membership has been *revoked*."

Again, those dark eyes flashed and pinned William with a sharp look, "I run a neat club here. The majority of my guests are decent men who come here for business. But that one," Bohart nodded, "That one was looking for trouble."

William stayed seated, watching the other man pace his office's length, Bohart's steps eating up the large room. Raising his hands and feigning indifference, William put the nail to the coffin, "Did he find trouble with the new Earl of Greystone?"

Bohart froze, his booted heels coming to a stop only a few feet from William. Rolling his eyes up to the hulking man who towered over him, William pushed on. To give Juliet a chance for her future, for a chance to be a part of her future, he needed this man on his side and his information in his hands.

Bohart's arms were tight, his body vibrating with suppressed emotions, but his vibrant blue eyes on William were surprisingly clear. "The Earl of Greystone," he said slowly as if feeling out the words as they left his lips. A dark chuckle escaped after, "He has been a patron of Blue Fiver since he was just the lowly Mr. Pinecrest. That man has more ambition than he does sense."

The way he said Pinecrest's name, the disgust filling every syllable, made William's heart skip a beat. At that moment, he knew he had an ally in Bohart and a valuable one at that. William gestured casually to the seat across from him again. Raising his chin, Bohart walked over to sit back down. As he did, William leaned forward, his elbows on his knees as a grateful smile taking over his face.

"Well, it seems we have a mutual interest in Marshall Pinecrest, Mr. Bohart," William said, "He is the stepfather of the woman I'd like to marry. Only Pinecrest isn't inclined to allow the match. Even under the circumstances that his stepdaughter and I met."

Bohart lifted one slender red brow and gave William a quizzical look. "Caught, unawares were we?" He said, his voice almost teasing.

William smiled but avoided his question; this was not the time for this story. He needed to convey the urgency situation. "I believe he means to marry Lady Juliet, his stepdaughter, to appease his extensive gambling debts, which Faber currently has hold of. I recognized Faber at the ball at Lakeview and wondered how he had weaseled his way into the party. Pinecrest has never been quiet about his financial issues, so when I saw Faber dancing with Juliet, it hit me."

Bogart's face was shocked now, his dark expression lightning as he narrowed his eyes at William. "Not even Pinecrest would stoop that low," he said softly.

William shook his head lightly, his fingers gripping a small letter in his pocket, pulling it out and smoothing it between them. Nodding to the folded note, "He has done it before," William growled, his anger leaking out into the statement.

"Not with Juliet, but he married widow Lady Elizabeth ten years ago, and I believe it was to stave off some bad luck at the tables that had been following him. Juliet claims that he has slowly been selling off bits and pieces of the old Greystone estate as well as small branches of their shipping company."

Bohart leaned back in his chair, pressing until the front legs lifted off the ground a bit. His face was pensive and thoughtful as he considered the statement. "That letter was found in Pinecrest's room when he left Lakeview, crumpled, and discarded. I have had my man keeping an eye on him after questioning his ability to make clear-minded decisions. Although I didn't anticipate finding this, it does make more sense," Bohart opened the small note.

In small, nondescript text read, "It's the money or a marriage, your debt is due Pinecrest. We need to talk." Bohart read it aloud once, twice, and then set it aside with a disgusted grunt.

"He is a desperate man, in a dire situation," William reminded Bohart, "I don't believe he is above a trade to clear his name, even if it does make him the lowest of low men."

Bohart nodded, his pensive expression making him seem far less thunderous and more thoughtful as he blinked slowly. Standing up, Bohart reached his hand out to William silently. William looked down at the offering, the same that he'd been snubbed at just minutes ago.

"I'm in. What do you need?" Bohart stated. William grinned at the man, gripping their hands together tightly. An ally.

Reaching down, William pulled a slim pamphlet of pages from inside his coat. "For starters, let's find out how much Pinecrest believes his daughter is worth. Then we will show him how much we believe he is worth it." A slow murderous smile creased Bogart's face.

***

The two men spent most of the days comparing notes from William's sources of information as well as tabs and bills that the club had kept from each of their patrons. William was impressed by the man's mind for numbers and the tightly organized business that was the lifeblood behind the poker and ponies that fed it.

They quickly discovered that even if Marshall had run up every possible tab at the Blue Fiver, he might have started to expand his addictions to other clubs in the area to be in the kind of debt that required Greystone's level of money.

Bohart believed there was only one that would have accepted a man with his reputation. Within moments, he had dispatched one of his crew to run to speak with them and get any intelligence available.

By midafternoon, both men were struggling to focus on the page and pages of tiny numbers. He knew enough to have confirmed that Marshall was in way over his head, and he feared that perhaps the formerly prosperous Greystone estate might have also taken on more of his damages than he had expected.

Pinecrest was a horrible gambler. You add that to his lack of friends, and it was apparent that he hadn't had much success in the city. The small shipping company, handed to him due to marriage to Lady Elizabeth, was floundering. The good credit of Greystone, which he had enjoyed profusely, was now being revoked all over town.

William rubbed his eyes. They felt like they had been blasted by a sharp coastal wind for several days, even though he knew it was merely from reading the tiny print over and over, trying to find a way to get Juliet out. Bohart was mirroring his action, his shirt sleeves were rolled up, and his jacket tossed over the back of a nearby couch. William gave him a tired look before pointedly nodding at the pile of paper between them.

"What does this all mean to you?"

"It means that I have a credible reason never to allow Pinecrest in my club again," Bohart said, a wide smile on his ruddy face. "So that makes me very pleased."

William groaned as he stretched his arms above, his joints stiff from the lurching position he'd been locked in, "How nice for you." He looked back down to find Bohart, giving him an appraising look.

"What is she like?" Bohart asked, his tone curious. He sagged his bulk back into his chair, waiting patiently, one hand mindlessly rubbing his stubbled jaw.

"Juliet?" William paused, his mind racing over every one of her qualities. His body warmed at the memories. Her smile when they had gone riding that day by the lake. Her body in that pink number at Lakeview.

He could share so many things, but at the same time, a large part of him wanted to keep everything to himself. Blowing out a breath, he relaxed into his chair as well, staring at the big red-headed man across from him.

"She is everything I didn't think I wanted. She's bold and strong, yet at the same time so soft. She rides better than most men, and she infuriates me. One moment I'm cursing the moment I met her, the next I find myself chasing her across a ballroom floor," William paused; his tongue felt thick with emotion.

"She makes me want to do more, to be better than my father was for my mother. Better than I am now," He looked over at Bohart, worried about how much he had exposed to this practical stranger, but the club owner remained silent for a moment before bursting out in laughter.

"You are a sorry case, my friend. Ruined." Bohart stood and, going to a glass bar cart, poured himself a finger's worth of scotch. Wagging the bottle at William, who nodded, he made a second glass. Dropping the drink in front of William, Bohart sat on the edge of his desk, his eyes bright with laughter.

"I know," William said, saluting the other man with his glass, trying to sound sad, but his body felt tingly, energized at his confession, and its truth. The girl who had burst into his room that night had quickly made herself at home in his heart as well.

"No one for you?" William asked, gesturing around them.

"No one, permanent," Bohart smirked, and William laughed again. They sat in mutually agreeable quiet for a few minutes, each sipping the deep brown liquid that burned its way through his throat and down to warm his belly.

"What's next?" Bohart finally said, setting his now-empty tumbler on his desk and eyeing William with something akin to excitement.

William stood, letting his empty glass swing from his fingertips as he considered the question. "We expose Pinecrest. But quietly. I don't want to do permanent damage to Greystone. Juliet would never forgive me," William announced, "But first we find proof that Pinecrest is in with Faber. Or that Faber is calling Pinecrest on his loans. Either way, we need to move quickly. It doesn't sound like Faber is keen to wait much longer for his debt to be paid."

Bohart extended a hand again, this time in friendship. "Let me look into them both for you," a devilish smile curled his lips, "My people know how to get more in-depth answers than yours did." William gave a knowing chuckle but took the man's hand, mentally noting to never get on the wrong side of Bohart's.

"I appreciate this. I owe you."

Bohart waved off the favor as if it were a pesky insect. "I was getting bored with the usual management lifestyle; this seems much more interesting." William nodded to him. While the big man talked like he was simply looking for a fight, William had seen the sincere interest shining in Bohart's face.

As he followed the man's assistant down the stairs and out through the deserted club, William got the sneaking suspicion that beneath the rough exterior, he had found a true friend and a good man in Montgomery Bohart.

CHAPTER TWELVE

Juliet had been home at Greystone for over a week, the towering buildings as empty as she had expected. Most days, she wandered the estate completely alone, the covered furniture and blank walls a stark reminder that Greystone was disappearing, piece by treasured piece.

It was already a ghost of the place she had called home, a shadow of the formidable family that used to stalk these halls. Now it was only her footsteps echoing, and as she stared up into the remaining family portraits, she felt the dark painted eyes following her, accusing her.

It seemed that it was with her generation that Greystone would fall. Juliet glared back into her ancestor's mahogany framed faces, her fists clenched. "Well, what am I supposed to do about it?"

There had been no messages from William, and only one from Marian. A simple note saying that Marian and her mother had made their way home to the Wain's family estate in Devonshire and that her little sister Laura was already making her completely mad.

She lamented that Robert had already disappeared into the pile of business documents waiting for him in the study, while the Wains ladies had been entertaining themselves pouring over the gossip columns in search of any mention of Nicholas' ball.

From what they found, the Summer Finale was considered the toast of the summer, and of course, the ton was obsessed with the Earl of Greystone's lovely daughter who had caught the eye of the handsome but brooding Marquess of Mansfield Park. Juliet had blushed reading that part of Marian's letter.

Juliet knew that she had been too awkward, too unsure of herself this spring when she first came out in society. But now, she felt like she was finally finding out who she was. And not just that, but who she wanted to be with. William was much more than she expected.

Marian assured her that there was no mention whatsoever of her late-night walkabout to William's room. So, while the small group who had been at Lakeview that night may be aware, Marshall must be keeping that secret between himself and Lord Faber for the time being. It was a double-edged sword.

To one end, it could, in his mind, help shame and control Juliet. But on the other, it may change people's opinions of her very quickly. Should the wrong people stumble into this secret, Marshall loses his power. It was a weapon he would have to wield carefully.

Marshall's anxiety over this was comical to Juliet. She didn't plan on that secret doing anything but hopefully becoming an embarrassing story that she and William could joke about in the years to come.

She wasn't sure when it happened, but how could she remain ashamed of the way she met the man who she cared so deeply for. It had only been a short time, but her heart, her body, her mind, they craved him. Most of all, she missed him.

Marshall had been away from the house since Juliet had moved back into Greystone. Her mother had raged the first day he was gone, saying that she hated being left alone in this enormous house while he got to go to the city.

Amelia, who had come back before Juliet, told her in loud whispers over breakfast that Marshall had left Greystone red-faced and angry, telling her that he was taking care of the estate business and she had to stay at home and be a wife.

Juliet's eyebrows had flown up, and Amelia had nodded enthusiastically, both of them fascinated and a bit surprised to see the supposed lovebirds fighting. And in front of a full house of curious staff.

Since then, Elizabeth had only appeared briefly for breakfast, her face drawn and pale before disappearing to her private suite where she would take her meals alone for the rest of the day.

That suited Juliet well. She roamed the house freely, spending her evenings reading in her favorite velvet chair in the library or out riding Sterling or Winsome as often as she pleased. The two stallions had to be separated by a stall, but otherwise seemed at peace with their bachelor life at Greystone.

Juliet had already sent a letter to her father's old business partner asking for his opinion on maybe restarting the small breeding operation here at Greystone stables. She felt like it would honor her father's memory and be a fun place to invest some of her allowances in. Coyly, Juliet hoped that William would like the idea and that perhaps he would be interested in partnering with her.

One-night, Juliet sat tucked up under a heavy woven blanket, a heavy book on business practices dangling from her hand as she doodled on another notepad she had brought in. The fireplace was crackling, throwing beautiful dancing shadows over the sitting room, making the gilded wall decor gleam.

In the warmth and quiet, Juliet's eyes drooped, and she felt herself nodding off to sleep, but startled when a hand reached up and gripped the blanket, attempting to cover her up more thoroughly.

Elizabeth didn't notice Juliet was awake, and her lovely face was naked of the coal, rogue, and jewels that she seemed to wear daily like armor. Her face was soft, almost loving, as she smoothed the fabric over Juliet's legs, carefully tucking in the ends around her toes. Juliet couldn't stop looking at her, and she could feel her heart tearing in two.

Who was this woman? She acted like the mother who had grown up chasing butterflies with Juliet and reading her bedtime novels, but she looked like the same one who threatened to abandon her just last week. The same one who called her naive and stupid when what she had needed was a shoulder to lean on, to cry on.

Juliet kept perfectly still. As soon as she was sure the blanket was carefully wrapped around her daughter, Elizabeth slipped silently from the room as if she were just another long shadow dancing in the firelight. When Juliet woke the next morning, on her position on the sofa, as she hadn't had the heart to tear back the warm blankets after her mother took the time to tuck her in so carefully, she couldn't help but wonder if it had all been a dream.

There was no Elizabeth at breakfast, and Juliet went about her day, as usual. She wandered down to the stables when she noticed the carriage horses had returned and were gently munching hay in their respective stalls. She tightened her grip on her riding crop as she knew exactly what this meant.

As if summoned by her dark thoughts, a thin male voice spoke out across the side yard. "Hello Juliet, we thought we might find you here."

Turning from the horses, Juliet immediately felt queasy. Not only was its Marshall, looking extraordinarily pleased with himself, but next to him stood an overdressed and paunch looking Lord Faber.

Although his face was again kind, there was something in the way his eyes boldly traced the lines of her body, stopping momentarily as if he got trapped on the curves.

Juliet curtseyed low, taking her time and offering him only views of her twisted hairstyle and the tops of her shoulders as she looked side to side, wishing frantically for someone to come walking by.

But other than the three of them, the stable area was empty. Dread curled in her gut, making her throat thick. Her head felt heavy. When she slowly straightened, Marshall and Lord Faber were both approaching her.

"You see, Henry, I told you she was a lovely rider," Marshall was saying to Faber, his face pale, focused on the shorter man who walked beside him.

"I would expect no less of a Greystone," Faber said good-naturedly, putting one hand in his pocket as they stopped before her. Bowing over her hand, his mustache tickling her knuckles, "It is nice to see you again, Lady Juliet." Juliet caught the fiery stare coming from Marshall, so while she desired nothing more than to yank her hand free and storm away, she painted a smile on her lips and allowed him to kiss her fingers.

"Thank you, Lord Faber. What brings you here today?" Juliet softly answered, ignoring the angry look that Marshall fixed on her. Lord Faber offered his elbow, which Juliet took obediently, and together they walked into the cobbled stable aisle.

Most days, the smells of hay and warm horses would've comforted her, yet she felt nothing but cold seeping into her bones. Marshall stayed where he was in the small courtyard, watching as Lord Faber walked her further away.

"I wanted to speak to you privately, Lady Juliet, about a deeply personal matter."

Juliet longed to recoil but allowed him to steer her over in front of his body, his small beady eyes focused on her face, or more specifically, her lips as he stumbled on.

"I've never married, you see, not for lack of desire, but for lack of time," Juliet fought hard to shove down her rising panic, "But now I find myself quite lonesome. My home lately feels too big, too empty. Bachelor life has been kind to me, but I'm ready for a change." His hand found hers, and as she looked into his hopeful face, her mind flew, trying to come up with a reasonable rebuke for whatever might come out of this conversation.

He rubbed his thumb over the back of her hands. The feeling left her feeling raw and uncomfortable, the furthest thing from a caress. Revulsion clouded Juliet's mind. Lord Faber leaned towards her, giving her a charitable smile, his belly dangerous close to brushing hers.

"Your father told me of your situation, my dear, and I'm prepared to make an offer for your hand. Mansfield Park be damned. I know that I will be a good husband to you, provide a good life for you," Juliet focused on not moving a muscle, clamping down on her lungs, anything that might qualify as a response to this statement.

"My stepfather…," Juliet corrected automatically, her voice trailing off. Lord Faber's face twitched slightly, displeased with her response to his announcement.

"Juliet, my dear, I'm asking you to marry me. Do you understand?" Lord Faber continued, his thin blonde brows lowering as if concerned she wasn't capable of following his train of thought. Her body screamed to breathe. Breath in, breathe out, she chanted internally.

Juliet peered down at her toes, the riding boots scuffed by a stumble earlier that morning. There had to be a way out of this, yet she just couldn't scratch through the fog of shock to find it. Her mind raced, desperate to find an answer for the man before her.

"You flatter me, my Lord," Juliet ground out, her jaw creaking as her stomach threatened to retaliate in the most unladylike of ways. To her horror, his face immediately brightened. Clearing his throat, Faber sent a sharp glance over his shoulder at Marshall.

As if waiting for this signal, Marshall turned abruptly and slipped out of the barn and out of sight. Juliet's eyes flitted between the two men, feeling a deep sense of foreboding settle in her breast.

Swallowing hard and forcing her voice to do something, "But I cannot accept your offer. I would never want to sully your good name with my scandalized one," Juliet closed her eyes and feigned embarrassment.

Lord Faber gave a dark chuckle, "That's not how I see you, Juliet. I know that your," he paused, and she could feel his stare again wander her person, "Morals, remain intact." Juliet blushed, feeling the humiliation of his statement heat up her face as she continued to tip her face downward.

"It would be my pleasure to shelter you from any misunderstanding, and if it is a question of rumor, I know that we can easily have that fire stomped out." He gripped her arm, clearly unaware of how uneasy she was with his hands on her body. "I am a powerful man, my dear, not a Duke or an Earl, but I have my ways of managing the fickle lot that the ton is."

Juliet felt faint, pressing a shaking hand to her stomach as she swayed a bit. Breath in, breath out, she began again. The fog in her mind cleared just enough.

"I am overwhelmed by your kindness Lord-," Juliet was stopped as Lord Faber held up a hand only a breath away from her lips, so close she could see the stitching of his lambskin gloves.

"Please," he whispered, his beady eyes straying again to watch her lips, "Call me, Henry."

Now hurrying, feeling as if her time for an answer was running short, Juliet blurted out, "Lord Faber, I cannot possibly accept such a proposal right now."

That snapped his head up, sending his prominent double chin-wagging as his face colored. Juliet scrambled to soothe his ire. She didn't fear this small, misinformed man. If anything, she felt pity for him; she was sure loneliness and desperation fueled his actions.

The lurking shadow that was her stepfather, however, was rotten to the core. If Faber were to storm out of here, angry, it would mean facing Marshall's fury. And that she was not prepared to do.

Juliet moved fast, her smooth, cool hands finding hold against the hot, ruddy, blotchy skin of his cheeks, effectively halting his actions. He looked at her longingly from between her clammy hands. It was almost enough to make her nauseous. In her heart, she knew that she needed to buy time, buy safety. Buy her and William a chance. She swallowed the bile in her mouth.

"Please. I just need more time. I've just had my heart stolen, broken by my silly impulsiveness, my Lord," Juliet kept her voice soft and coaxing. Faber's eyes narrowed. Juliet changed tactics, looking for the answer he craved. "As a woman, I've never known how to express my desires." Juliet watched as Faber stiffened, his eyes dilating as her tactic took hold.

"Your desires," Faber spoke slowly, the words garbled as he gazed at her.

"Yes. I need time to understand. To come to grips with the new man in my life." It was true, except for the part about which man was the new one in her life. That role belonged solely to William. If there had been any doubts in her mind, she knew that she would never, and could never be happy married to the man standing before her.

Lord Faber flushed deeply, his face growing warm and sweaty under her palm. His face filled with adoration, he turned into her arm, inhaling against the soft skin of her wrist. While repulsed, Juliet was too frightened to do anything but hold entirely still.

"I completely understand, Juliet," his intense gaze was plastered to her face, watching as he used her given name freely. Juliet tried to smile, but suddenly Faber rushed forward, sealing his lips over hers.

Surprise froze her for only a moment, feeling the sloppy, wet pressure of his mouth pulling at her, before gasping, she shoved him off. Her chest heaving as she wiped at any trace of his lips, unable to bear the feeling of his mouth branded on her skin.

Faber looked at her hard, his face again tinged with embarrassment, but also a fierce victory. Juliet knew at that moment that this man, who acted so friendly, so kind, had a much darker side to him that she had barely scratched the surface of. The silence between them grew, growing sharp and ominous as she struggled to find the right words. Breathing hard, Juliet pressed a shaking hand to her chest, her frantic heartbeat pounding beneath her palm.

Shaking his nearly bald head with a short cluck of his tongue, Faber finally broke the silence. "Please do not mistake my pleasure at you being my potential wife for an excuse not to give me what is due to me," his face twisted, his eyes flickering behind him briefly, where she knew Marshall waited for them.

"I know what kind of woman you are, Juliet, desires, or no, I will not be denied. I have already waited a long time for you. You can consider this if you'd like, our official engagement because whether you like it or not, our wedding will be taking place very soon. You can count on it.

With that, Faber spun deftly on his heels with a jolt and left her standing, sputtering and shivering in the middle of the stable. The moment he disappeared from view, she heard her stepfather's voice, it's slick, charming tones working their magic on Faber's frustration.

Inside the aisle, Juliet found herself able to take only a few steps before leaning against the first solid surface she found, a dilapidated stall. Sterling and Winsome were both silent in the foreboding chill of the day and watching with their curved ears pricked forward to their distressed mistress. Her body crumbled against the stall door.

"What am I going to do?" she cried thickly, her voice cracking as she leaned her forehead against the rough edge of the stall, the prickling of wood against her skin grounding her in its pain. The pain kept her eyes open and focused even as the tears flowed. But neither horse answered, and while Faber and Marshall's voices had long faded.

Juliet straightened, looking out into the yard as a pair of sloppily dressed Greystone footmen cared for Faber's sweat lathered carriage horses. She was certain that Lord Henry Faber wasn't going anywhere. As he had said, he wasn't used to being denied, and what he wanted most now was Juliet. Her fear was tangy in her mouth.

Although she had promised herself and Marian that she would leave William to his business in town, she was desperate to update him with not only the pressing marriage but at the fact that Faber was here in residence at Greystone. She had faith that William's plan, whatever it was, would keep her out of Faber's arms and into his.

But now, the timeline was moving too quickly. William needed to hurry. Ducking into the barn office, she found a small scrap of paper, an inkwell, and quickly wiped the tears off her face, not wanting to let them run into her words and alarm William. Shaking her head to clear her thoughts, she quickly scribbled a note to William.

He has proposed, and I can't say no. Please hurry.

Juliet folded the letter, deciding to leave off her signature and William's name, just in case it fell into the wrong hands. Hurrying across the yard, Juliet cut through the kitchen, finding the butler and begging him to find a way to post her message as soon as he could.

Her tear-streaked face must've shocked the entire room of Greystone cooks and staff members who had gone silent during her pleading. She hadn't cared a single bit at the wary expressions or whispers that followed her, so completely focused on getting the message out.

She quickly escaped out the back stairs to her bedroom. That is precisely where Amelia found her hours later, curled in a tight ball under the blankets.

"Oh lovely, please don't cry," Amelia said, perching her weight on the edge of the bed so that she could lean over and look into Juliet's hair-mussed face.

"You weren't there," Juliet said softly. "He all but claimed me. Like some kind of auction prize." She sniffed hard then attempted to cover her head with the blanket again, hiding from Amelia's kind, searching eyes.

"I've heard all about it, Juliet. What I want to hear now is what you are planning on doing about it," Amelia said the words gently, but the fierceness that lurked in that voice was something to be admired. Juliet peeked out an eye.

"What do you mean?"

"What I mean is that the girl I knew, the girl I raised, she is the daughter of a powerful Earl and a force to be reckoned with all her own. Auction prize is damned, I say."

Juliet rolled her eyes, feeling like the past few days of solitary had destroyed the meager confidence that she had built up while staying at Lakeview.

"My father is gone, I'm going to be married to a man twice my age, and the man I love is all the way in London," Juliet blurted out, frustration threatening to bring more tears as she turned her head into the softness of her pillow.

Breathless, Amelia gave a soft laugh. "So, you've figured out that you love him. I'm so happy for you, my dear."

Juliet withdrew her head to stare at Amelia, and the only maternal influence she could remember in her short life. Amelia's eyes were shimmering with unshed tears. Leaning forward, Amelia brushed her hand, tenderly over Juliet's tear-dampened cheek. "It was clear since that first day that you two were made for each other."

She straightened in the bed, hands going to smooth the covers habitually. "Now, let's talk about how we can keep you single enough to accept that gorgeous boy's proposal when he does finally get here." Juliet laughed, her voice muffled. But slowly, surely, she turned to look at Amelia, swiping harshly at the remaining tear marks.

"Did you have any ideas?" Juliet whispered, sniffling, her heart in her throat. Amelia's wise face lit up conspiratorially. Juliet couldn't help but smile back, so grateful to have someone in Greystone who was on her side.

"Oh, do I," Amelia said, standing up and whipping the blankets off dramatically away from Juliet, who laughed. Feeling a bit more like herself as she leaned into Amelia, waiting to hear what the maid had cooked up for Lord Faber.

***

While Lord had initially told Greystone staff, he meant to stay the entire week. His bright eyes had crawled over her skin as he announced he wanted to get to know his future bride better. Elizabeth had glowed with pleasure, clapping her hands like a small child given a glittering present. Marshall, too, had been pleased, whisking Lord Faber away to celebrate his engagement to Juliet with a mid-day cocktail.

Juliet had stood quietly as they had clapped and smiled, absorbing everything, a smile on her face. A smile that didn't waver because she knew in her heart that she was ready to fight back, that she had something to fight back for. Turning, she went to find Amelia. It was time to put their plan into motion.

Over the next two days, Faber began to change his tune. It seemed everywhere he went, especially to be closer to Juliet, he ran into *issues*. First, the hunting dogs were accidentally getting locked in Lord Faber's room left to wreak havoc on his wardrobe and bedchamber. Then when he attempted to join Juliet on her morning ride, and her father's old horse, Winsome, took him for a ride that he wouldn't soon forget.

By the third day, he announced that he needed to make an early trip to London and be back as soon as possible. He gave Marshall a knowing look as he stomped out the door. Juliet would've been worried, but she was a little sad they hadn't gotten to use any of the other ideas Amelia had thought up.

Marshall and Elizabeth had gotten into an enormous fight after the man had fled. At the same time, Juliet had secretly celebrated the victory. She knew that time was still short and hoped William would make his appearance soon.

The day after Faber left, Juliet sipped her tea and read through a list of pedigrees that her father's dear friend and former businessman. She hoped to present William with a list of beneficial matches for both Sterling and Winsome's first crop of foals. The broodmare's names were foreign to her, but she was determined to learn everything she could. And it helped to distract her from her restless heart.

Juliet glanced up as her mother swooped into the room, entirely made up and wearing a spotless navy gown, the picture of an aristocratic wife. No wonder Juliet always disappointed her and Marshall.

Juliet sat on the chair in the most casual dress she had, it's soft blue tones complimentary to her figure and coloring but did not scream to the universe her bloodline and nobility as her mother did.

Looking down at the horse's pedigrees before her, she set it aside roughly. She hated the look in her mother's eye when she explained any of her business ideas for herself or Greystone. The disappointment, the confusion there, would bring Juliet to tears long before words could.

"What are you reading?" Elizabeth said, brushing past Juliet to find a place on the chair beside her and placing a delicate piece of nearly complete embroidery on the table.

"Nothing of importance," Juliet responded brusquely, folding the letter up into her other notes and turning to look at her mother, her elbow sliding the documents out of reach.
There was no need to cause waves now, not when the time was short. If everything went to plan, her letter to William would've been delivered yesterday. While she felt no regret in secretly calling for William, Juliet felt compelled to explain to her mother. Perhaps there was still time to make her see.

"Mother, I need to speak with you."

With a sigh, Elizabeth pushed aside the embroidery she had brought with her and looked up at Juliet with the same flashing copper eyes as her daughters.

Swallowing, Juliet refused to balk at the stalk look. "I wrote to William. I asked him to come here."

Elizabeth's finely arched brows flew up, her lips pinching in stark and obvious disapproval.

"The Marquess of Mansfield Park? Why would you do that?" she said incredulously. "You know that your father is never going to allow you to marry that rake? Especially after your little show at Lakeview. Look at what he almost did to your good name! Our good name."

Juliet felt her temper flare. Unable to stomp out the flame of her anger, she slammed her hands against the table, silencing her mother. She felt the bite of the wood smart against her palms. "First, mother, allow me to remind you. He is not my father. Second, it was me, me, who sullied William's good name or at least attempted to. And you know what, I'm not sorry that I did it."

Juliet pulled herself up to her full height, her chair screeching backward against the hardwood floors. She stared down her nose at the woman who continued to deny her love and support, even after all these years.

"If that is what it took for me to have met William, then no price is too high. Even if you and Marshall try to ruin this for me, for us, I know that at least I made that one decision on my own. And that being with him was wonderful. I know my worth, Mother, and you or Marshall no longer define it."

Juliet gathered her scattered papers with deliberate slowness and strode from the room, her dress sweeping out behind her with the force of her steps, as if carried by an invisible wind. She didn't look back, and her mother didn't call out.

The day from there turned gloomy. Rain threatened as Juliet looked out into the darkening sky, the dark rumbling cloudbanks mirroring her mood. She was already dressed to ride, planning an evening ride on Sterling to clear her mind before the sinking sun went down and the chill in the air became too much for her thin cloak. She sighed, pressing her face to the window, feeling the weight of her fight with her mother drag at her shoulders until she wanted to collapse to the ground.

Biting her bottom lip, Juliet decided that even a damp ride was better than spending another moment in this vacant, depressing house. A ride would brighten her spirits, and she could always cut back across the property if the rain started up.

She dashed down the stairs, boots tapping merrily along the steps, past a scolding Amelia who carried in her arms a bundle of fresh towels. Laughing, Juliet made her escape to the rain scented day, her nose tingling with the weather change.

Juliet made quick work of tacking up Sterling in the deepening chill, and using a nearby fence line, climbed easily into his back, astride. The majority of the stable hands and barn manager had been among Marshall's first cut from the staff, so she was all alone as she ventured out, the fog shrouding the pair as Sterling's hooves softly beat against the earth.

The sky continued to look ominous, but seeing as the rain was holding off, she and Sterling marched off across the overgrown property yards towards the front roads. His heavy steps carried her away from the stresses inside of Greystone.

Leaning her head back, Juliet yanked the pins from her hair, letting the dark mass free to sweep over her shoulders like a cape. With a sigh, Juliet closed her eyes and tried to soak in some peace.

She was planning on using the dirt roads to cut through to her favorite galloping track since the wooded paths were obscured with branches. Not that it was anyone's fault, the smaller gardening staff had more than enough work to maintain just in the estate's garden, let alone on the expansive riding trails that crossed across the grounds. Juliet sighed as she stared up at the sky, rolling her shoulders as she felt the tension slowly recede from her form.

Sterling was thrilled to be out and pranced lightly along the roadside, his ears pricked with the black lined edges eagerly pointed towards the deserted roadway. They had gone maybe a half-mile when Juliet felt the first raindrops splash against her cloak. At first, just the occasional drop, but soon the sky opened up with a deep rumble, and Juliet cursed loudly as the rain grew heavy.

Squinting into the downpour, Juliet spotted the stone-lined groundskeeper cottage on the corner of the Greystone property. Marshall had only recently let the groundskeeper, Albert and his wife Susana, go. After almost twenty years of Greystone service, Juliet had cried when they had packed up to leave, another victim of Marshall's poor management skill.

Swallowing the lump in her throat, Juliet steered Sterling towards the path to the empty cottage. There would be a porch on the side that Sterling could step under, as well as plenty of firewood still stacked up inside if Juliet were to need it.

Giving Sterling his head, she squeezed her legs on his sides, urging the reluctant, rain-drenched horse forward. "Come on, boy, it'll be dry there," Juliet found herself shouting at the horse, as the wind had suddenly picked up all around them. Gripping his mane in her slick riding gloves, she leaned over Sterling's thick neck to try to avoid the worst of it as they walked into the thrashing wind, her thin cloak whipped back behind them both.

In a flash of brilliant light, the sky split open with a keening cry, lightning crashing to the ground in the large field on her right. The lightning sent Sterling into a scramble, rearing again and again, and even as Juliet tried to keep her seat, the big horse backed up quickly, preparing to flee from the lightning when his hooves slipped in the mud of the road.

With a squeal, the pair began to go down, the uneven edge of the road falling away under the torrent of rain. Juliet clamped her eyes shut, her hands fisting into Sterling's mane to hold on, and for a moment, she wondered if the stallion would be able to keep his feet.

A breath later, the world went topsy turvy. The last thing she remembered was her leg being pinched under Sterling's heaving sides and cool darkness settling over her mind.

***

Juliet's eyelids fluttered open, her mind feeling hazy as she tried to ascertain what had happened and how long she had been out. The rain was still steadily coming down, and Juliet could feel the spongy texture of the muddy soil beneath her left side.

The same side that was effectively pinned to the ground by Sterling's mass. The great horse had gone down on his side. Because of the angle of the ditch, they were now stuck where he fell. Sterling was surprisingly calm, his breathing ragged but his eyes quiet, as if waiting for her to wake up and get them out of the predicament.

Juliet took a quick stock of the rest of her body, moving her hands over her limbs. Nothing seemed broken. She may have been fortunate this time. The rain had soaked the ground all under her, providing a way to cushion her pinned leg against the weight above it. Stroking the sodden, hot neck of her mount, Juliet tried to sit up to slide her leg out, using her hands to push back against the saddle. Nothing happened. With a grunt, she tried again with little success. They were very stuck.

Tears threatened as she realized how far she was from home and that even if someone bothered to come looking for her, there were a hundred other more logical spots to look before checking the main roads that surrounded Greystone. Juliet leaned back down, hating the thick, paste-like mud that clung to her elbow and shoulder, the chill of the rainwater chilling her to the bone.

"Help!" Juliet shouted, leaning towards the road and trying to project her voice as well as she could. Nothing but the falling rain responded to her, drowning both her voice and her hope.

"Is anyone out there?" She tried one more time, her throat sounding hoarse against the steady downpour. Frustration blurred her dark eyes, and she went back to fighting the saddle, frantically pushing this way and that, trying to free her leg from under the bulk of the horse.

Suddenly Sterling's body quivered, and he took an enormous breath, letting it out with a screaming neigh. Juliet covered her ears as well as she could in her awkward position, flinching away from the severe sound.

Sterling's head was as far off the earth as it could get, and his ears were pricked forward, flickering slightly towards the roadway. With another deep breath, he repeated the screaming neigh. This time a less hysterical, nearby whinny responded to him. There was another horse up there.

"Help! Help us!" Juliet shouted. Patting the shifting horse, "God bless you and your big mouth."

"We're down here," Juliet yelled again, her eyes searching the swirling grey sky, her eyes narrow against the attacking raindrops, waiting to see if anyone would step into view. But there was nothing.

"Please," Juliet cried, feeling desperate. She leaned back down, resting on her mud-caked elbow, closing her eyes as she began to shiver.

"Juliet!" shouted a deep man's voice, worry apparent in its pitch. Juliet's eyes flew open; she recognized that voice. A dark horse and rider were halted at the top of the ditch, the horse's legs several inches deep in mud. Within moments, the rider threw himself off the horse and slid down the ditch to her side. The hands upon her face were warm against the clammy feel of her skin.

CHAPTER THIRTEEN

William's heart felt like it might pound out of his chest. When Athena had first returned the mysterious horse's call, he had been irritated at the piercing noise and legged her on. He was drenched to the skin, his heavy clothing plastered against him. He wanted desperately to get to Greystone, to get dry and warm. But most of all, he wanted to get to her.

Receiving Juliet's letter had almost broken him. He had immediately postponed his last meeting with Bohart's sources and ridden out of the city. The weather hadn't been kind as his mare had gamely pushed through the frigid rain. He was so close now, and all he could think about was the doe-eyed girl who had turned his world upside down.

That was until his mare had stopped in the downpour, and he had looked down to see his worst nightmare unfurling at their feet. Juliet curled at the base of the roadside's ditch, trapped in a sodden divot with the massive grey stallion trapped directly over her.

Her eyes had been closed; her face a shocking shade of pure ivory. He was out of the saddle and down the slope before he had time to register any of it. When he had gotten to her, she had opened those incredible amber eyes, and when she had seen him, well, it had changed everything, the way she looked at him.

"Juliet? Easy now. What's hurt?" He asked roughly, his throat was tight, and the emotions building in his mind from seeing her like this threatened to overwhelm him. Forcing them down with a swallow, he pushed a comforting smile to his lips. His hands floated over her body, looking for any sources of pain or injury.

"My leg is sore, the one under him, but nothing feels broken," Juliet answered, her voice a little too breathy. Her lips were beginning to turn blue, and he knew that between the cold and the shock, he needed to get them both right-side-up as soon as he could. There was no time to ride to Greystone for help, even if he could bear to leave her in this state.

"Okay, I think I have a plan," William said, "I need to go back to Athena for a moment." But Juliet's hand shot out as her face crumpled.

"Please don't leave me here," her eyes wildly looking from him to Sterling and back.

"It's okay, darling, you have to trust me," he whispered, pressing a kiss to her forehead and feeling her chilled skin under his lips. Carefully he pulled his hand out of her grip, and she lay there quietly as he stood, then sprinted the few strides up the slope again to his mare.

The thick mud pulled at his legs as he clambered to the top, his blood heated by urgency. In his saddlebag was Athena's tie-downs for when they had made camp the night before. It would be long enough to do what he needed.

Looking down at the trapped horse and rider, William could see exactly how he needed to free the large animal. Once freed, he would be capable of rising on his own and leave Juliet safely on the ground.

Thankfully, Sterling remained quiet, his body crooked, but nothing looked damaged from Williams' quick overview. Quickly William made a harness and wrapped it around the saddle before sliding down just far enough to catch one of Sterling's back hooves. Setting a loop around that leg, William let his body slide the remaining distance back to Juliet's head.

She smiled at him when he came into view. "Are you going to pull us out?" Her voice sounded doubtful.

"Not quite," William answered. "All I need you to focus on is making sure your foot, this foot here," he pointed at the leg under the horse, "is free when he gets up." He tried to smile at her.

"Otherwise you'll end up hanging from the side of him like a monkey," he joked. Juliet's pale lips quivered as if a smile tried to appear but didn't quite make it.

She nodded, and he watched as her long delicate fingers gripped a bit of the rein, her knuckles a ghostly white under the skin, preparing herself for what might be a lot of violent movement from Sterling as he attempted to right himself.

William climbed back up and onto Athena, facing her in the direction of Sterling's errant legs. Patting the rain-soaked horse, he clucked and squeezed his legs hard against her, "Go 'Thena, go."

The mare was a riding horse, not a cart or plow horse, but she quickly realized what her rider was asking. She dug in, the slick mud deepening around her hooves. Within moments, she lunged forward, yanking Sterling hard enough that his hindquarters dropped off the ledge that had been keeping him from getting up on his own.

The moment his legs felt the solid ground, the big grey lurched to his feet. "Juliet, kick free," William shouted to her. He didn't need to, though, since Juliet had immediately thrust her foot out and now sat upon the ground cringing, watching as Sterling shook himself like a wet dog.

William again flew down from Athena. Sliding deftly down the slope, he knelt beside Juliet, his handsome face filled with worry. "Juliet, Juliet," He said deliberately, her face stared at him. His hands raced down her muddy leg, tracing the lines for obvious signs of pain or discomfort. When he found nothing obvious, the relief nearly choked him.

"Let's get you up. We need to find shelter and get you warmed up now." Juliet nodded dumbly, taking both his hands in hers and attempting slowly to stand. She flinched hard, pain filling her lovely face and settling it into a scowl as she gently kneaded one hand into her left thigh, the one that had borne both of their weights.

"Here, let me," he shifted until he could put his arm under hers and prop her up.

"It's not bad," Juliet breathed, "Just some rather significant pins and needles." But regardless, she leaned her head against his shoulder. Together they carefully made their way up to Athena. Sterling followed obediently, giving William a chance to assess the horse's soundness visually. While the animal looked fine, William wasn't eager to put Juliet back on a horse just yet.

Looking about them, he saw the cottage just off the main road. Jerking his head towards it, "What is that?"

"It's part of Greystone, vacant for now."

"Well, that's where we are going then," William said, relief in his voice. Reaching behind with the hand not secured around Juliet's body, he looped Sterling's mud-soaked reins over Athena's saddle. Then whistling to the mare, he began to walk towards the cottage, sticking to the high road until the last possible moment.

Juliet kept up with him hobbling a little on her leg as she went. Her bottom lip was in her teeth as she focused on maintaining her pace. He squeezed her waist, trying to reassure her as she made their way up the sloppy path.

Thank god that they had been within easy walking distance to the groundkeeper's cottage, William thought as together William and Juliet stumbled through the doorway. Rain dripping off the clothes and creating a long line of mud and water on the dusty hardwood floors. Stopping just inside the door, Juliet saw a chair.

"You can set me down here," Juliet murmured, her teeth starting to chatter as the icy rainwater settled against her skin. Carefully William lowered her until she could sit down, her water-laden skirts dragging behind her as if they'd been dipped in lead. William quickly dashed back out to secure the horses under the overhang to dry, making sure to grab the leather bag from the back of his saddle.

William reentered the cottage, his heart skipping a beat, this time not in fear, but adoration. Juliet was slowly walking across the kitchen area, every line in her body filled with stiff determination. She was a force to be reckoned with, that he could tell.

"I don't think you should be up and walking quite yet my love," his voice softened as he closed the door behind him, the endearment slipping out.

Juliet glanced over her shoulder, her eyes warming at the sight of him and the gentle affection. "I'm alright. I can feel the numbness receding." Subconsciously she ran dirty fingers of the drying mud on her hip.

William looked around them. The cottage was sparsely furnished but had been occupied recently. Gratitude for the monstrous stone fireplace filled his body. Juliet had been in the cold and wet for way too long; William was still worried about her going into shock.

Thankfully, the fireplace already had a small stack of logs in it that looked dry and ready to burn. Striking a match against the stone chimney, he dropped the match into the prepared kindling. Juliet sighed gratefully and dropped to her knees against the fireplace edge.

William followed her with his eyes, wracking his mind to come with a polite way to tell her that she had to get out of her soaking clothes, and he probably needed to as well. The storm outside continued to rage, heavy rain pounding down against the little cottage windowpanes. He ducked into the first-floor bedroom and took stock of blankets folded in a deep cedar chest at the base of the bed. He grabbed several and headed back to the main room.

"Juliet, we need to get dried off. Both of us are going to end up sick staying in these wet garments. I say we swap out wet clothes for a mountain of blankets and let our bodies warm up a bit. There are plenty of clean ones in that bedroom. You can get changed there if you'd like. I'll keep the fire going out there." He held up a small stack he had claimed for himself, tossing them onto the rug behind him.

Juliet's eyes widened, and he couldn't help but smile that she blushed at the implication. Sure, he was direct, but it was a serious situation as well. He wasn't going to sit here, freezing, covered in mud while they could easily undress and sit in warm, dry blankets just as easily.

"You are right. It seems like we will be here for a while longer. We should get more comfortable," Juliet said, walking towards him, her formerly pale cheeks now pink with a pretty blush.

Her riding habit was molded to every inch of her body, and her sodden hair had fallen loose of its pins and now tumbled down her back in a wild mass of dark curls. She stopped only a few feet from him and turned, reaching back to slide a hand through her loose hair and exposing her back to his view.

"Would you mind? I remember you being good at this," She said sweetly, laughter clear in her voice. William grinned, even at this moment, this situation, this woman was trying to drive him mad. He remembered vividly that stolen kiss the night of his arrival. He had no place putting his mouth on her, but God, it had been worth the world of pain he had been in since. Every time he thought of her, it was like a fierce burn covering his mind and body until he could think of absolutely nothing else.

His smile dimmed as his blood heated slowly, wondering at how her skin tastes now. Would it taste like fresh rain? Or how she had that night? Like the last drips of summer's honey.

Then Juliet shivered, hard, and guilt overwhelmed him. She might be teasing him, but he was the gentleman here. It was his job to keep them on the right path. Or at least that what he told himself, over and over. And over as he quickly freed her laces, letting her riding habit slide off one shoulder.

Juliet caught the wet garment, holding it against her body as she smiled at him over her shoulder. Was it his imagination, or did she seem a little disappointed? The thought sent a spark of heat straight to his already throbbing groin. As she walked from the room towards the bedroom, he took several deep breaths in as he tried to calm back down, shaking his head to clear all visions of her silken skin from his memory.

***

Juliet let the sodden riding habit fall to the floor and began to peel back the other layers. Her chemise, corset, and pantaloons followed quickly, all landing in a wet pile that she quickly set about draping across the small room so that they might dry. She was shivering in earnest now, quickly grabbing another of the thick, sweet-smelling blankets and wrapped it around her body, relishing in the softness of the quilt against her chilled skin.

Knocking on the door between them, she raised her voice over the sound of the rain, "William? Are you decent?"

A laugh sounded on the other side, and she took that as permission to enter. When she did, William stood by the fireplace, a wide grin on his face, another quilt like hers spread over his body.

"You, of all people, ask to enter the room?" Juliet blushed brightly but also grinned at the joke, relieved that they were to the point where humor was the best explanation for their first encounter.

"Well, I knew that it was a one-time mistake, my Lord," Juliet said tartly, stopping directly in front of him and tilting her face up to his. She gripped her quilt tightly in front of her breasts, keeping the blankets held firm so that she was modestly covered.

Biting her lip, she chanced a look at how William had used the blankets as a makeshift wrap. The top acting like a cloak and a kilt-like knot around his waist as well, leaving long feet and part of his calves exposed to her eyes.

How did the man manage even to have pretty legs? Juliet wondered to herself, wishing she could slow her racing heart and calm the ache that spread from her belly downwards. In the dimly lit space, the sharp planes of his face flashed into shadow as she stared at him, drawn to him like a moth to the flame.

His eyes had grown dark, sensually, lazily looking her over as well. First, her face, then at the quickly warming skin left exposed across her shoulders, her collarbone, and the tops of her breasts. They seemed to swell, grow tight under his examination, and lust flashed over his face, making her breath quick in her lungs.

"A one-time mistake? What a pity," William growled.

"Unless you'd like otherwise," Juliet said, trying to sound seductive, but a smile slowly taking over her full lips. William threw back his head and laughed loudly, his partially dry locks flopping over his eyes.

"You must've hit your head when Sterling went down. No man in his right mind would ever turn you away, least of all me. You've been slowly driving me mad since that night, and I'd be disappointed if you stopped now," William finished, a coy smirk pulling her in.

"Oh. Well. That is good to know. I think," Juliet said softly, watching the firelight backlit his face, making him seem mysterious. However, bold her words, she didn't have any experience to back it up if he called her on her flirtation.

Looking at him, though, Juliet was pretty sure that he knew those things. That she was more inexperienced than she wanted to admit and that she loved being bold and forward with him. Not all men would appreciate her newly found sharpness.

She shivered again, her blanket was finally chasing away the lingering cold, but her body still felt sensitive, over-stimulated. Memories of their last night at Lakeview together, what William had done to her body overwhelmed her mind.

William caught her movement and immediately stepped towards her, worried, "Come here," he said softly, guiding her to sit on the pile of blankets he had brought in.

As soon as she was seated, he sat behind her and pulled her against his chest. Even with the layers of blankets between them, Juliet sighed in pleasure. As she turned her head, her cheek met the smooth bare skin of his chest, and it took her breath away. Hot, smooth, and she could practically feel the power beating through those veins.

She was safe here. In his arms, the rest of the world faded until it was just the two of them together. His heat leaked into her, sparking her body awake. Juliet felt restless against him, unsure how to calm the firestorm in her veins, the throbbing in her body.

Taking her restlessness as something else altogether, William pulled her closer, murmuring soft, comforting noises against her ear. "Shhh. It's okay now." His deep voice rumbled over her shoulder, sending another tight burst of sparkling heat through her body. Juliet opened her mouth, sighing loudly.

"Thank you," Juliet said. She turned in his arms to look at him, her eyes serious. She knew that her blanket had slipped just a fraction, exposing inches of formerly hidden skin just above her breasts. Keenly aware of the roughness of the fabric against her sensitive skin, she welcomed those silvery eyes as William's gaze followed the line of the blanket.

"You're welcome," William said, his voice chipped, his face drawn as if he were in pain. Yet he leaned forward, close enough she could smell the rain on his swarthy skin, his eyes focused on her lips. Seeing that, she habitually bit down on the bottom one, her white teeth pushing into the pink.

"You'll be the death of me yet," he said, his voice quivering as his flint eyes turned to granite. William's hand reached between them, his thumb brushing against the lower lip she tortured with her teeth.

She stopped kneading her lip and instead boldly met his eyes as she turned a little to kiss the palm that had stroked her cheek. With a groan, both of his hands shot out, burying themselves in the thickness of her hair as he crashed his lips against hers.

Her sound of surprise only opened her mouth for his plunder, letting his tongue sweep in and soothe the abused spot on her lips before sliding across her own tongue, tormenting her into more action.

Juliet's hands were knotted in the blanket she was wearing, but somehow, she managed to stand up on her knees and slide one over the top of his split legs, bringing their blanket clad bodies into a sharp awareness of each other.

One of his hands dropped to her lower back, where he rested her for a moment on her bottom before slowly pulling down and around the back of her knee, deftly moving her second leg over his. She now straddled his wide torso on her knees, her face tilted up to his.

William released her mouth for a moment, his breathing ragged, and his thick, muscular chest exposed. Juliet felt like her hands acted on their behalf as they reached out to touch his jaw, and then inch by inch made their way lower. First down his stubbled jaw, past the corded muscle at the base of his neck and to his chest, which was covered lightly with soft, black hair that she let her fingers tease through.

Now it was William who seemed to be breathless, his head falling back as he revealed in her hands' attention. She briefly wondered if he could feel the heat pooling at her core, making her feel like she might come apart at any moment. Dropping down lower, she gasped as her inflamed skin brushed against the blankets between them.

She could feel the hard, eager length of him just below her, and it sent spasms of pleasure and power through her body from her core straight to her tight nipples. She might be a virgin, but she wasn't uneducated. Letting her hips fall a little, she instinctively ground against the firmness she felt there, moaning at the contact that made her thighs quiver in anticipation.

William let out a chuckle. "Temptress," he gritted out, his hands now gripping her hips hard, his fingers digging in as they rocked against each other.

Juliet couldn't tell if his hands meant to hold her away or pull her to him again. Whichever it was, she didn't want him to stop. Pinning him with her eyes, she searched his face before a devilish smirk snuck across her own.

Rising a little, loving the little sigh that came as their blankets sliding down her body, she then let her hips roll against him, torturously slow. While she meant to please him, she couldn't control the moan that came out of her mouth. Every movement, every touch made her feel like a great crescendo was building inside of her, and William was at the center of it.

With a growl, William pushed her off of his lap, their legs tangling as he overtook her, laying her out on her back against the blanket-covered floor. His mouth captured hers, and he moaned softly as she experimented with her tongue, shyly returning his bold touches with her own.

Juliet's mind was wild with passion, with the feel of this amazing man in all of her senses. He released her mouth only to gently trail his mouth down her neck, his wickedly hot tongue swirling on her shoulder. Juliet instinctually bucked her hips towards him, practically lifting them from the blanketed floor.

"William, please," her hands were in his hair, combing it back as his mouth continued to taste his way across her collarbones. When he reached the top of her breasts where the frayed edge of the quilt ran across her body, he hesitated. Juliet felt his forehead lean onto her neck, the pants of his breath hot against her skin.

Her blood hummed, and her mind screamed at her to make him keep going; she lifted a leg, trying to urge him forward, but her knees were trapped beneath layers of pesky quilt. She felt his hand press down on her hip bones through the thick fabric.

Juliet tried to remain still, but her body quaked in unease. His face was so serious as he stared down at her. Gripping the remaining blankets that covered her body, he yanked them back to expose her.

Cool air surged over her bare skin as his eyes closed, his head dropped back as a sigh of pleasure escaping his lips.

"You are perfect." The words were only a whisper, but every part of Juliet felt them. Curling her toes, she found herself preening under his stare. But there was so much more she wanted and needed. She raised her arms, unabashedly asking for him to rejoin her on the floor.

"Come here," Juliet's voice was strong, certain.

"Are you sure? Because I can stop right now. We can stop this right now." William's soft voice skimmed across her aching body.

"You would do that?" Juliet felt her throat tighten as she pushed the words through her lips.

"Of course. You are worth waiting for," came the easy response. William was on his knees above her, wrapped only in a blanket. She could see the muscles of his chest and belly contract as they stared down at her, waiting. He was again, giving her the chance to choose.

She couldn't think of anything she wanted more.

"William? I want you. More than anything." At her words, his face flushed, his incredible lips swollen from her own. Just the sight of him sent another almost painfully intense streak of desire down her body, straight between her legs. Her breath came short in her lungs as he crawled over her, letting his delicious weight settle onto her body.

"You undo me, my lady," he said slowly, his voice ragged. Propping himself up on his elbow, he looked down into her face, his eyes brightening as he stared down at her. Juliet felt his fingers tangle lightly in her hair before his hot mouth planted kisses down the column of her neck and across her chest before coming to a stop just above her breasts. Her nipples puckered in the chill of being exposed.

With deliberate softness, William's fingers trailed across the dark pink skin. Juliet felt her body tighten further, her hips shifting restlessly under William's weight, pressing against him.

Suddenly the hot, wet heat of his mouth took her breast, his tongue a silken pull against her nipple. Juliet arched her body into him, her hands diving into his hair to hold him against her. Moans tore from her throat as he suckled first one breast, then the other. Finally, he pulled away to trail down her body, his nose and tongue painting a path over her ribs, across her navel, and straight down to her hips.

By the time he reached her pelvis, he reached out to cup her hips, to calm them as he pushed back, ducking down to drop a kiss over her most intimate place. With a cry, she rose off the floor. Planting one of his heavy hands across her belly, he pressed her earnestly back into the blankets, urging her to let him continue.

Her find fogged with pleasure as she felt his hot breath on her folds. With such delicate sweetness, he slid a single finger along her crevice

"William, please," Juliet begged again, her voice bold.

"Please what?" William said softly, pressing a chaste kiss against her core. Juliet cried out, tugging his thick, dark hair between her fingers.

"More, I need more." Juliet barely finished the words before William took her with his mouth, sucking lightly on her core before sliding his tongue out to taste her rapturously. Her body arched in desperation to be closer to his lips, his hot mouth. She felt her body beginning to spiral as his tongue probed her body.

William suddenly moved away, rocking back on his heels and throwing aside the blanket that had been caught between them. Juliet's eyes immediately fell to the erection jutting from his body, the thick shaft bobbing against William's taut belly. He gripped it in his hand, staring down at her, watching her, gently palming himself. Curious, Juliet sat up on an elbow, her body still humming with desire, with need, and boldly laid her hand over his.

William inhaled sharply as he let his hand drop, hers remaining where she stroked his swollen organ, her eyes staring up at him. He was magnificent, every part of him. She knew that more than anything, she needed him inside of her.

Gasping, William finally gripped her wrist, chuckling as he urged her to relax back. "No more of that, or this show will be over before it even begins." Juliet smiled, pleased that she had brought him even a small measure of the pleasure that he continued to show her.

Taking her mouth with his, William's lips were sweet against her. They pressed her into the blankets as his hand reached down her hip down to her bottom, where he pulled her thigh up against this. Juliet broke the kiss, panting, as she opened up to his body. With the smallest movement, she and William would be one.

Instinct drove her to raise her hips, begging for the pleasure she knew awaited her. The slick head of William's length pushed against her. Butting her with his nose, William kissed his way across her face, even as his fingers on her thigh tightened. In a smooth, possessive move, William thrust forward, filling her with all of himself.

Gasping, Juliet clutched at his shoulders, crying out quietly as she buried herself in his arms. William froze, his body completely still, as he allowed her body to adjust to his invasion. He swept her face with soft kisses.

After catching her breath, Juliet found herself returning his kisses with more of her own. Pressing her hands into the small of his back, she reveled in the feeling of being completely, uniquely one.

Carefully watching her with his nearly black eyes, William began to move, rocking his hips back and forth. At first, Juliet braced herself for pain, but the slick slide of his body against hers began to rekindle the fire of passion that quickly consumed her body. Digging her nails into his skin, Juliet begged him for more, her body meeting his thrust for thrust.

His lips captured a nipple, tugging on it lightly with his teeth as his hips continued to set a rhythm against her body, his body glowing in the firelight. Juliet felt herself going mad, her mind filled with the pleasure he was giving her. Biting down on her lip, she gave herself over to the passion, the instinct, letting her hips rise to meet every thrust, her eager body begging for release.

William's motions were speeding up, becoming less gentle as his torturous lips again captured her breast. Tugging gently with his teeth, he wrung a cry from her lips, teasing the peak with his tongue. She was so close to oblivion; she could feel it threatening to overtake her with every surge of his body. William's voice panted in her ear as strong hands urged her to wrap her legs around his waist.

"Fall with me," he rasped, the sound rumbling through her body as he reached between their bodies. Finding where her core hummed, his fingers circled it, rubbing, even as his thrusts filled her.

Juliet shouted his name as her body shattered below him, clenching tightly around his shaft as the waves of exquisite pleasure rolled through her again and again. Distantly as if from far away, she felt William curse darkly, his powerful body straining against hers as he threw back his head in his climax.

As Juliet came back down to Earth, her limbs turning to a delightful languid state, she trailed her curious fingers over his heaving chest, his wide, powerful shoulders. She smiled coyly as his skin jumped, twitching at her gentle touch. William watched her actions through heavy-lidded eyes, dark hair loose and wild around his face. Finally, Juliet untucked her legs from his waist, letting her legs fall to the pile of blankets.

William lowered his face, brushing affectionate, light kisses across her lips even as he continued to stare into her eyes. Juliet's body was sated, but her heart trembled at the open adoration that he looked at her with. Sliding from her body, William pulled Juliet to his chest, pressing her body against him, as if unhappy that any space dare separates them. She didn't mind.

"I didn't know it would be like that." Juliet blushed, her eyelashes fluttering against the warm skin of his chest.

"Neither did I." William's fingers traced patterns down her back.

Glad that he wouldn't see her face, Juliet couldn't resist asking, "But haven't you been with other women? It's not uncommon."

His chest rose and fell before he answered. "I've been with other women, Juliet. Some I regret. But it has never felt, even a bit, like what we just shared. That was something else entirely."

"Really?"

"I wouldn't lie to you," William chuckled, tightening his hold on her body. "You should rest for a bit, my love. I'll wake you when the storm passes."

William gently wrapped his arm around her shoulders, tucking her into his warmth. Not getting a response, he leaned forward.

"Juliet?" She was fast asleep; her lips parted in a dream as her body curled around his own. His silver eyes crinkled at the corners as he leaned forward to press his lips to her forehead, covering them both with part of the quilts. And that is where they stayed. Juliet was dozing against the head of his body as they let their clothes dry.

"Hello beautiful," William's rich voice settled over her, rousing her gradually from her dreamlike state. She raised her eyebrows. Based on the hunger she felt that it must be past dinner by now and the darkness was settling over the estate.

"The rain has stopped. We'd best get a move on." William said, gingerly getting to his feet. He did not bother to cover his naked body, and Juliet's eyes immediately drank their fill. William's body was striking.

Long, well-muscled arms and legs from his riding were drawn together by a thick, powerful chest and torso covered by a fine layer of silken dark hair that matched what was on his head and between his legs. And speaking of that part, his body seemed aware of her eyes as it began to thicken and grow.

Juliet swallowed, stretching her body as best she could without letting her quilt drop. Even still, she blushed when she felt his hot eyes on her again.

"You're right." Standing quickly, she dashed to the bedroom, where her clothes were drying. As she got to the door, she heard his voice.

"That's probably best. If we stay here any longer, I might be convinced to ravish you again." She trembled at the heat that flashed through her body at his words. Taking a deep, steadying breath, Juliet stepped into the tiny bedroom and quickly closed the door, leaning her burning face against the cold wooden door. Laughter bubbled in her chest, even as she pressed a hand to her face, letting her fingers wander across the seemingly permanent smile there.

CHAPTER FOURTEEN

It took more time than even she'd imagined getting dressed in her still damp clothing, the heavy fabrics sticking to her warm skin. By the time she yanked her clothing into place and exited the cottage bedroom, it was dark outside. William stood by the door and smiled at her when she walked in, his whole face lighting up at seeing her. Which, of course, made her face pink up in pleasure.

Walking slowly to her, she boldly let herself lean against his side. Without breaking his gaze out the window, his arm curled around her, hugging her tenderly. "It's time for me to go."

"What?" Juliet said sharply, her upturned face searching his.

"Only, for now, love, I don't think that being found haphazardly dressed in an abandoned cottage will do much in our case to say that I'm the best choice for you," He said, his finger gently brushing an errant curl away from her face.

"It would keep the other suitors away?" Juliet pushed back, her heart pounding at the prospect of him leaving already.

William chuckled but stepped back from her. "Not the one we are worried about, it won't. I'm going to go just back down the road and stay at the closest inn." Juliet's brow wrinkled as she waited for him to explain.

"Then tomorrow, I will come to Greystone and surprise you," William said with a wink. "I'm hoping that shortly after my associate will be here with everything, we need to assure your engagement to Lord Henry Faber is over."

"Your plan worked?" Juliet whispered, her voice sounding frantic as William adjusted the damp cloak of his shoulder. "You know we can convince Marshall?"

"Faber's offer for your hand is not only inappropriate but invalid," William finished, his face growing dark. "We can approach Marshall, as you call him, together. Talk some sense into him. Maybe he will change his plans without having to get any authorities involved."

"Authorities, William, what is this all about?"

"I promise I will reveal everything tomorrow," he said.

"But tomorrow, Faber will be at Greystone as well. He arrives first thing via carriage," Juliet pulled a face. "I scared him away the other week, but I worry he's grown tired of Amelia's tricks. He won't be so easily fooled into leaving this time."

A cunning smile crossed William's face. "That, my love, is what makes it all the better." He walked to the door, turning back, his face still clouded. "I'm sorry to keep you in the dark, but know that everything will come together as quickly as possible. And I've called for reinforcements during Faber's stay."

Juliet gave him a tight-lipped smile, crossing her arms and rubbing the flesh of her arms vigorously as if to ward off the idea of a marriage to Lord Faber. "I trust you, William."

William strode back to her with a curse, pulling her tightly against his body in a rough embrace. "I-," his voice cut off gruffly, "I-I know you do. Stay safe and stay away from your stepfather. I will be back before you know it." William set her back, his expression solemn.

Juliet nodded, her traitorous eyes filling with tears. "Goodbye, William. For now." He walked out into the inky fall evening; his boot steps muffled against the wet leaves on the ground. She heard him slap his leather saddlebags across Athena's back, and then the gentle jingle of the metal bit in the mare's mouth.

And then they were gone, carefully picking their way back up to the main road. She waited by the door until she could no longer hear the rhythmic hoofbeats taking William back down to the local Inn. Juliet shivered, already missing his warmth, his voice.

Juliet gathered the quilt back around her body and went to recline by the fireplace, her fingers running over the wooden floors where just hours ago she had been laying beneath William. The thought brought tingles to her belly and a smile to her face. She knew she could ride home, but she and William had decided that feigning a small injury might be the best explanation for the time that had elapsed since she had left that afternoon.

She bought time milling around the house, finding some pins left in a drawer, she attempted to smooth her hair. She had liked the old groundskeeper, Randolph, and wished that they had been able to keep him here.

With a pang, Juliet realized how badly she wanted to free not just herself from Marshall's reign but the entirety of Greystone. It weighed heavily on her shoulders as she listened to the darkness of the night.

She was refolding up one of the heavy quilts when the front door flew open with a deafening bang. Marshall stood in the doorframe, his usually coiffed blonde hair unruly around his wind-whipped face. Seeing her, he strode up to her and grabbed her upper arm in a rigid gloved fist.

"We have been looking everywhere for you," he snarled at her, spittle flying, "What are you playing at?"

Juliet wrenched her arm free, twisting away with a flourish of her skirts, "I wasn't playing anything! Sterling and I fell. We just came here to dry off," she shouted back.

"We?" Marshall growled.

"The horse and me. We." Juliet said, sarcasm slipping into her voice. If possible, Marshall's face grew redder.

"Do you have any idea how important you are?" Marshall's voice rose, filling the cottage. The volume made Juliet want to cringe away, to retreat, but she planted her feet against the onslaught. She would not give him the satisfaction of cowering.

"Important to you? Or important to Faber's offer?" she spat back at him. His face blanched, and he seemed to freeze for a moment. Breathing deeply through his nose, Marshall looked down at his mud-splattered coat, straightening it with jerky motions.

"I have no idea what you're talking about," he said, eerily calm.

"Don't lie to me. I know I've never been anything but a payout for you. And the only reason you would deny the Marquess would be if Lord Faber has made a better offer," Juliet twisted her face, her heart cold. "That or if it just pleases you to continue to deny me a chance at real love."

Marshall stood above her, looking down his long nose at her. Whereas she had always seen the vain, handsome but hateful man her mother had married, she realized now that all she saw was a monster. The man who changed her family changed their home and spent the past decade isolating and ignoring her.

Raising her chin, even as it quivered, she turned and brushed past him and out of the room. Walking to a dry but muddy Sterling, she heard Marshall slam the cottage's door and join her on the porch. Looking him straight in the eyes, she clambered onto Sterling's back, unflinching, even as a variety of pains tightened her chest.

Without a word, she steered the stallion down the path and up to the road and past a small group of riders who had accompanied Marshall on his quest to find her. Juliet nodded deeply to them, recognizing them as household servants from Greystone. She appreciated them coming, even if they had been ordered to do so.

By the time she got home, her anger had faded into exhaustion and more than a little soreness. She handed off Sterling to a footman who promised to give the horse extra care and made her way into the house.

Not surprising, but still disappointing, her mother wasn't anywhere to be seen. But as soon as she mounted the stairs to her room, a warm, comforting hand found the small of her back, and she turned to see Amelia standing beside her. The older woman's kind face was red, and her eyes were glassy with tears.

But in her usual no-nonsense way, Amelia urged her upstairs, "Let's get you to bed, my lady."

Juliet nodded, her own eyes filling as the overwhelming events of the day hit her like a boulder to her chest. Letting Amelia guide her, she climbed to her room, where she was stripped of her cold clothes and dropped into a steaming bath. The last thought she had before she dozed off that night was that tomorrow everything would change.

***

Juliet felt stiff the next day, but she remained unencumbered by her fall for the most part. She had hurried to the stables to see how Sterling fared, only to be equally pleased by his recovery. The only long-term damage from the day before was her completely, wonderfully ruined modesty. Which, in Juliet's mind, was more than worth the tradeoff.

By the time breakfast was served, Juliet had made her way downstairs, eager to see what the day would bring. She was alone in the dining room when she heard the distinctive creak of carriage harness and wheels pull around the front drive. Laying her fork carefully to the side, she dapped at her lips with the napkin.

Lord Faber was early; she thought to herself. Smoothing anxious hands down her dress, Juliet quickly slipped out of the dining hall and across to the entry. As she expected, she would be the only family member available to receive Lord Faber at this hour.

Bringing William's image from yesterday, his body glowing in the cottage's firelight, to mind, then held onto it tightly, her belly clenching at the memory. Blushing slightly, she walked through the foyer and nodded to the tall, slim butler who opened the front doors wide.

Juliet only had a moment to react before a slight, warmly wrapped body ran straight into her. With an "oomph," Juliet stumbled back a step, looking down and seeing an abundance of bright blonde hair peeking out from a woolen scarf.

"Did you miss me?" Marian squealed, uncharacteristically loud in the echoing entry of Greystone. Juliet's mouth was working hard, but no sound came out as she stared first at Marian, then at the open door, as if expecting Lord Faber to pop out at any moment.

"Well, of course! But what are you doing here?" Juliet said, dropping her voice low as she turned them from the door. Marian's eyes grew serious.

"William said you could use an ally, and I'm already feeling more than a little insane cooped up with Laura and my mother at Devonshire." Marian smiled at her, bright eyes illuminating a kind heart. Juliet had to bite her lip to keep back the wave of tears that threatened her. It had only been two weeks, but she had missed her friends badly.

Marian squeezed Juliet's hand tightly between her gloved hands. She shrugged out of her overcoat as the butler came and retrieved it, his face a slate of stoic indifference. "Come. Invite me in, and we will talk all about it."

Juliet led the way to her favorite sitting room inside the library, where Amelia quickly brought them tea and freshly iced ginger biscuits that Marian eagerly devoured as Juliet caught her up in hushed tones.

She told her friend everything, about Lord Faber's engagement, about her suspicion of her stepfather, about William finding her and Sterling. She did glaze over the part in the cottage, those memories were still hers to hold tight, but she was sure her friend noticed the blush.

"William said he has evidence coming that will free me from any possibility of marrying Lord Faber," Juliet said, setting her teacup down and turning to look at her friend, a bright smile on her face.

"If there is anything I am completely sure of is that William always finishes what he starts. I'm sure he has a way to explain to Marshall why you two belong together," Marian nudged her friend's knee, "Because you two certainly do. I mean, the sparks flying at Lakeview, and now the letters from him. I believe he's falling in love with you, Juliet.'

Juliet blushed furiously, and Marian leaned back again against the cushioned settee, giggling maniacally, her hands covering her face.

"When I saw you two together at the summer's end ball, I think I knew it too," Marian said softly. Juliet peeked between her fingers. "The way he looked at you, like nothing in the room could compare." She sighed dramatically, but Juliet heard the honest, wistful tone in her voice too.

"He is," Juliet stopped, staring off for a moment, "When I'm with him, I just feel complete. Probably for the first time in my life." She shrugged her shoulders as Marian took a sip of her tea, then added more sugar.

"Ah, yes. It doesn't hurt that he's devastatingly handsome and carries one of the oldest titles in England either?" Marian murmured, her bright eyes laughing at Juliet over the brim of her teacup. Juliet swatted her affectionately.

"You and I both know that had nothing to do with it. I don't need a title. I never have."

"I know, but had to point it out in case you'd forgotten you can use that to your advantage too," Marian looked at her sideways, "Why any father, or stepfather in your case, would forego the chance to see their daughter happily married. And married to a Marquess, no less, is beyond me. I can't even imagine how my father would act if I came to him, half in love with a marquess. I would've been married before the ink dried on the newspaper."

Juliet shrugged her shoulder. Trying to find a way to change the topic to something more lighthearted, Juliet stirred her tea, smiling widely at her friend. "Since we have a moment, I don't suppose we could bring up the way that you and Nicholas look at each other? Hmm? Maybe I'm not the only one at the Summer Finale who stumbled into love."

Marian calmly put her tea down, leveling Juliet with a sharp expression on her pretty face. "He is handsome and ridiculously charming, but it just doesn't feel like there is something there."

She shrugged a little, her eyes downcast. "Besides, I'm practically an old spinster at this point, and I don't want to interfere with his chances of finding a bride. And at this rate, he and Robert will be old and grey before they are ready to settle down."

Juliet patted her friend's forearm, "You are no spinster, Marian. Someone perfect is out there, waiting to find you. I know it."

Shaking off the mood, Marian quickly changed courses, poking Juliet's shoulder, "Maybe I should just wait until someone visits and jump them in their bedroom."

Juliet's jaw dropped, and she feigned horror at the statement but secretly enjoyed the rousing jokes and fun. She had been alone so much of her life; having someone who understood her so thoroughly was a true pleasure.

They spent the next hour catching up, laughing, and then Juliet took her friend on a short tour of Greystone, or at least of the rooms still open. Much of the enormous manor had been closed down, cloaked in billowing sheets to protect the remaining furniture pieces.

While Marian had surely realized the family was in severe financial distress, she didn't mention anything, focusing on admiring the luxurious rooms as they explored.

Before they returned to the main part of the house, Juliet heard it, another carriage making its way up the pebbled drive. This one a four-horse, which would've been needed to travel as quickly and as long as Lord Faber would've had to.

She looked at Marian and saw a clear understanding in her eyes. As they halted in the empty foyer, Marian reached out and gently gripped Juliet's hand once. She wasn't going anywhere, the gesture said, and its soothed Juliet's pounding heart.

In the final moments, before the butler marched over to open the front doors, Juliet saw her mother and Marshall appear from their wing of the home. They were dressed in the pinnacle of fashion, yet her mother's elaborately beaded cobalt blue frock looked horribly of place.

Juliet fought her desire to roll her eyes, a cold drip of dread sliding down her spine at their presence. Juliet focused her eyes on the open doorway as Lord Faber slowly climbed the stairs, his squat form taking up the width, but in no way the height, of the frame.

"Henry!" Marshall moved them forward, his green coat making the pair of them look like a peacock. He gripped Faber's arm, even as the shorter man's eyes were trained on Juliet.

"Yes, yes, good to be here," Lord Faber said passively, giving the lady of the house a brief kiss on the hand as he turned towards us. He shook off the chatter of Marshall's greeting with a wave of one meaty hand. His eyes were skimming over her body with a frankness that raised her hackles.

"Lord Faber," Juliet ground out, dropping into a curtsy as Marian mimicked her obligingly. Standing, Juliet looked to Marian, "This is my dear friend Marian, of Devonshire." He looked over appreciatively, but Juliet almost laughed at the expression on her friend's face. Something akin to a scowl, but deeper and more resolute. Juliet clamped down on her laughter, glad she had told her friend of Faber's unwanted kiss in the barn.

Turning from Marian, Faber refocused on Juliet, his meaty neck quaking as he swallowed hard. "It's lovely to see you again, Lady Juliet."

Uncomfortable, Juliet gave him a small, nervous smile. "Please, won't you come in?" Faber moved loudly past the pair of young women and into the parlor. When Juliet glanced back to her mother and stepfather, she noticed a small group of people who had joined Faber. Her brow furrowed, she remained where she was, and the latest guests didn't approach her either.

Marshall led the flock of guests from the room and into the parlor after their coats and bags had all been handled. When Juliet and Marian stayed put, he made a clear gesture with his hand that they would be required to join them. Sighing, she sarcastically offered her elbow to Marian.

"If I have to go, so do you." In response, Marian groaned loudly but slipped her slender arm through.

"Onward then," Marian said, tilting her head back and all but dragging Juliet out of the room, one hand covering the giggles that threatened. William had been right. She had needed an ally.

***

It was afternoon before William would finally make his presence known. To Juliet, it felt like years had passed. All-day, she had laughed, smiled, and made painfully drab small talk with her supposed fiancé. Marian had stayed true by her side, acting as a chaperone, much to Faber's chagrin. By the time William's horse trotted up Greystone's drive, frustration dotted Faber's face as he again attempted to speak to Juliet alone.

Juliet's heart raced as she took a step away from Faber to face the entryway, her thoughts consumed by the excitement of seeing William again. She knew that Faber would see the longing in her look, but she could not stop, couldn't make herself care. Not anymore. The somber-faced Greystone butler, who was getting more exercise today than he had for years, marched into the room, clearing his throat loudly.

"Announcing, Lord William Huntington, Marquess of Mansfield Park," the butler bellowed to their group, before turning sharply and striding back out of the sunlit room. Juliet flew to her feet as William strode powerfully into the room.

He was immaculately dressed, no trace of his muddy attire from their meeting the day before. His fine navy waistcoat, brilliant white cravat, and buff breeches were spotless.

Every strong, muscular inch of him screamed prestige. Not to mention that his handsome face appeared bored at them already; the smirk that graced it was casual and cunning. Juliet almost laughed at his carefully constructed camouflage.

Marshall stood, sending an icy stare at Juliet before moving to greet William. While the title was higher than William's, there was no doubt in her mind which held power in the room.

Juliet watched the two men size each other up, dark and sharp William, to Faber's soft blondness. William nonchalantly offered the lower-ranked man his hand as he got closer, the picture of well-bred manners and refinement.

"Pinecrest, what a pleasure," William said, his voice graveled, sensual, as his silver eyes snuck past Marshall to find Juliet. "I hate to intrude, but I need to speak with you. Alone if you'd please," At those words, Faber also rose, his paunch belly even more prominent after the large meal they'd watched him consume. The older man appeared nervous, his mustache twitching as he took in the Marquess' cutting figure.

"That can wait," Faber said loudly, "Come join us, William. Tell us what news you bring from Mansfield Park. Or is your family's estate still boarded up?" He gestured to a wingback chair across from his own. "After your father's death, I'm sure it was easier to leave that place closed up, eh?"

William nodded a little, his eyes never moving from Marshall's face. Tucking his hands behind him, William brushed past her stepfather and into the room.

Always the gentleman, he stopped first to greet her mother, offering her a stiff bow, and then moved toward Faber. But instead of stopping, he moved purposefully to the other side of the man and gripped Marian's slim fingers and, with a wide smile, pulled them to his lips.

But even as he held Marian's hand, William's eyes were trained on Juliet. Every part of her body had grown warm the moment he arrived. She resisted the urge to fan herself lightly as she melted into his glinting eyes, loving the way they traveled possessively over every inch of her face and lower. As he released Marian, he purposefully shifted so that he was blocking Juliet from the others' view.

"I couldn't stop thinking of you," he whispered hotly against her fingers, for her ears only. The words sent a dart of pure desire straight in her core and turning her legs to jelly. She smiled back; her cheeks flushed. Those stolen moments in the cottage were only a taste of what could be between them; she knew it.

"What brings you here, William," Faber said bluntly from behind the pair, repressed anger lurking in this voice.

William rolled his eyes, giving Juliet's knuckles one last brush of his lips, and turned to face Faber, bringing himself up to his full height as he walked back to the man.

"Just some business with Pinecrest, I'm afraid," William said, shrugged as he sat on a settee beside Juliet's chair, "And I had heard that you would be here."

"So, you decided to stop by?" Faber said, his face clenched in anger.

"Yes. I have a vested interest in making sure that Lady Juliet is happy and safe." William practically hissed the last part.

"How chivalrous of you, my Lord Marquess," Faber ground out, a glistening sweat breaking out on his forehead. He wiped it with his handkerchief and looked meaningfully over at Marshall, who was seated beside his wife.

Both Marshall and Elizabeth looked uncomfortable, pale, their pasty skin standing out sharply against their bright clothing. Had it been any other person, Juliet would have been concerned for their health. But not this time. What she was seeing was merely the ramifications of her family, making deals with bad people.

William made himself comfortable, settling his length into the deep cushions and watching Juliet with openly adoring eyes. Marian watched the two with a small smile on her face, her eyes darting over to wonder at how Faber or the rest of the party might react from this show of interest from the Marquess.

Elizabeth finally spoke up, her hand resting lightly on Marshall's knee. "My Lord, you will have to stay the night. It would be far too late to leave after dinner." She rose from her seat, holding out her hand. "Juliet, will you join me? We will prepare Lord William's room for him."

Juliet moved slowly, her eyes staring into her mother's quietly smoldering brown eyes; she rose and made her way dutifully to her mother's side. Stiffening as she felt her mother slip an arm around her waist, Juliet dared to cast a glance back into the room, seeing both Marian and William looking at her with concern on their faces.

Juliet plastered a smile on her face to convince them, as well as herself, that she would be fine. Juliet and Elizabeth swept down the narrow hall, slipping down the kitchens to supposedly talk to the housekeeper.

As soon as they got out of hearing range, Elizabeth stopped short, dragging Juliet around to face her. Holding her hands tight, Juliet looked down into her mother's face. It was twisted into a mask of rage and disbelief.

"Mother." Elizabeth looked everywhere except for her daughter's eyes. "Why didn't you tell Marshall that William was coming?" Juliet's voice was tight, spoken through clenched teeth.

"Why didn't I?" Elizabeth asked, her face was trapped in a sneer. "Because it would've done no good. Just like it will do no good to have him here. It will only fan the tempers of Marshall and Faber. And while I know he acts cold as ice, I know that William won't be the one to step down either. You have created a monster of your own making. Now I'm going to sit back and watch you be devoured by it."

Her grip tightened until she could feel her mother's sharp nails against her palms. The older woman continued.

"And then you will do what is best for your family. Perhaps for the first time in your entire life," Elizabeth mused, her cruel face twisting into a smile.

"Do you hear yourself?" Juliet finally got out. "Are you completely blind to what Marshall is doing? Are you both bargaining me away for money? You must know that. Why else would Marshall be so obsessed with Faber? Do I mean nothing to you? Papa would be so disappointed," Juliet hesitated, waiting until her mother's angry eyes rose to meet her own. "Mama, I think I love him. I have a real chance for a family with William. For a future with him."

Elizabeth's eyes stared through her, and Juliet took a moment to continue.

"I know it was a mistake back at Lakeview, but I got the chance to talk to him and to know him. And Mama, there is so much there. He lost his family too. Together, we could show each other what it means to be family. You want that for me, right?" Juliet's eyelids fluttered, she swallowed hard.

Elizabeth's sharp gaze was unwavering, her fair skin blotchy with red spots as she stared at her only child.

"You have to let me have this chance, Mama," Juliet finished, softening her voice as she pulled her hands from Elizabeth's chilling grip. Stepping back, Juliet knew she had said everything she could.

Elizabeth coiled like an offended snake, "Juliet, do not make me the bad person," her eyes flickered around the empty hall, then back to her daughter, "This is how it works for every woman of noble birth."

"Not against her wishes," Juliet insisted, "And we are Greystone's, who says we can't buck the tradition."

Elizabeth's eyebrow rose slightly.

"I simply mean that in my opinion, however small, I believe William is worth it. What we have, together, is worth that. And I wanted to tell you."

"But what about me?" Elizabeth said, practically shouting, "Do you think I wanted to marry your father? No! But I did because it was my duty as a daughter." She turned and paced a short distance to and fro in the hall, her skirts swirling around her like angry waves in the sea.

"And you will do yours. It's what's right." She stomped her slipped heel against the hardwood floor, reminding Juliet of an angered child.

Juliet watched her mother's breakdown, her body shaking a little as she tried to calm herself. Where she thought she would find anger at her mother, she only found a pity.

Pity that she had such a small view of the world. Without a doubt, Juliet knew that any daughter she had would never feel a single moment of the disappointment or distrust her mother demonstrated towards her.

"I'm sorry, Mama," Juliet said softly. "I'm sorry for everything you've been through, but I'm mostly sorry for what you will miss out on."

Elizabeth's pretty face turned to a snarl again. "You have no idea what you are saying," Juliet shook her head, but Elizabeth held up a finger, swishing it back and forth in her face, "When the moment comes, you will honor your pledge as a Greystone, as your father would've wanted, as I want."

Juliet felt her blood run cold. "And if you don't, Juliet, I know for a fact that bad things will follow you. You and that puppy-eyed Marquess you've ruined."

Juliet recoiled at the subtle threat, clenching her jaw shut as she stared at the creature her mother had become. Not just a stranger, but someone filled with hatred and fear.

CHAPTER FIFTEEN

Leaning against the cold harshness of Greystone's smooth painted walls, Juliet let herself slide down until she could curl into a small ball, her knees to her chest. Only then, when she could muffle the sounds of her crying straight into the folds of her dress, did she let the tears that had been threatening for weeks fall.

Finally, she felt her tears slow to a stop, leaving that all too familiar, gritty void. Lurching to her feet, Juliet shook her sleeping limbs into action. Making her way down the hall and away from where there would soon be a flurry of activity, Juliet trudged to her room.

The autumn sun was low on the horizon, and she knew that soon she would be expected to attend dinner with the man she wanted to marry and the man who wanted to marry her.

They were two different men, for two very different versions of herself. One was the dutiful daughter who longed for her family's acceptance: the other, a Juliet who had a taste of passion and the chance for a life of love.

The halls, doors, and stairways passed in a blur until finally, she made her way to her room. Stepping inside, she was startled to find not only Amelia, as she expected, but also William. He was reclining by her small fireplace, his leg casually crossed at the knee, smiling and talking to a flustered looking Amelia.

However, one look at her face had him bolting from his seat and to her side. "Juliet, Juliet, what happened?" He said, his hands rushing over her face and shoulders as if checking her for injuries.

She looked up at him blankly. Barely feeling his warm, gentle hands on her body, the angry, disappointed voice of her mother still pounded in her ears. Juliet looked at him, his worried expression, his sharp features filled with anxiety over her silence.

"Nothing," Juliet said curtly, "Nothing's wrong." She stepped away hard, putting an obvious amount of space between them. William's bright eyes flitted over her face, confusion now tainting his worry.

"Are you sure?" He said slowly, his deep voice low and soothing.

"Yes, I'm sure. I need to get ready for dinner," Juliet said, turning and walking over to her window, showing him her long, tense back. If she had looked over her shoulder, she would have seen the sorrowful gaze that Amelia and William exchanged before he quietly walked to the doorway.

"Whatever you'd like, Juliet, I'll see you at dinner."
William's voice was laced with sadness, and moments later,
she heard her door close gently.

"My lady, what has gotten into you? That man came here to
stop your marriage to a well-dressed toad. The least you could
do was treat him with some respect! Never mind that he is
head over heels in love with you," Amelia's voice scolded her.

Juliet wished more than anything that she could turn and
fall into her soft breast and pour out all her sorrows to her
closest confidant. But every time she tried to open her mouth,
she saw that face, the one her mother had made, screaming at
her to finally do what she was told.

Juliet stayed still, her hands clenched to her sides, staring
out her window, praying she would have the strength to
decide what she needed to do. And what she should do.

***

Dinner that night was shaping up to be a festive event. The
table was elaborately decorated, the beautiful tableware
gleamed. Juliet habitually smoothed her hands over a soft
lilac-colored dress that she hoped would bring some color to
her cheeks.

To her, the face in the mirror had remained pale, lifeless, as
she prepared herself mentally for what would come next.

Amelia had been silent the entire time she helped Juliet into her dress, which she didn't blame her for. Now, as Juliet stood in the foyer between her mother and Marian, she could practically feel herself wilting in shame. Shame for the way she had talked to William after he had come to help. Every part of her wished she could run to him, kiss him, claim him for her own in front of everyone.

But it was not that simple. If she married Lord Faber, she would have a life of luxury with a husband she could barely stomach being around. It would sustain her family, sustain Greystone's proud name, her father's legacy. But at what cost?

Juliet knew that life would William would be filled with stolen kisses, horseback rides at dawn, and a chosen family who loved her. She would leave this shell of Greystone behind.

The choice seemed obvious. Her whole life she had longed for the ability to choose her path, yet now she was terrified. How does one choose between honoring your family and following your heart?

When she raised her eyes, they immediately found William, walking with Marian. He was hunched over, leaning down so that he could hear her better, a casual and friendly smile on his striking face, his white teeth flashing as they shared a laugh.

Juliet felt every inch of her wanton body come to life. From her fingers to her toes, she ached for him. Her heart, her body, her life, it was his. There couldn't be another way. Now she just had to find a way to make it official.

They came to a stop in front of Marshall and Juliet's mother, Marian dropping dutifully to a perfect curtsy, and William offering a polite bow. While his eyes stayed on the floor, Juliet tried to catch William's attention but succeeded only catching Marian's. She quickly came to her friend's side.

"What did you do to William? The man is seething," Marian whispered, moving them to stand behind two dining chairs side-by-side.

"What do you mean?" Juliet said, sniffing hard and looking away from her friend.

"William came to me, looking for all the world like a beaten puppy before dinner. I know for a fact that he was coming from your rooms," Marian hissed at her, "Coincidence? I think not."

Juliet's chest ached; she swallowed once, twice, trying to get a grip on her emotions as they galloped away with her.

"I was angry with my mother," Juliet began when Marian cut her off.

"I'm sure you were, but don't forget that we are only here because of him. And he is only here for one thing. That would be you." Marian finished with a flourish of her long-sleeved cream-colored dress. The Greystone staff arrived and helped them both into their chairs.

Juliet clamped her eyes shut, taking a deep breath to soothe the desire to again run to William and apologize. To try to explain the storm of emotions that had battled in her mind.

"I'm sorry," Juliet murmured as the rest of the group slowly entered the candle-lit dining room and began to be seated. "Please forgive me."

Marian patted her arm quickly, "It's not me that you owe an apology to," but she smiled kindly, "But thank you regardless. I know you didn't mean to hurt anyone's feelings."

"I did not," Juliet looked around, quickly taking in the two other guests that had accompanied Lord Faber, arriving silently midday today. So far, she had only seen them wandering around the manor after Lord Faber like lost ducklings or hiding out in their rooms.

She suspected one was a type of security for Faber, big as a mountain, with a face sprinkled with scars and a crooked nose; he didn't look like the type anyone wanted to cross. Faber had simply introduced him as Demetri.

His black eyes reminded her of the cool, dead eyes of the fish in the pond out behind the manor. She shivered as his eyes passed over Marian. Beside her, she could feel Marian stiffen as well. Neither of them relaxed until he found a seat away from both of them.

The second man had spent most of the afternoon napping, but it had done very little for his energy level. Even now, as he sat alongside Faber, he seemed only moments from dozing off.

His starched collar reminded Juliet of a man of the cloth, but he didn't wear a pastor's habit, nor did he turn down the very large glass of wine passed his way, so she discarded that idea quickly. Perhaps he was just a conservative-minded associate of Lord Faber.

Juliet could picture him enjoying every part of the paperwork aspect that it must take to run a banking institution like Faber's. As the first courses went by quickly, Juliet was able to pick up on the sleepy man's name, a Mr. Redding, who did indeed work for Faber.

William was seated diagonally from her, and while his somber grey eyes found hers throughout the dinner, she was already thinking through the conversation she wanted to have with him. She wanted to start with an apology.

Then move to a thank you. And finally, Juliet wanted to wrap her arms around William's neck, press her body against his, and show him exactly how glad she was that he was here at Greystone. Juliet smiled to herself. She knew exactly how to welcome him to her home.

"Juliet? Did you not hear me?" a hoarse voice stole her away from her seductive thoughts. Faber had been talking to her, and his eyes bulged in their sockets as he scolded her lightly. Marian snorted into her napkin, pretending it had been a cough as Juliet painted on a thoughtful smile.

"I'm sorry, Lord Faber, I was thinking about how delicious this dinner was," Juliet lied clumsily, but Faber seemed grateful for any kind of response and quickly grinned boyishly back at her.

"I'm glad to hear it, my dove since this is an important dinner. One that you will remember for the rest of your life." Every head turned to look at the plump man who conspicuously stood at his chair, his breath uneven and wheezing.

He raised his glass of wine, his third by her count, and waved at the others to join him. Begrudgingly the table joined in his toast.

"To Juliet, my beautiful bride, who has continued to enthrall me during our short courtship," Faber took a rasping breath, a manic grin stretching his face, "Happy wedding day, my darling girl."

Juliet froze, her fork clattering to her plate as her numb fingers lost their grip. Beside her, Marian went still as well. Juliet looked for her mother, hoping to see a shred of understanding, only to find Elizabeth keenly watching her husband as he rose slowly beside her.

"Marshall?" she began, her voice low and discreet, the voice she used when she didn't want people to know she was unhappy. "What's going on?"

The silence twisted around them like a vice on Juliet's heart. Fear forced her mind to race as somehow everyone's faces seemed to turn to hers, awaiting her reaction.

Juliet turned back to Lord Faber, watching as the man drank heavily from his wine glass, smiling expectantly.

"Well, Juliet, what say you?" Faber said, guffawing at this sleepy-eyed friend beside him who seemed to rouse himself enough to return the clink of glasses.

"You must be kidding?" William's dark voice broke across the room like a thunderclap. He stayed seated, his wine untouched as he glared across the table at Faber.

"Oh, not at all, Willy boy, I'm dead serious." If William bristled at the absurd nickname, he gave no outward reaction. Yet Juliet knew to watch his eyes as they slowly grew darker by the moment.

Demetri, Faber's guard, strolled over to stand near his master, fists crossed over a powerful chest as if sensing the tension. Juliet's eyes flitted over him before coming back to rest on Faber. She was shocked to the core.

"Faber, you can't imagine me ready to marry you, tonight, at Greystone?" Juliet opened her mouth to continue when Faber let out a growling response.

"Yes, Juliet, I do."

Juliet felt her hackles rise at the undertone in his voice. The man meant every word, and they were in very real trouble. "I don't know you; I don't love you."

"Love comes with time, and we will have plenty of that once we are wed." Faber leered at her over his glass. Even Marshall cringed, and William rose to his feet, an angry shadow at her side.

"Please, I'm begging you. This isn't right." Juliet felt the panic rise in her throat, pressing against her tongue. She had directed her words to Faber but kept her eyes trained on the man who planned on giving her away, Marshall.

For once, Marshall looked ashamed, almost apologetic, his throat working hard before finally saying, "Juliet. Lord Faber was able to procure a special license before coming here today. And since the season is over, there is no reason to delay your wedding for another six months on account of being fashionable."

Juliet felt like ice had been poured over her body. This was truly happening.

"A license," she said. Distantly, as if from a great distance, Juliet saw her mother rise, her face clouded with genuine surprise.

"Yes. For our wedding, my lady." Faber said, his voice smug. The words crawled over her body like unwanted insects, leaving trails of fear across every part of her.

Shaking, Juliet pushed back her chair, maintaining eye contact with Marshall as she did. Gripping the back of her chair for stability, she held back the tears that threatened to spill. "You can't let this happen," Juliet whispered, but in the utter silence of the room, everyone could hear exactly what she said.

Marshall sniffed and looked down, brushing invisible lint from his pants as he said casually, "Like I said, Juliet, this is done. It is time for you to do your duty. Not just for yourself, but Greystone."

Her throat closed, and her vision swam as she considered fleeing. She snapped back to reality when she realized that William was confronting Faber, demanding to see the license, his face glowering as he shouted at Marshall.

"You can't be serious? Be reasonable, man. What kind of man does that to his family?" Juliet shut her eyes, the tears streaming out of them as she backed away from the table, feeling Marian's slender hands gripping her body, steadying her, grounding her, amongst the chaos.

When Juliet looked down, her tiny friend looked as fierce as a lion, gnashing her teeth at Marshall's approach, who continued to drone on about the impossibility of Juliet finding anybody else that would be a better match.

William had lost control now, his words loud and angry as he stood in front of Marshall. "How can you say that? After the letters I sent. The meetings you never showed to. I gave you every inclination that I wanted to be with Juliet. I won't let this happen."

Juliet closed her eyes as Marian wrapped her arms around her as the room seemed to erupt in anger, voices were shouting, the staff was running here and there, unsure what to do with the guests.

"Everyone, shut up!" Suddenly bellowed a deep, strange voice from the doorway. Juliet turned and audibly gasped. A positively enormous, red-haired man filled the entire doorway, his finely cut suit doing nothing but making him seem even more intimidating as it clung to the muscular planes of his body. His face was flushed as he stared in at the dinner party in disarray, his great chest heaving as if he had just run a long way.

Not a soul moved or breathed for several moments, staring at the newcomer with wide, confused eyes. Juliet slowly looked at Marshall, but he looked just as confused as the rest of the group. However, when she looked at William, she saw that his face was painted with relief.

"You lot have gone positively mad," the newcomer shouted, his powerful voice cutting through the room like a hot knife through butter. Marian released her to stare at the mountainous human but maintained her place between Juliet and Faber.

Faber's double chins were quivering with distaste as he looked down his nose at the man, or as much as he could when he was so significantly shorter than him. He also elbowed Marshall in the gut hard enough to make the man flinch.

"This is a private event," Marshall said, in response to the elbow, his hand protectively laying over his ribcage. "Who are you?" Like a sullen shadow, Demetri rose and went to lurk over Faber's shoulder.

"Private party, eh? Well, it's a good thing I was invited then. I love weddings," the man drawled, sauntering towards the table and the group of diners.

Marshall looked confused, his nose wrinkling in dislike at the casual tone. "I highly doubt that. I am the Earl of Greystone; I didn't invite you here."

William moved towards the newcomer, his arm extended in friendship and greeting, which the mountain of a man shook enthusiastically. "I didn't know you highbrow threw such entertaining dinners. I would've been here earlier if I had known."

Marian snorted in front of her, a sound of laughter or horror, Juliet wasn't sure, but the redhead's deep blue eyes glanced her way with a slight smile curling his luxurious lips.

"And risk missing your entrance. Not likely," William's words with light, but his tone was deadly. The redhead's eyebrows went skyward, and he quickly smoothed his red curls back from his face, as if to dress up the situation. Had her future not been hanging in the balance, Juliet might have been tempted to laugh. The man had a dramatic flair for sure.

"This is my associate, Mr. Montgomery Bohart. He has been a valuable asset to me while we looked into some personal matters regarding *the Earl*.' William swept his hand from the bowing redhead to the rest of the room.

"This, Bohart, is an uncomfortable mix of Juliet's family, friends, and people who are marrying her without her consent," William said to Bohart, angry sarcasm lacing his voice. Juliet looked at him, wondering why on earth he could be so confident. Who was the man?

Faber hissed and Demetri, moved around his master with careful, predatory steps, eyes on William and Bohart.

"You have no idea what you're talking about," Faber snarled. Marshall was shifting back and forth on the balls of his feet, clearly uncomfortable. Elizabeth had approached them too, standing beside her husband, looking onto the debate, her beautiful face vacant of all emotion.

"Hold on there, big man," Bohart said, stepping into the circle, his hands raised towards Demetri. "Not that I'd turn it down, but I didn't come to fight." Bohart looked over his shoulder and whistled sharply.

"Jenkins, get yourself in here." A tall, skinny man poked his head around the edge of the doorway behind everyone. He shared Bohart's red hair, but that's where the resemblance ended. He was skittered into the room, his arms laden with stacks of papers, all bound together with string.

As soon as he reached Bogart's side, the larger redhead picked up one and pointed at Marshall with it. "You, Pinecrest, are in far more trouble than being banned from my club. I have here records from several establishments in London who are all looking for you. It seems that it's time to pay your debts."

Marshall went white as snow, his Adam's apple bobbing as he stared at the booklets. He didn't look at his wife, who now stepped forward as if to take the papers before she stopped herself.

"However, I have here, in my possession, an account from Lord Henry Faber's financial institution that says, pending, paid in full at the conclusion of the wedding." Bohart looked at William. "You were right, my friend." William almost sagged in relief, but Juliet was still confused.

"That could mean anything?" Faber sputtered, spittle flying into the air at his angry words. "You can't scare me, Bohart. I've known you too long."

Bohart stepped towards the man, his expression deadly, "Usually, the longer people know me, the more scared they are. So, allow me to change your perspective. When William brought this idea to me, I was quickly able to find records in the books, the debts, the general dirty business. It was easy, to be honest," Bohart stopped, his eyebrow quirked at William for a moment.

"But what did my source find? Even more interesting. It seemed that there was another already investigating you both. How convenient for us all." Bohart's eyes were solemn as he looked at the group, which remained silent except for the raspy breathing coming from Faber.

"It took minimal effort to convince him to step forward and help us. As his mistress is already here as well." Juliet startled, looking immediately to Marian, who shook her head just once, eyes wide and engrossed as Bohart spun his tale.

Bohart whistled one more time, and a stiff, bald man bustled through the door, his dark hat pressed against his chest as his nervous eyes jumped about the room. He seemed happiest to lurk in Bohat's shadow as he faced each of them.

For a painful minute, no one moved. Juliet longed to rush to William but stayed where she was, desperate to know more.

"Tell them what you have," Bohart said finally, nudging his newest companion with an elbow. The shifty character took a step towards the group, clearing his throat as he moved.

"I have proof, hidden somewhere safe, that implicates not only Marshall Pinecrest and Henry Faber in illegal gambling operation but also in the attempted coverup of the same crime ten years ago that took someone's life." His voice grew louder with every declaration. "It was the cover-up that left the Earl of Greystone dead."

Gasps filled the space. Juliet's head felt light as she stared around the table.

"Thank you, Volland, that will be quite enough," Elizabeth said sharply, half the room jumping as she moved confidently into the middle of the room. With all eyes on her, she raised her brow, looking down at the same man.

"Of course, mistress," Volland said, shifting his weight from one foot to another nervously as the room stared at the two of them. Then as one, the cluster turned to look at Marshall and Faber. While Marshall was looking down at his feet, Faber was fidgeting nervously, getting closer and closer to Juliet, angry curses spilling out under his breath.

Juliet's mind was racing, her eyes finding Williams and latching onto them for strength. Faber and Marshall had killed her father? And why did the investigator answer to her mother?

"You have no idea what you are talking about, you rat," Faber said, his voice practically a growl, his face sweating profusely now. William and Bohart both took a step towards the banker, his crazed expression clear for everyone to see.

"I didn't hurt that man. That was Pinecrest! He owed me. Just like he owes me now!" Faber shouted, his arms whirling in the air in his fit of passion. "He's too dumb to do anything at the tables. I'm not sure how I ever trusted him to do something as simple as drive the correct person off the road."

Faber turned to Juliet, licking his lips sloppily, one hand smoothing down what little hair he had left. "I had no qualms with your father, Juliet; it was supposed to the Duke in that carriage. An honest mistake. Don't you see?"

Juliet felt her heart pounding in her ears even as her legs carried her forward. One more step and she would have him, and she was going to land her hand right across his hideous, murdering face. This man, this monster, had killed her father over nothing—all for being in the wrong place at the wrong time.

"Juliet I -." Faber took one more step forward when Marian, who Juliet had almost forgotten about, launched towards the frantic man. Her tiny fist balled up, she punched him straight across his left cheek.

For a moment, time stopped. Then it erupted. With a roar, Lord Faber launched towards them, throwing Marian harshly to the ground in his haste to wrap his hands around Juliet's neck.

Bohart let out a shout of his own, staggering towards the pair in step with William, whose face was dangerously dark. Juliet gasped at Faber's clammy hands on her body, crumbling away from him when she suddenly felt a cold metallic press into the side of her neck.

Bohart and William immediately halted, their faces twin deadly looks of anger. Elizabeth stood over Marshall, who remained sitting at the dining table, his hands in his hair. Her mother's face was one of horror.

Juliet realized that the man she had once danced with at Nicholas' Summer Ball was gone or had probably never existed. This man, Henry Faber, was neither harmless nor kind, he was dangerous and vindictive, and he was the one responsible for her father's murder. Now he held the long neck of a pistol against her throat.

"Easy, Henry, what are you doing?" William said, his smooth voice low and comforting.

"What do you think I'm doing?" Faber shouted hysterically. "I'm leaving. And she is coming with me!"

"No, Faber, she's not," William said in that same quiet voice. Juliet realized then that he was using that voice for her. She stared straight at William, biting down on her bottom lip, trying to convey in a look what she wanted to say a hundred times over.

Faber tightened his hold on her neck, yanking her body against his swollen belly. Forcing her body to bow out around his, inadvertently acting as a shield between her father's murderer and the one she loved most.

Bohart took a moment to reach down and, as if she weighed as much as a kitten, slung Marian up and into his arms. Stepping back, Bohart nodded to William, offering support but not interference as Faber continued to unravel. Juliet could tell that her captor was losing his grip on both his sanity and his grip on the weapon.

Taking a deep breath, she thought back to her father, to his lessons. William was still trying to ease his way closer to Juliet and Faber as Faber backed them into the main foyer.

When Faber hesitated at the door, Juliet knew her moment was staring her in the face. Silently mouthing, '*I love you*' to William, she balled up her fist, and using her other hand Juliet thrust her elbow as hard as she could into his gut.

Faber let out a startled grunt, stumbling back, and as he did, Juliet threw herself forward and away from him. Moments later, William tackled him to the ground, quickly wrestling away the gun and tucking it into the back of his trousers. At first, Faber continued to flounder under William's body, bellowing out his anger and vengeance at all of them.

Echoing in from the dining hall came the sour voice, "Oh, do shut up, Henry. You're embarrassing yourself."

It had been Marshall. And while everyone was surprised to hear it, his words did silence Faber, who lay quietly now, bloodshot eyes trained on Juliet as she stumbled to lean against the banister.

Bohart spoke up sharply from behind them.

"The constable will be here shortly. Might as well enjoy what time you have left."

Marshall raised a wine glass from where he sat and quickly downed the entire thing, reaching for another leftover from dinner. William slowly stood, letting Faber roll to one side and sit up, his chest heaving in exertion.

"Sit," William growled before walking away. Bohart had placed Marian safely on a chair in the attached parlor and returned, crossing his massive arms as he stared down both Marshall and Faber. Demetri seemed to have disappeared in the foray and accusations.

William strode up to her. His face was serious, his eyes wild as he put both hands on her face, staring at her intently.

"Are you okay?" he whispered urgently, his fingers gliding across her skin, "Truly?"

"Truly," Juliet said softly, leaning her forehead into the warmth of his body. Then, to lighten the mood, "This is the worst wedding I've ever been to." His half-hearted chuckle echoed her own.

William stroked the small of her back with one hand, the motions soothing. Not believing her earlier statement, he clearly remained frightened that she might collapse at any moment. But really, he might be right; Juliet felt like her head was so full of these fresh, vivid memories that there wasn't room enough for the basics like breathing or thinking straight.

Forcing herself to try more deep breaths in an effort to calm the blood singing in her veins, Juliet gathered her scattered wits and managed pride. She had something she had to tell him; she would never be caught holding back again.

She tilted her head up to look at the man she loved that she desperately wanted to tell about her feelings. But she caught sight of her mother staring at them, her dark, unreadable eyes filled with tears. Volland, her investigator, hoovered just off her shoulder.

Elizabeth stared straight at her daughter, with excruciating slowness, her red lips parted in a loving smile. After a moment, her mouth formed the silent words that Juliet had longed to hear for as long as she could remember.

"I'm sorry."

That was the last thing Juliet remembered before the starry vision turned to black, and a pair of strong arms swept her up to carry her away from this nightmare.

CHAPTER SIXTEEN

When Marian opened her eyes again, it was late in the night, and she was in her bedroom. She immediately saw William standing by the window, his tall frame outlined in the soft apricot glow from the fireplace.

Even from here, she could see the worry, the concern on his face. Pushing up on one elbow, Juliet let her body acclimate. But unlike earlier, the world stayed level, and she slowly sat up.

"Juliet," William rushed to her side, immediately joined by Marian, who had been sitting curled by the fire. "How are you feeling?"

Juliet raised her eyebrows, and William flinched, while Marian snickered softly. "How do you feel considering the situation?" William amended, his handsome face drawn and pale.

"I feel alright," Juliet said, a half-smile pulling at her lips. "About all of it. Or at least the part I understand." She looked down at the bedspread and gasped, her fingers tracing the bulky bandage wrapping Marian's right wrist and hand.

"Marian, what happened?"

Marian flushed, picking up the injured hand, and attempted to wiggle her fingers for her friend's amusement. "I do not have a very good right hook. Mr. Bohart said it was a valiant attempt, but pitiful execution."

Juliet grinned at her dear friend. "I thought you were magnificent." Marian pinked even further.

"Not like you, Juliet, you were so brave, standing up to that awful man."

Juliet's head snapped to William. "What happened to Faber? To Marshall?"

"The constable was here a bit ago to pick them up. They will be taken down to the courtyard and charged for their crimes. Vollund, Bohart, and I turned over all the evidence we had."

"How did you know?" Juliet asked, she and Marian looking at William inquisitively.

"Honestly, we were originally operating under the assumption that Pinecrest had been blackmailed into promising you to Faber. But the further we got, the deeper the story went. And when Bohart told me he had found a valuable source, I knew that we had to act sooner rather than later." William said, his fingers gently stroking the top of her hand on the bed.

"I'm sorry we kept you in the dark, both of you, but we didn't know what kind of people we were dealing with and didn't want anyone to be in danger." William finished, his face sheepish as he looked at Juliet.

"I understand, but please, let's never do that again," Juliet said.

"Do what specifically?" William said, grinning. "The impromptu wedding? The pistol plays?"

"Not tell each other things," Juliet answered promptly, her eyes sliding urgently over his face, absorbing every minute detail of who she treasured most.

"Oh, goodness, you two are ridiculous. This is where I take my leave," Marian said, smiling and standing to go to the door, her bandaged hand raised to eye level as she pretended to shield herself from the sight of them.

"Marian. Better get that hand looked at again; I think some of the bandages might have shifted." William said after her, his silvery eyes flashing.

"What? Are you sure?" Marian looked over the immaculately wrapped appendage, her face serious.

"Yes, I'm sure Bohart would like to take one more look at it," William said, his voice full of teasing. "The first two rewraps were clearly not up to snuff."

"Oh, you!" Marian scolded, her face blossoming into a brilliant shade of red Juliet had never seen. Stomping out of the room, the blond woman threw vulgar curses over her shoulder as she went.

Juliet raised her eyebrows at William, who laughed. "Bohart? Really?" Juliet asked, shifting slightly on the bed so William could make himself more comfortable alongside her.

"He's a good man. Maybe even a great one." William was pensive, his gentle fingers tucking a wayward brown strand behind her ears. "Besides, crazier things have happened. Once I was visiting a friend, and the daughter of an Earl accosted me in my bedroom."

Juliet swatted at his shoulder, blushing prettily at his knowing smile. "But then even crazier was how I couldn't forget her, and now I find myself not wanting to be without her."

Juliet's heart thumped in her chest, her chest aching at the love that filled her every void. William's face grew serious, almost studious as he looked into her face.

"I know that this day has been a wild ride. But Juliet, seeing you in his arms, afraid I might lose you forever, it would've killed me." William leaned forward, brushing his warm lips over hers in a caress so sweet that made her heart clench.

"Marry me, Juliet. Choose me. Love me, the way I love you." William said passionately, his voice quaked.

Closing her eyes, she let her forehead fall against his chest, biting her lip hard as she choked back hot tears. "I thought you were supposed to get down on one knee. Present me with a ring?" Juliet looked up at him, her fingers feeling their way up to his chest to his face where she cupped his jaw, gently stroking the rough skin there.

William snorted. "And do things that usual way? Absolutely not." His fingers moved her face upwards so that he could look directly into her eyes. There, he waited, his handsome face filled with love and adoration.

"Yes," Juliet answered softly, moving her lips up to his. "I choose you. Yes. I love you." With a strangled groan, William swept his arms around her, his lips taking hers in a gentle, loving kiss.

Hooking her leg around his, Juliet dragged him down into the bed with her, determined once and for all to give him the welcome she had been craving. For once, no one dared to interrupt them.

CHAPTER SEVENTEEN

Three months later

The first rays of the sun shone brightly across the bed. Juliet groaned, shrinking away from the glaring flares of light. Ducking back against her pillow, Juliet felt the heavy, warm heat that was William. With practiced precision, she tucked herself under his arm, laying her cheek on his chest, letting the steady beat of his heart soothe her ragged heart.

It had been a busy season. First, there had been an intense and lengthy discussion with her mother, where finally, after all these years, Juliet had gotten the full story. How her mother had fallen in love with the handsome, charming Marshall Pinecrest, only to grow increasingly suspicious of her new husband as time passed.

Elizabeth had employed Vollund to clear away any confusion about this motive for their marriage but quickly found her concerns to be the truth. She had spent the following years in bed with the man who killed her first husband, frantically gathering research to prove the murder.

Juliet had listened with rapt attention as Elizabeth finally told her about her father's death and apologized for the destruction her grief-stricken actions caused.

She had truly believed marrying as quickly as possible was the best solution. The older woman repeatedly apologized, begging for another chance to show her a parent's true love.

Juliet had forgiven her. The weight of bearing that kind of toxic relationship would've continued to smother her. At least now she could look forward to rebuilding a new relationship with her mother instead of wallowing in the past.

And then, of course, there had been the small matter of her wedding to William. They had plans, big ones, for both Greystone and Mansfield Park, and after he proposed, Juliet had taken the lead on preparing his childhood home for permanent residence again. They would create new memories, happier memories, in the homes they loved.

Nicholas, the Duke, Marian, Robert, Lady Eloise, Lady Catherine, and even a gruff Mr. Bohart had made the trek one snowy day in November to see William Huntington, Marquess of Mansfield Park, marry the Lady Juliet Sonders in the historic chapel at Greystone. Following the heartfelt vows, the Mother-of-the-bride, Elizabeth, threw a wedding feast to put all others to shame.

Juliet had been a stunning bride, deliriously in love with her groom. William had been the picture of masculine beauty, his eyes glued to the dark-haired woman who owned his heart. They had lasted through only the first course at dinner before sneaking back to their rooms, laughing, barely able to keep their hands off each other.

And now, just a few weeks later, they were here, in Mansfield Park, thoroughly wrapped up in each other. In this life, they were creating. Juliet let her devilish fingers trail down William's bare stomach, feeling his rumbling breath under her cheek as he awoke.

"Wife, you are playing with fire."

"And what if I am?" Juliet responded playfully, her leg sliding up his so that in a quick shift of her hips, she found herself straddling her husband's torso. Grinding her hips lightly against his, Juliet coaxed a whining groan from his lips.

"Why are you always such an early riser?" William threw one muscular arm over his eyes, feigning anger at her. His other hand followed the line of her body down where he could cup her hip.

"I'm not the only one," Juliet replied saucily, feeling his body hardening beneath her.

"So crude," he scolded, rolling her onto his back and under his body. Nose to nose, William stared down at his beloved wife. The woman who challenged everything he thought about love. And who had given him a future he secretly craved by erasing the pain of the past.

Juliet kissed him softly, feeling his fingers trail down her form to rest just above her belly button. Her belly was still flat, taunt, but he rested his hand there as if he could feel the heartbeat of his child from where it grew within her body.

His eyes fluttered shut as a wave of overwhelming peace, of happiness, took him. Juliet pressed her forehead against his.

"I choose you," she whispered against his skin. "Always."

The End

Thank you for reading!

I hope that you enjoyed reading about Juliet and William's love story as much as I enjoyed sharing it. If you did, I would appreciate you leaving a short review on Amazon or Goodreads. Reviews are so important to authors and sharing your thoughts would be much appreciated.

You can find more books by Anna Macy on Amazon.

She Ruined the Marquess
A Lord's Redemption (Coming January 2021)
Heart for the Holidays (Coming November 2021)

Note: The novels in the Unexpected Love series are stand-alone stories meant to be read individually. If you would like to read in chronological order, please see the list below.

Coming January 2021

A Lord's Redemption: A Historical Romance

After his fiancé broke their engagement to marry another, Robert is desperate to put as much distance between himself and love as possible

She's the beautiful daughter of his family's biggest rival.

When Robert Wains meets Georgiana Conning at the theater one night, his mind and heart are on two very different pages. His heart still aches for the chance at happily ever, but his mind is done taking risks, especially in matters of love

Georgiana is the only daughter of Robert's biggest competitor. Their families have been battling in business for as long as she can remember. When she stumbles into Robert's arms, she finds herself falling straight into love with the only man in London she couldn't have.

Robert cannot deny the growing attraction between himself and Georgiana, and as feelings grow deeper, the tension between the two families grows. When this rivalry threatens to drive them apart, Georgiana and Robert must choose the love they feel for each other or their duty to family.